THE RENEGADE

By

Randy Lee Eickhoff

The Renegade
Published by *Cane Hollow Press*
Copyright © 2015 Randy Lee Eickhoff
All rights reserved
Cover art: Timothy Truman

The Renegade is a work of historical fiction. Many of the important historical events, figures, and locations are as accurately portrayed as possible. In keeping with a work of fiction, various events and occurrences were invented by the author.

and memorable work. Don't miss it.

-William Martin, New York Times Bestselling Author of *Cape Cod* and *The Lincoln Letter*

With this relentlessly gritty page-turner, Randy Eickoff proves he belongs among the ranks of the great novelists of the American frontier. Laced with political intrigue and spiritual mystery, *The Renegade* takes the reader on a wild journey from the back alleys of old Philadelphia to the long houses of the Senecas. His characters virtually reach out from the page and grab you!

-Mike Blakely, best-selling author of *Comanche Moon* and *Moon Medicine*

An extraordinary story that rings of truth, and it rings beautifully. *The Renegade* is a painting of early America, when the first white men in this country wove a tapestry of the wild land, their own ways, and Indian ways into a uniquely American life. A pure treasure.

-Win Blevins, Bestselling author of the Author of the Rendezvous Series, *Darkness Rolling*, and *Stone Song*

The language of *The Renegade* is staggering in its beauty. In the hands of this master, Randy Lee Eickhoff, the story of the earliest time of white people in our land floats like a mist above the people, the animals, and a mysterious world. A timeless story of solid friendships and those that waver … yet still live in our hearts. The story is in time, of time, and timeless.

-Meredith Blevins – author of *Darkness Rolling*

"... he views
The dismal Situaton waste and wild
A Dungeon horrible, on all sides round
As one great Furnace flam'd, yet from those flames
No light, but rather darkness visible"
Paradise Lost
John Milton

MEPHOSTOPHILIS: Why, this is hell, nor am I out of it.
The Tragical History of Doctor Faustus
Christopher Marlowe

for Lucia St Clair Robson
a rare find—beautiful, talented, kind, wise,
and adventurous. *Nemo melius ornateque dixisti
amicum peteret.*

The Renegade   by   Randy Lee Eickhoff

Origo Mali

A blood moon ran red over the top of the dark and silent trees. The cabin door burst open, and Old Man Girty staggered down the narrow lane to the spring house perched by a deep cut of the Susquehanna River. His blood-shot eyes probed the cool darkness of the bricked well until they found the stone jug filled with two-month-old whiskey. With a satisfied grunt, he pulled it from the well. Heavy cold drops of water beaded its sides. He lifted it to his ear and shook it: at least half-full.   He smiled happily and lifted his bearded face to the darkness. "Po-cheen! Po-cheen!" he cried, a peculiar yell of Bluestock mountaineers from Donegal as they poured forth from the public houses, brandishing pistols and pikes high in the air, threatening the moon with cries of vengeance against King George II and his Sassenachs and *gombeen* men, a challenge to mortal combat, their strength the strength of the moonshine.

He pulled the cork from the neck, tilted the jug, and drank deeply, his large Adam's apple rising and falling rapidly in the cords of his scrawny neck until the raw spirit caused him to gag.   He lowered the jug hurriedly and gasped for breath. Distorted images, half-forgotten dreams of nights drinking and riding with the Ribbonmen and Whiteboys, flickered through the whiskey haze of his mind.

"Po-cheen! Po-cheen!" he cried again, cocking his head to one side, listening for an answering call. But the only sounds in the night came from ghosts riding on the wind. He shook his head sadly and slumped back against the wall of the spring house. He looked out mournfully through the door to the darkness of the woods a few yards away. Light from the moon touched the leaves of the trees with a secret brush, painting them with crimson highlights.

"The times, the times," he said sorrowfully. "Ah, and where have they gone, the Ribbonmen and cony-catchers? And the wild Tralee women and the fair lads from Donegal? Even a good Cork man cannot be found. All buried by the gobshite men a-chasin' after the Whiteboys. Where ha' they gone?" He cleared his throat, washing it clean with a taste of the whiskey, and began to sing, thumping the side of the jug in place of the bodhran to keep time:

> "Be it right or wrong,
> these men among
> on women do complain;
> Affirming this, how that it is
> A labor spent in vain
> To love them well;

> for never a dele
> They love a man again:
> For left a man do what he can
> Their favor to attain,
> Yet if a new to them pursue,
> Their first true lover than
> Laboreth for naught;
> for from her thought
>   He is a banished man."

His voice, harsh and strained in the night, broke on the last line, his thoughts not of the nut-brown maid of whom he sang, but of Ireland. He stopped to take another drink then froze, the jug half-tilted to his mouth as a shadow moved across the moon. Slowly he lowered the jug, lungs caught in half-breath, eyes straining through a blear of whiskey to see the apparition suddenly manifest itself from the dark woods.

"Whis-kay," a deep voice commanded. The outline of an eagle feather curving away from a lean jawline broke the blackness of the silhouette. Girty laughed at the trick the night had played upon him.

"There's no drop here for the likes of you," he said. "Go away. We'll trade tomorrow." He raised the jug.

"Whis-kay," the voice said again. A bronzed hand reached through the red light of the moon for the jug.

Girty jerked away and staggered to his feet. "Fish, you heathen savage! Go away, I tell you! This night belongs to me! To me! We'll trade tomorrow."

Again, the hand reached for the jug. Girty held the jug out of the Indian's reach behind him and, seething with whiskey anger, lifted a brawny fist and clouted the jaw just visible in the red light. He grunted with pleasure as he felt the jolt through his arm to his shoulder. A warm glow suffused him with fond memories of past brawls. He bent to carefully place the jug safely against the wall of the spring house, then rose to the battle-surging of his blood. He saw the flash of the silver crescent in the red light but never felt the blow as the hatchet cleaved his brain pan.

From the doorway of the cabin, young Simon watched the Indian seize the jug of whiskey and flee to the dark of the woods. He waited long minutes before walking down the path to the still figure of his father. He squatted and closely studied the wound: in the night, the pool of blood looked black. He placed a forefinger in the blood and raised it to his lips, tasting it. He leaned back against the wall of the spring house and stared at the woods where the Indian had disappeared. When morning came, he rose and walked into the forest. He did not return for six days and six nights. No one ever knows what happened during those six days and six nights. Years later, those in the Ohio River

Valley claimed he had made a pact with the devil and became Satan's scourge.

Often I have thought about these words as Simon told them to me. There is not much else to do at my age, at this place. I remember the fear in people's eyes, in their voices when they spoke half-fearfully in stage whispers to guard against the words reaching his ears. Eventually, even those whispers ceased as people worried about their words being carried to him on the wind.

I remember Simon well. All too well. Perhaps the Devil did have a hand in his making. Not every man knows everything about his friends or enemies. People place far too much emphasis upon the Devil these days.

Except here. Here, I sit. And wait.

Jonathon Francis Huntington

Chapter One

The last few days I've been thinking, thinking of
the fall in my country I dare not return to across the
water from my cabin by the shores of Lake Huron. The
time goes very slowly—I cannot get it to pass as
quickly as I want—for a great sorrow, a great regret of
my past, lies heavily upon my heart. I do not want for
anything here on St. Joseph Island save that which I
cannot have; that which is so close that I can see the
golds and russets of fall maples and oaks across the
shoals just after the rising of the early morning fog.

At times, a great bitterness wells up inside me,
and I feel the familiar throbbing in my temples. A gray
mist falls across my eyes in rage at the injustice done to
me. I pace angrily back and forth along the pebble and
shell-strewn beach below my cabin and fling stones and
curses across the waters towards my country until the
fit passes. Other times, a restlessness descends upon
me, and I take up my rifle and powder and shot and
head deep into the woods behind my cabin, at times
staying away for days until, weary and aching from
arthritis and half-a-dozen old bullet wounds, the peace
of the forest cleanses me, and I again limp home to
spend my days among my books and pens and papers.

The Renegade   by   Randy Lee Eickhoff

Twenty years ago, time passed very quickly, making a blur of summer and fall, slowing only (and then briefly) for the winter before leaping into spring. A year was gone before I knew its passing. I have forgotten many things that happened then for I scarcely thought of them, looking eagerly ahead for what the new day, week, month, year would bring, living only in the present and future. Many things seemed curious and unnatural and sometimes a bit frightening but always I found something to look forward to. Alas! The youth I was found too many and forgot them as quickly as they happened in his impatience for the new. Now, I remember only select items: certain nights clear like day; people strange enough to earn a lasting niche in my cliff of memory; the odd meal after a time of hunger; crisp, cool mornings in the woods; a partridge on sudden rise; a deer frozen, one leg lifted, next to a pond. Isolated memories, meaningless in their solitude, but all that I have. Sometimes, I will see someone paddling a canoe with a raven painted on its prow or an elk swimming in the lake, and the ripples on the water bring back a sudden surge of memory, and I reach feverishly for pen and paper and write furiously to keep the memory alive for the cold hours of winter when memory lies dormant and I feel only the cold and smell stale scents of old buckskin and Hudson Bay blankets needing airing instead of the rich odors of roots and leaves and the marrow-like sachet of fir-sap.

The Renegade by Randy Lee Eickhoff

I am alone except for my dog Esau, a large mastiff a soldier at the fort on the other side of the island gave me. At times, I talk to him about how comfortable we are inside the cabin with the roaring birch fire in the stone fireplace and the wind howling like the lost souls of Satan outside.

"What d'you think, Esau? A haunch of venison for the night?" I ask.

And he licks his massive chops and blinks knowingly while I spit the venison and lay it across the cauldron hooks in the fireplace.

When we are both fed, Esau stretches out in front of the fire, propping his chin on my slippered foot, and waits patiently while I light a pipe and pick up my journal of memories to read him to sleep.

Many a night passes in this manner.

Chapter Two

Yesterday, a small packet arrived from Fort Malden in Upper Canada. I opened it and found a finely-beaded belt in light and dark blues bordered in gold. No letter or signature accompanied the packet; only two eagle feathers carefully wrapped in oilskin but enough for me to identify the sender: Simon Girty who, like me, lives an outcast from his country across the border. I have received many such packets—presents, actually—but I send nothing in return. Although the day differs each year due, I am positive, to the lagging memory of Simon, the season remains constant: mid-fall, the anniversary of our first meeting as prisoners of the Senecas.

I had been with the Senecas for three years before the Indians brought Simon and his family to the Deleware Indian town of Kittanning on the eastern bank of the Alleghany. Prior to my capture, I had been a young schoolmaster in Philadelphia, bored with trying to teach Latin to young infidels who preferred to run wild through the cobblestone streets to the taverns on the outskirts of the city where the backwoodsmen gathered to trade furs for powder and shot and swap stories. Actually, I couldn't blame my young charges

9

for I, too, often wearied of the staid lectures in Philosopher's Hall and the pretentious preening of my self-confessed elders who had grudgingly admitted a youth of seventeen into their august body. I had not only a gift of numbers, but literature as well, having received intense instruction *ab incunabulis* from a widowed father with nothing else to offer his only son save the benefits of his position as dean of the college endowed by John Harvard. My childhood playmates were the dead Copernicus, Plato and Aristotle, Homer, Galileo, Shakespeare, Spenser, Borelli, and Isaac Barrow. Upon my father's untimely death from a chill contracted one cold December night after forgetting himself while walking in deep thought along the bank of the Charles, I was thrust by necessity into the practicality of provider instead of dreamer.

With the help of long-time family friend Benjamin Franklin, I found placement despite my youth, at a small academy in Philadelphia. Mr. Franklin also arranged rooms for me in the house of a Mr. James Street Hall, the husband of a young lady eighteen years his junior and the father of a daughter a year younger than his wife by a previous marriage. Both were anxious to initiate me into the mysteries of pleasure that had been sadly neglected during my tenure among my father's books. I remember the day well when I awoke to find Mistress Hall and her step-daughter snuggling tightly against me, my manhood rising willingly to their caresses. To their delight, I proved an eager learner, quite willing to explore all aspects of pleasure between a man and two lusting women. I became an avid pupil, and they became my family, of sorts. All loneliness disappeared.

I believe now that Mr. Franklin had anticipated my need for companionship while making his selection of my rooms. It was his sponsorship as well that brought me into Philosopher's Hall, the home of the American Philosophical Society. A grudging admission, I admit for many of the stodgy old fellows displayed an arrogant reticence—could I call it "intellectual snobbery?"—upon my admission. But following my argument over composition of energy, they swallowed their opinions.

By all social standards, I quickly became an acceptable Sunday guest in Philadelphia homes and my future secured. But I was not content. The city stifled me with each passing day. I eagerly looked forward to the end of the terms when I could journey to the deep woods and rest among the quiet, soothing glades hidden from prying eyes, safe from societal demands.

At the end of the second spring term, I accepted the offer of a brief summer appointment to a Moravian Mission in the north. I left Philadelphia for Lake Erie, promising to return for the following winter term. That term found me instead a prisoner of the Senecas with Simon Girty in the Deleware town of Kittanning.

The Renegade   by   Randy Lee Eickhoff

Chapter Three

Rain and storm—not much to last in man's memory. Such are the melancholy days when one sits before a clear pane in a window to watch the tossing of the trees, the bursts of jagged lightning—the Devil's breath—accompanied by glowering masses of thunderheads.

The rain had come on suddenly, driving all of us inside the Long Houses at Kittanning. I crouched in one corner close by the door—the relegated spot for slaves—humming a little tune to pass the time and to entertain a little girl sitting on her heels a short distance away, solemnly sucking on a piece of leather soaked in berry juice. Between us lay four or five dogs. Suddenly, they leaped to their feet, hackles raised, legs stiffly locked, low growls rumbling from their throats. I stopped humming and listened warily as did the warriors, hands casually draped over weapons, at the back of the lodge. Then I heard voices grunting in that peculiar clicking of the Seneca language. I relaxed. Another party of visitors, I thought, then recoiled as the door burst open. A party of six whites stumbled in and stood blinking in the dim light of the lodge. Their captors silently filed in behind them on either side of the Long House. The mother wearily held a four or five-year-old boy child draped sleeping over her shoulder. Behind her stood two gangling youths and another, about fifteen, a long shock of gleaming black hair falling over his broad forehead towards gray eyes above high cheekbones. His nose was aquiline, lips thin and hard, chin square and thrust out defiantly at the world. Broad shoulders strained the seams of his homespun shirt, muscles bulged the sleeves.

"Where are we?" the father asked, words clicking like pebbles in the silence. His eyes flickered uneasily around the Long House at the Indians watching silently.

"The Delaware town of Kittanning," I said cautiously, keeping an eye on Rides-the-Moon, my "benefactor." Although I had been given the privilege of being allowed in the Long House, I had to be careful not to overstep the unspoken rules of prisoners and slaves.

"A white man?" he asked, peering uncertainly at me in the dim light. I wasn't offended: after a year living with the Senecas, I appeared more Indian than white. My hair, normally dark-blonde, had become sun-bleached almost white, my skin tanned nut-brown, and my clothes, long-reduced to tatters by brambles, had been replaced with castoff, greasy buckskins.

"What is left of one," I said dryly. "I am Jonathon Francis Huntington."

14

"By God! Can you help us?" the man asked hoarsely, clutching at my arm. "I'm afraid these saveges mean us great harm."

"I'm a captive, too," I softly answered. "There is little that I can do. At least, for now. If nothing happens before tomorrow, then I might be able to drop a hint or two. Maybe they'll keep you as a slave."

"Do you think so?" he asked. Hope shined desperately from his eyes.

"No," the broad-shouldered youth said softly, turning to face us. "No, I don't think there's much hope for that.

I studied him for a moment, surprised at the calm mask settled upon his face. I could see no resignation, no fear, just acceptance of his fate. "What makes you so sure?" I asked him.

"I wouldn't give it in their place," he said quietly.

"Be quiet, Simon!" the mother exclaimed. She turned to face me: a handsome woman, not quite pretty. Long black hair lay in abandoned ringlets across her wide shoulders. Almond-shaped eyes carried a suggestion of excitement in their dark depths. Heavy breasts strained the front of her dress. Demeter, I automatically thought, then caught the thought and wondered at its origin.

"What can we expect, Mr. Huntington?"

I inclined my head in lieu of a bow and said,

"Usually, the complete opposite of what you hope. But, even that is an expectation, so I will have to say: I don't know. The Indians have a certain barbaric simplicity about them that is entirely unpredictable." It had been so long since I last spoke the King's tongue that the words felt awkward, uncomfortable upon my tongue.

"Savages, savages!" Turner said gloomily. "Damn Captain Edward Ward to eternal hell!" He saw the question in my face and hastened to explain.

"We had heard about a war party moving up the Juanita River," he said. "So, a bunch of us got the families together and headed into Fort Granville for safety. The fort wasn't ready for us. The supply trains hadn't come through yet, so Captain Ward decided to gather the grain from crops we left behind. He took his Pennsylvania provincials out despite our pleas. A couple of scouts had come in with a report of a French and Indian force under the command of Neyon de Velliers coming down upon us from Fort Duquesne. But Ward wouldn't listen to us and took his men out. They never came back. De Velliers surrounded the fort and laid siege to it. We did the best we could, but," he shrugged. "Finally, a group of Indians crept low along the banks of the Juanita until they got within range to shoot flaming arrows into the stockade. With the fort burning down around our ears, we had little choice but to surrender. I let down the heavy bars to the stockade gates to allow the Indians to come in."

16

"You were in command?" I asked sharply after he finished his story. He nodded, his face suddenly bleak, sharp planes and angles.

"Yeah. That ain't good, is it?" he said.

"No," I said shortly. ""But, maybe. . . .""

I never had a chance to finish. Rides-the-Moon suddenly stood and barked a guttural command. Three braves seized Turner and dragged him roughly from the Long House. Rides-the-Moon made a gesture, his face a grim mask. I knew that look well. With sinking heart, I faced Turner's family.

"I am afraid that you all must follow," I said apologetically.

"Why?" One of the others—Jim Girty, I discovered—asked.

"To make us afraid," Simon said softly. He walked through the door behind the Indians dragging Turner. The others stared bewildered at the door for a moment, then resignedly followed his lead. Rides-the-Moon jabbed me sharply in the side. Reluctantly, I walked from the Long House, my gorge rumbling. Yet, I found myself strangely fascinated as well by the youth who walked silently behind the Indians leading us down the path through the center of the village. His movements were graceful and confident, almost as if he *knew* that nothing would happen to him; that he had a further destiny to fulfill.

We followed the yelping band carrying Turner

17

between them to the nearer bank of the Allegheny outside the village. Curses spilled in a frothy foam from Turner's lips as he fought them hard. One brave reeled away from the melee, cradling his jaw tenderly in both hands. Another let out a scream of agony and pulled away, blood pouring from an open wound in the middle of his face where his nose had been before Turner bit it off. But there were too many of them. They stripped and spread-eagled him between four tent pins driven deep into the earth.

"What . . . what are they going to do?" his wife asked. She clutched the young child hard against her breast.

"You'll see," I grimly replied. "God help you, but you'll see."

She watched in horror as warriors slowly advanced on the tied figure, carefully holding red-hot gun barrels by wooden stocks. His screams began immediately as they pressed the gun barrels against him, burning tiger stripes on his naked flesh. The stench of scorched flesh rose from his charred body and drifted over us. She gagged, the whites of her eyes rolled up. She crashed forward in a dead faint over the young child. I wrenched my eyes from the tortured figure and looked at Simon standing calmly five feet from his step-father. A slight smile played around his lips, one of weary acquiescence. His throat worked as he swallowed his fear. Behind him, his brothers tried to avert their eyes only to have them involunterily drawn to the horror of the writhing figure on the ground. Two braves stepped forward and dumped blazing faggots from damp birch bark upon Turner's stomach. Another slipped a scalping knife over his skull, sank his fingers into the long hair, and wrenched it free with a fearful yell and a wet *plop*!

For three hours, Turner screamed in agony as the women slipped forward to jab pine splinters under his flesh and set them on fire, as knives slashed long strips of flesh from him, castrated him, and cut a small hole in his belly to pull out his intestine for the dogs that savaged it, fighting and snarling with each other as they pulled the rest from him. Slowly his voice lost all human resemblance, until harsh mewling sounds, like those of his primitive ancestors, escaped from his bloody lips.   At last, Rides-the-Moon stepped forward to end his agony with a war axe.

I felt Simon's eyes upon me and raised my own to meet his over Turner's body. I felt myself being drawn into their depths. Primitivism, I thought, the true splendor of barbaric simplicity. An eyebrow lifted silently in question. My God! Could he read my thoughts? He nodded slightly at me and turned away to follow his captors back to the Long House. Two of his brothers helped their mother while I carried the young child, bringing up the rear, my thoughts for the first time in my life a chaotic jumble void of logic, of reason.

Chapter Four

That night while the Shawnee, Deleware, and Seneca argued over the prisoners, we rested under guard in the Long House. Simon seemed unconcerned about his fate, sitting cross-legged in front of the fire, staring deeply into the glowing, golden-red embers. I waited for him to show a faint interest in his future, but he ignored me and the mutterings of his brothers as they milled uneasily around the narrow window near the door, watching their fate being decided by heated argument around the flickering flames of the council fire. At last, I spoke to him: "Aren't you even the least concerned?"

He raised calm eyes to mine. "Why should I be?" he asked. He smiled, teeth flashing whitely in the firelight. He placed his hands behind him, arching his back. "Is that what you really want to know?"

"Not really, but it will do for a start," I said.

He silently laughed, his eyes burning with the heat of the stars. "God's balls! Well, then, in answer to your question: No, I am not concerned. I cannot help what they," he nodded at the doorway, "decide to do. But, I do not think we are in any danger."

"Why not?" I asked. "Remember what happened

to your father?"

"Stepfather," he corrected. "And, yes, I do remember. I shall never forget it. But if they planned the same for me, I would have been tied next to him."

"How do you know that?"

He grinned and shrugged. "It's the way I feel."

"You do not seem to feel much remorse about the death of your stepfather," I ventured.

"And this upsets you?" He seemed surprised at my comment.

"I do not understand why you are not," I countered.

He shrugged. "I don't know," he answered. "But that's not important. It is over. There is only time now for the living. Besides, his life was filled; he had received everything he wanted." And, he proceeded to explain, giving for the only time since I have known him, a brief look into his past.

Girty, the second son of Old Simon Girty, an Irish immigrant, had been made fatherless by the Indians the first time when his paternal father refused to share a jug of whiskey with a warrior named The Fish. John Turner, with an interested eye cocked towards the comely Widow Girty, tracked The Fish to a small solitary camp above Sherman's Creek and killed him. The Widow, Mary, more than a few years younger than her slain husband, joyfully accepted the scalp of The Fish from Turner's bloody fingers and Turner's body in

22

her bed still warm from her first husband's memory.

I was surprised at the calmness Simon exhibited while relating his story. At first, I filed it away as one born of youthful bravado. A few years later, I was forced to revise my opinion When I again met his mother—still comely if a bit long in the tooth and still eager for a romp with a man in whatever tick was available. (I don't believe that she suffered greatly "the pain worse than death" at the hands of the Indians who abducted her but accepted her lot with the joyful resignation the handmaidens of Circe greeted the sailors of Odysseus.)

He finished his narrative in the same quiet tone in which he started, staring into the fire, waiting patiently for the end of a council that had yet to decide his fate. I think he knew whatever decision came from the council that night would be the right one. I wonder now if he wasn't equally sure that our fates were woven from the same thread for he showed no surprise when Rides-the-Moon sent James with the Shawnee, and left Mary, George, and the infant with the Delewares. Rides-the-Moon took Simon with us the next day when we left Kittanning to return north to the Seneca village that was to be our home. Here, Simon forged the ties that would give him the right to sit in the council of the confederacy the Senecas had formed with the Iroquois, Ononodagas, Canandaiguas, and Mohawks. From that council, he would build an army that would link his

23

name with the one who was without a doubt his spiritual father: the Fallen Angel.

Simon's stoic response to his stepfather's torture struck some response in our Indian captors. His ability to keep his feelings submerged beneath an ice-cold exterior pleased them. When we arrived in the village that was to be our home for the next couple of years, Simon remained silent despite the probings and poking of the women who jabbed him continuously with sharpened sticks. Strangely, though, the village dogs who normally nip at the heels of white men brought as captors either left him alone or befriended him.

This did not go unnoticed by Speaks Thunder, one of the ancient prophets of the village who leaned heavily on a gnarled stick, clutching it with fingers swollen from arthritis, watching Simon with glittering black eyes that peered from beneath a map of wrinkles as deep as ravines. Speaks Thunder had long abandoned hunting and war parties; his crippled legs would not allow him to slip unnoticed through the forest. But wisdom hung around his shoulders like a rich mantle and when he spoke, men and women alike listened reverently to his words.

One day, Simon was being especially mistreated by a young woman who repeatedly jabbed him with an ash stick sharpened to a wicked point that had been fire-hardened. Badger Woman (for that was her name) repeatedly stabbed Simon for not bringing wood to her fire, sinking the ash point into his flesh until thin trickles of blood curled around his arms and torso. He bore the torture stoically without wincing. At last, Speaks Thunder hobbled forward.

"Stop this," he commanded.

"But this slave is disrespectful," Badger Woman complained.

"No, it is not disrespectful to refuse to share your pallet when your husband is hunting," Speaks Thunder said.

"Are you accusing me?" Badger Woman blustered, aware of the eyes of others upon their confrontation.

"There is no accusing," Speaks Thunder said firmly. "Do you think I do not have eyes? I do not have ears? I saw you yesterday in the chokecherry bushes when you tried to get this man to come to your lodge. Shameful! Shameful!"

He turned away from her and looked at Simon. Their eyes locked for a long moment, then a tiny smile turned Speaks Thunder's lips up into the mass of wrinkles in his cheeks.

"Come," he said. "You will work for me. No other."

A muttering rose from those around for never had Speaks Thunder allowed another to enter his lodge. He had remained alone for as long as those there could remember, an ancient man who had outlived his generation and another besides.

Simon silently followed him to his lodge. They became as one, Simon following beside the old man as he hobbled around the village and into the forest, listening to the words falling softly from the old man's lips. Simon cooked for the old man and swept his lodge clean. He washed his clothes beside the stream, drawing laughter from the women who washed the clothes of their families—except for Badger Woman whose looks of hatred followed Simon wherever he went after her husband stripped her naked and forced her to run through the village, exposing her shame for all to see after he heard about Speaks Thunder's words.

Occasionally, I would come upon them in the forest, Simon sitting cross-legged in front of the old man as he lectured to him.

One hot, summer day, I came upon them deep in the forest next to a stream. I crept closer, slipping into a stand of willows, silently working my way down close to them to hear their words.

The old man sat comfortably on a blanket, sipping water from a gourd. In front of him, Simon sprawled, drawing strange designs in the dirt with a hazel wand. I slipped back into the shadows of a beech tree and stretched out, watching, listening.

"Why do your men give the women the power they have?" Simon asked. "This I understand they have, but this I do not understand."

Speaks Thunder laughed. "Your heart is beginning to become Seneca, but your mind still thinks like a white man, Worm," he said affectionately. "It is not so difficult as you try to make it. Think what a woman is. What a woman really is and not what a man would like her to be or thinks her to be." He pointed to a walnut tree growing behind Simon. "What is the purpose of that tree?"

"To give nuts for those who need them," Simon replied.

"And who needs the nuts?" asked Speaks Thunder.

"The squirrels. Man," answered Simon.

"Is that the only purpose of the tree?" the old man asked.

Simon furrowed his brow, thinking. "It does give shade," he said doubtfully.

"Ah," answered the old man. "Yes, it does. It comforts us in the heat of the day. Its wood gives us warmth in the winter. When it dies, it returns to the earth to help other seedlings grow. So, what is the purpose of the tree?"

"All things," Simon said slowly. "Everything."

"Yes," Speaks Thunder said. "And since you have answered so well, you may gather some of the nuts and some berries and I will show you how to make a paste for pemmican tonight. But before you do that, perhaps it would be a good idea to take your friend who lies in the shadows of the willows behind us and see if you can catch any fish for our dinner."

I rose, blushing from my place on the ground and came forward. A slight smile tilted Simon's lips.

"I am sorry, Speaks Thunder," I said apologetically. "I was only curious."

"That is the first step towards wisdom," the old man said. "One can know many things, but using that knowledge is a gift that few have. But tell me: wouldn't it be easier to join us than to hide in the shadows?"

"Yes, it would," I said. "But I did not wish to intrude."

"There is no intrusion if one wishes to learn," he said. "Only if one seeks to disrupt is there intrusion."

"I will remember that," I said.

"Good." His eyes twinkled as he looked back and forth between us. "And while you are catching fish and picking nuts and berries, you might walk a bit to the south where there is a dead tree and see if you cannot bring life from it."

"Of course," Simon said. He nudged me and I turned to follow him from the clearing as the old man leaned back contentedly against the oak behind him.

"I'm not Christ," I said to Simon when we had gone a safe distance from the old man so that I knew my words would not carry to him. "How are we going to bring life to a dead tree?"

"We're not," he said. "You weren't listening. He

said to bring life from it. There's a difference."

I held my tongue and followed him to a small clearing. A dead oak stood in the middle, its top half split and jagged from a lightning bolt. Bees buzzed around it.

"I think I understand," I said dryly. "Honey, correct?"

"Yes," Simon said. "And how are we going to get it?"

"Smoke," I answered, adding, "and fast feet. We'll make them sluggish with smoke, but we won't get all of them. We'll have to run for the creek before they come around."

He grinned and began gathering dead moss, piling it around the base of the tree. On top of that, he piled green moss, then took tinder and steel and struck sparks. The tree was hollow inside and drew like a chimney. Soon, we were sticky from honey, our hands filled with the comb as we raced for the creek. I paused to drop my burden on a small hummock of green grass before diving into the creek and swimming under a small bank overhang. My back smarted from a dozen bee stings and I rolled against the mud of the bank, relishing the coolness against the hot needles. Moments later, Simon joined me.

"Many stings?" I panted. He laughed.

"A couple," he admitted.

"Do you suppose we're not thinking of

something?" I mused.

"Probably. But isn't that part of learning? Getting stung? We'll figure another way next time."

"Hmm. I think I already have," I answered. "We'll get somebody else to get the honey like Speaks Thunder did."

He laughed and swam away, deep under water, drifting down the stream. I kept pace with him, twisting like an otter.

Many days passed in this manner as I joined Simon and Speaks Thunder during the day. Not long after this, Simon asked Speaks Thunder about the Confederation of tribes.

"Once," the old man said, settling himself against an oak tree, "we were always fighting. Bloody and endlessly, constantly fighting. It was not good, but no one could see a way to stop it. Many women cried for a long time in their lodges for their sons and husbands killed in one battle or another.

"But one day, Deganawidah, a holy man who was born of a virgin mother, spoke out against the horror and outrage of the war that he saw with his own eyes. That night, he went to sleep under a Tree of Great Peace, much like this one under which we sit now. There, he had a vision in which he saw the Five Nations drawn together. The Iroquois, Deganawidah argued in council after council, must cease fighting with each other. They must unite under the sheltering branches of the Tree of Great Peace and live in harmony and justice by forming a law that all would obey.

"There was a Mohawk named Hiawatha who became Deganawidah's follower. He spread the message himself, traveling from one tribe to another among the Nations. Finally, all agreed with Hiawatha and a great council for all the chiefs of the five Iroquois tribes was called.

"The laws and customs that were to be maintained were agreed upon and each of the Five Nations clasped the hands of their sister tribes so firmly that a falling tree could not sever them.

"Thus, the Confederacy of the Iroquois was born among the Mohawks, the Oneidas, the Onondagas, the Cayugas, and the Senecas. At the first council, it was decided that the Onondagas would be the fire-keepers and from that time on, all the great councils would be held at Onondaga. These people were to call in the other tribes each year to discuss their differences, and maintain the Great Peace.

"The Onondagas also became the wampum keepers, that which was made to be given to show the truth and peace of one's heart," he added.

"How long ago did this happen?" I asked.

"A long time ago," he asked. "Long before your people came to this land, long before the first great ships came. And each tribe had its own land that it worked and cared for. And longhouses for each clan

31

that they covered with elm bark. First, there were the clans, the Eagle clan, the Heron clan, the Wolf clan, the Beaver clan. From this, the women gave birth to the men and gave them the power to rule over their clans."

"And that is why they are the ones who elect the Council?" Simon asked. Speaks Thunder nodded.

"Oh yes. Men rule, but only as much as women will let them," he said, smiling. "It is the women who elect and dismiss the Council. But that is only right for it is they who bring life into the world. Therefore, they should rule that life. They are the ones who take care of the fields as well for when it is time for the earth to give birth to beans and squash and sunflower, there is the need for a woman to deliver the birth."

"I see," Simon said. "Then, why do not the women hunt and kill?"

"Because they are bringers of life. Man is the destroyer," Speaks Thunder said patiently. "Now, I am tired and this is enough for the day. Go, and gather some wood for tonight. I feel that there will be frost in the morning and my bones do not like the cold anymore." Obediently, Simon and I rose and went into the woods to gather dead wood for Speaks Thunder's fire.

Those days that were filled with teaching and learning were happy days. I felt fortunate to be included in Simon's teaching. But I did not know what secrets the old man taught him during the night. Ancient secrets.

Chapter Five

A tall gray stone stands outside the door to my cabin. On summer days, I like to rest against it, feeling the warmth through its hard surface. Its hardness is comforting, and I know it as an old friend. When I leave, it is like leaving an old friend behind who will vigilantly watch over my cabin and be waiting there to welcome me upon my return.

Sometimes, I do not find any game in the woods and am forced to return, tired and hungry, to my cabin. My spirits are immediately lifted when I see the stone, and I know the next day I will find game.

Out on the lake below the knoll upon which my cabin stands, the waters roar, turgid and wild, great whitecaps furiously rushing towards the shore to crash forcefully upon the land, battering it with the ferocity of a vengeful army, flinging up in its mist figures of dancing horses and fluttering pennants. This is how I like it: wild and unspoiled. Ships trying to navigate the shoals at such times are doomed to die upon the jagged rocks barely visible in the boiling mist.

My soul is at ease.

I feel that by staring into the seething cauldron, I am staring into the bowels of the earth and seeing the past laid out before me.

Esau grows restless and whines in his dreams as his great paws twitch in desire to be free of the cabin and roam the woods. He needs no reason; the rain and the wind, the sun and the moon, the grass and the trees, all are reason enough.

I wish I could enter his dreams, but I am too old, too old. My dreams belong in the past. I look towards the East, but I see only the gray wall of the squall moving over the lake. Beyond that wall is my former world, a world of memories, a useless exercise in nostalgia. But, that is how it should be for if those memories ever again become reality. . . .

I pull my book of memories from its niche beside the fireplace. Esau opens one eye at my movement, recognizes the book in my hands, and grunts with contentment as I open the book and begin to read aloud to him. . . .

Game was in abundant supply in those days on land or in water. One usually had only to travel a few miles from anyone's camp to replenish the larder—a rabbit, deer, trout, or bass. If one was good enough, one could swim underwater to snatch the odd mallard or goose from beneath the waves. When game began to thin out in one area, the Indians formed hunting parties to go on long treks to hunt and bring back the game.

Morning   mist   and   fog   dampened   the

mountainsides. A cathedral quiet made one feel in deep communion with an omniscient being. All creatures seemed hushed in prayer. From far away, one heard the quiet gurgle of running water singing an endless paean to pagan and Christian alike.

A little over a year after Simon came to the Senecas, we were allowed to accompany a hunting party to the North. Although each of us had previously accompanied smaller hunting parties on overnight trips, this would be the first time we had been allowed together on a long hunt. Simon and I anxiously waited for the moment to get away from the camp even though we knew that we would only be the butchers for any game the party found.

We hurried from the camp, eager to get deep into the cool woods among the oaks and ashes. We climbed the mountains and descended the other side. Lower down in the forest, we came upon an old trail along a large creek that twisted around ancient bedding grounds past a salt lick. A sense of freedom filled our spirits. The air smelled cleaner, the colors glowed brighter, and we began to move slowly, rambling more than trekking, through the woods. Far away, a grouse called and we waited eagerly for our first sightings, but we saw no game that first day. We were not concerned for we knew it was to be a long hunt. But after the third day and having found nothing but old spoor, the hunters' humor began to disappear. Our provisions had begun to run out. Simon caught two fish with his hands in the creek and I managed to knock a squirrel from a tree with a rock, but two fish and one squirrel are not enough meat for a hunting party of twelve men. Our bellies began to ache with hunger even though we tried to keep them full with nuts and berries and cold water from the creek.

The sixth day we worked our way along a small feeder stream. Suddenly the leader paused and raised his hand. A certain thrill rapidly spread through the group. Then I heard it: not game, but the solid *chunk!* of an axe settling into wood. With a sudden bitterness, I knew what had happened to the game.

Slowly, we crept up to a clearing and peered through a tangle of vines and leaves at two cabins in a small clearing. The wind blew in our faces, keeping our scent from the dogs. The men and older boys worked on the far side of the clearing, cutting back the forest. The women chattered among themselves as they dipped candles while the young children tended a fire under a large kettle.

I stared at the clearing for a long moment as anger slowly built a raging fire inside of me. A fog seemed to creep over the clearing, and I felt I was looking upon my own death, each cut of an axe into the trunk of a tree a slice gouged from my own body, my own soul. Suddenly a scream seemed to surge from my lungs. Only it wasn't my lungs but rather the lungs of our group. They leaped into the clearing, war axes and hunting knives gleaming brightly in the forest light.

Within moments, it was over, and I found myself standing dazed in the center of the clearing, torn bodies turning the gray of the day into a crimson nightmare. I heard a whimper through the ringing in my ears and looked down at a young girl fearfully clutching my buckskin-clad leg. A bloody smear on her forehead gave her a barbaric look. I glanced around the clearing and suddenly found myself looking into two burning pits of hatred: Simon's eyes. With an effort, he pulled himself back from whatever hell he had entered. He glanced around the blood-spattered clearing and gestured weakly, a frown creasing his forehead.

"I heard it," he said lamely.

"What?" I asked.

He looked uncomprehendingly at me and shook his head. "Her. Screaming."

"Which one?" I asked, glancing automatically around.

"No. No," he said. He made an impatient gesture and shook his head. "This. Everything. Her death cry. Her wails." His eyes clouded and slowly, I realized he was not lamenting the deaths of the settlers.

"You heard nothing?"

"No," I said cautiously. "I heard nothing. Only the beating of my own heart."

"Yes," he said. "Yes. That's what I mean." He pointed at the Indians who had led the charge now wandering aimlessly around the clearing, their eyes slowly fading to dullness as they tried to comprehend what had happened. "I think they heard it, too."

I shuddered and looked away, knowing I had just looked into the deep abyss of my soul.

Logic escaped me. I could not comprehend the mystery that had just taken place. For the rest of the hunt, I moved silently with the hunters through the dark woods, afraid for the first time of what could be around me. Once, my heart nearly stopped when I looked off into the gloomy shadows and saw a wolf staring at me, his lantern yellow eyes glowing eerily. Another time I thought I saw the humped shoulder of a bear disappearing around a large boulder followed shortly by a panther, his gleaming skin rippling in the dappled shadows of the trees. But I could not be sure.

When we returned to the village, I kept a close eye upon Simon, watching carefully as he worked hard at the tasks given him. Slowly, the men took notice of his diligence, of his attention to even the most menial task given him, and began to take him for walks by the creek that ran by the village, curling its way deep into the forest. I began to follow them whenever I could sneak away from my chores.

Chapter Six

A ship almost capsized last night as it tried to brave the shoals during a spring storm that suddenly swooped down from the North following a cold spell. I watched for hours before the skipper gave up and came about to head for deeper waters.

Sometimes, I think I would rather be buried at sea than stuck in the earth as fodder for blind worms, but then I recall the fish and am heartened that at least my body will still be working in the mulch left in the earth by worms long after the dung of fish has joined the sterile sediment on the sea bed.

The earth began to smell a little today; a sweet, rotten smell from the piles of dead leaves in the forest. A couple of squirrels build a nest in the trees at the rear of my cabin. A flight of geese heads north to their nesting grounds. The lake seems higher from the winter run-off. Even Esau feels spring stirrings for he paces restlessly from the hearth to the door and back, breaking the silence with pathetic little whines as he casts longing looks at my rifle and powder horn hanging above the mantle.

Yesterday, John Keogh, my soldier friend visited to see how I had weathered the winter and left a smoked ham. I am grateful; not simply for the food, but for the visit and conversation. He listens patiently while I tell him about the thoughts and ideas I have developed over the winter. He is also my *"Gazette"* and supplies me with the news I have missed. Esau enjoys his coming, too, but makes a point of staying close to my leg during the whole of the soldier's visit.

I think he fears the soldier will take him away.

"Well," my friend says, sinking into the chair across from mine. He reaches for the glass of wine I have poured for him. "And how have you been?"

"A bit alone," I say, smiling and relaxing against the fur pelts forming a cushion on my chair. I motion towards the parcels he has dumped on the table: a few books, a couple of jugs of wine and brandy, a ham. "Thank you for the supplies."

Keogh laughs and looks around the cabin at the shelves crammed with books. He cranes his head, reading some of the titles: *The Farmer's Alamanc, Aristotle's Masterpiece* (pornography not published by the philosopher), *The Life and Memorable Actions of George Washington, The Wild Irish Girl, Salmagundi: Or the Whim-Whams and Opinions of Launcelot Langstaff, Esq.* haphazardly piled on top of others: *Paradise Lost, Paradise Regained, Samson Agonistes,* the plays of Shakespeare and Christopher Marlowe. I read for there is little else for an old man to do.

"You're welcome," he says. A grin tilts the

corners of his lips. "But, you've paid for them many times over."

I wave away his reference, feeling a bit of embarrassment. Keogh's father had taken ill while he was assigned to duty here and I had pressed a small bag of gold upon him to help with expenses. He had tried to refuse it, but I pointed out that I had little use for it. Since then, he made it a point to visit me often, bringing me little things in appreciation which I valued more than the gold.

"And, what news do you have?" I asked.

He laughs, his eyes twinkling. He stretches out his legs towards the fire and sips from his wine. He rubs his hand over his red hair, tousling it.

"Well, let me see." He pretends to think, then says, "The French have been driven out from Portugal. A bad thing for Napoleon. We hope, anyway. Perhaps that will take a little pressure off the government back home."

"Why?" I ask. "What's wrong?"

He sighs and shakes his head. "We're having a bit of trouble with workers. Or," he amends, "those who were workers. I'm afraid that steam engine and the power looms are causing a bit of a problem in Manchester."

"Oh?" I gesture towards the bottle on the table and he nods. I stretch across the small space separating us and refill his glass, then mine. "Watt's engine is causing a few problems after all?"

He smiles ruefully. "You predicted that one, you old rascal. How did you ever do that?"

"Simple," I answer. "You must always ask purpose. We knew that the steam engine had been built, but having an engine serves no purpose unless it can be utilized. What better, than to make it do the work of an animal? Or person?"

"Well," he says grimly, "in this case, it is causing havoc back home. Some people have built power looms that can weave cloth much faster and cheaper than the women can in their cottages. . . ."

I wave away his explanation. We covered that during his last meeting when I had suggested that the loss of income for the farmers who had depended upon the cloth their wives and daughters wove during the winter months would be disastrous. It had been all too predictable from the flying shuttle made by John Kay to the steam engines developed by James Watt and Matthew Boulton.

"And?" I prompt.

"A group of workers calling themselves 'Luddites' have been raging around the countryside, rioting against the factories," Keogh says glumly.

"Let me guess," I say. "They have been destroying machinery under the presumption that they'll be able to return to the old ways."

"I suppose," he says, shaking his head. "Their

reasoning has been clouded by their rhetoric. And what we have been getting at the post is sketchy at best."

"Then, you have to use your imagination to fill in the gaps," I say absently. I frown. "So, Napoleon's defeat in Portugal is giving England a chance to draw her breath. Hmm."

"Napoleon has big problems," my soldier friend says. "He is not invulnerable after all."

"No," I say absently. "But, he is brilliant. Twisted, perhaps, but brilliant nevertheless. Watch for him to invade Russia next."

"What?" He shakes his head in amusement. "Now, why would he do that?"

"To secure one flank from attack," I answer. "Otherwise, he'll have to spread his armies too thin to do him any good when he renews his war with England."

"Ah, Jonathon!" He laughs gently. "We should hire you for His Majesty's Privy Council."

"I wouldn't take it," I say firmly. "I'm retired. I only speculate, nothing more."

"Oh, I almost forgot," he says. "His Majesty King George has been declared insane. The Prince of Wales is now ruling in his place as regent."

"Oh?" I frown. "That should cause some changes. The good Prince has been making strange friends of late, if what you told me at our last visit is correct. I wonder what he'll do now? He needs to get backing if he wishes to continue to rule."

"Continue? After George is declared insane?"

"Rulers have always been a bit insane," I say. "That is a luxury for them and a need. It shows their total domination over their people."

"This is a bit different, I suspect," Keogh says, finishing his wine.

"Perhaps," I say. "But the problem is that kings are not ordinary people; they have the faith of their people behind them; a faith supported by Divine Right. George may be imprisoned for now because he is insane, but do not look for that to last. The people want a king, not a regent. And, the prince's friends are not the king's friends. I think you will see George suddenly cured of his madness."

"We'll see," he laughs, rising. "I have learned to respect your speculations. You've been right too many times in the past for me to second-guess you on this. May I bring you anything on my next visit?"

I shake my head as I follow him to the door. "You do enough by bringing me the news," I say. "Although I reject the world, I still find a bit of comfort in knowing that it hasn't disintegrated during my absence from it."

I watch in envy as he moves quickly and lithely along the path leading to the fort. I once could walk that same path with the same jaunty step, the same confidence. But now, now I must be content with ambling, conscious of my steps to keep from falling.

For some reason, the forest seems to be calling me. I walk as far as the stream and think about setting a fish trap while Esau chases butterflies. But, I never move a finger to work save to peel the bark from a limber willow switch to occupy my hands while a strange restlessness makes me nervous.

Suddenly, Esau bounds to my side and stares back towards the cabin, hackles raised, a low rumble emitting from his deep chest. Alarmed, I let the willow stick slip between my fingertips to the ground. I kneel beside him, tangling my fingers deep into his fur to keep him close as he strains forward.

"What is it, Esau?" I whisper. "Where?"

Boughs rustle at the far end of the clearing. Esau pulls harder against my fingers, growls growing louder, becoming rage. My fingers slip from his fur as the figure steps into the clearing. I catch a glimpse of the black cassock and yell, "Esau! No! Hold!"

Esau's hundred and thirty-odd pounds catch the priest square in the chest, driving him backwards to the ground. But the mastiff holds, paws pinning the priest to a pile of dead leaves, lips drawn back in a throaty snarl, strings of slobber dripping onto the startled face.

"Back, boy," I command as I hurry forward. Reluctantly, Esau moves backwards, stiff-legged, eyes hopeful that the figure will try some mischief to justify another attack.

"Are you hurt?" I ask anxiously. Silver-rimmed spectacles lay a-skew across a heavily-tanned broad face with a light dusting of silver in black hair. A faint tracing of veins maps its way across his heavy cheeks and bulbous nose.

"Faith, by God!" he gasps and raises thick fingers to re-settle the spectacles. He takes a deep breath. "Aye. At least, it's after thinking I am although me breastbone is nigh married to me backbone." He peers accusingly at me. "And why would you be wanting to set the hound upon me? 'Tis not very hospitable you are."

"I didn't," I say. I move back away from him to sit on my haunches. "Esau! Down!" Reluctantly, he moves to lay beside me, a quiet, warning rumble still rolling from his chest. "We do not receive many visitors in the woods," I explain. "Those who approach without warning are usually plotting no good. Wicklow?"

Bushy eyebrows shoot up in surprise. "'Tis a keen ear you have, Lad."

"Stop it," I say in irritation. "I am at least twenty-five years older than you, and I am not Irish. Nor am I in a mood to humor faith-found bog-trotters seeking to bring my soul to an act of contrition. You are trespassing. In more ways than one," I add. "I do not need, nor do I want, any of the fish-foundering tales you feed the poor, ignorant savages to bring them face-to-face with bread masquerading as the flesh of a god.

47

Did you ever consider that you were bringing nothing new to these people with your Christian cannibalism? They've been eating the flesh of their enemies for years."

His face flushes darkly at the insult. "Apostate from hell," he sputters angrily and lapses quickly into silence as a warning rumble rises from Esau's chest.

"Foolish. Where else would an apostate come from? And," I add as Esau inches closer, "I would begin to act a bit more friendly if I were you. Esau's quite protective. Who are you?"

"Father Sean O'Meara," he says sullenly, casting wary eyes at Esau. "I was just after paying a wee friendly visit."

"Jesuit?"

"Aye. Will you be calling off your hound?"

"Um. Bad. That's bad."

"What?"

"You being a Jesuit. I have little use for them. Let him up, Esau. Down!"

O'Meara cautiously rises, his eyes never straying from Esau. Erect, he brushes off his cassock awkwardly. Esau ceases to growl but still watches him carefully.

"And what," he asks, "will you be having against the Jesuits? What harm has befallen you from their presence?"

"Their zealousness," I answer. "They strengthen

their souls by robbing others of theirs in the name of salvation. They do not realize that man's soul is in a state of grace until he recognizes there is a god."

"Sure, and wasn't I told you were an educated man? But what they are not telling me, Jonathon Francis Huntington, is the mysticism of your belief." He crosses himself and eyes me suspiciously. "Is it sedition you'll be preaching? or theosophy?"

I laughed and stand. Esau moves protectively in front of me, forcing the priest back a step.

"Ah, yes," I say, feeling delight bubble up within me at his discomfort. "I was brought up in the service of the one in whose army you so diligently serve, but soon saw that the world I belonged to did not do Him service from love, but from fear, secretly betraying Him the moment the priest pronounced the week's last 'amen.' Here, in the forest, no man cowers before a false altar; no man dares to profess to be what he is not. Here, our prayers are secret prayers that come from the heart for a natural Master and friend and our prayers are answered in the game He sends us, the fruit He breathes life into, the seeds He raises from the soil. Can your God do as much?"

As I speak, his lips grow thinner and thinner, twin lines of distaste appearing between his eyes. He looks sternly upon me and says, "Be careful, John Francis! 'Tis close to blasphemy you are preaching! Is it a belief in the Devil you are professing?"

Suddenly, I am tired with the banter. A great weariness begins to descend upon me. "Would you care for a cup of coffee?" I ask, hearing a giant tremor in my words. Esau turns his head and looks anxiously at me. I rub my fingers reassuringly through his hair. He whines uneasily.

"Are you feeling ill?" O'Meara asks, concern edging his words.

He moves closer, peering intently into my eyes. His words seem faint and distant. A darkness enters the edge of my vision accompanied by the beating of a thousand bat wings. A low keening rises from the depths of the woods behind me.

"Simon," I whisper as the keening grows louder. I pitch forward upon my face. I smell the sour earth and feel the press of dead leaves upon my cheek as the beating bat wings become a roar and darkness rushes over me.

Chapter Seven

I gag. A burning draught drips down my throat. Weakly I push at the hand holding the vile potion to my lips.

"Drink!" a voice commands gently. Obediently, I open my lips and feel the burning again, this time tasting a familiar afterbite: brandy, and a far better vintage than I had in the cabin. I open my eyes and stare into the concerned eyes of a priest, bright blue beneath bushy eyebrows like brambles. For a moment, my mind reels in confusion as it tries to register the reality against the impossibility of heaven. I feel the familiar softness of Hudson Bay blankets beneath me, and a wet tongue lapping the side of my face. I turn to look at Esau, and the priest's name jolts simultaneously into place.

"How," I ask hoarsely, pausing to try and clear my throat. "How did you get me here?"

"I carried you," he says matter-of-factly. "How do you feel?"

"Poorly." I look at the plump frame beneath his cassock and wonder at the strength it hides to carry the dead weight of a six-foot man nearly two hundred pounds a couple hundred yards through a dense forest.

Esau whines and drapes a huge paw upon my chest.

"Has this happened before?" O'Meara asks.

"No." I try to smile. "But I've been expecting it. Thank you."

"You're welcome." He ducks his head and looks around the cabin to hide his embarrassment. I wonder: all the other Jesuits I have known strutting arrogantly around the Indian camps, spouting suppurating supralapsarianisma were more than eager to claim credit for having done someone a service for a two-fold purpose: one, to put that person in debt and, two, to count off another credit on the rosary beads they wore as a brave did his belt of scalps. Maybe, I think, I have done this man a disservice by looking only at his robe and not at the man beneath it.

"A fine place," he says. I can tell from the warmth in his words that he means it. "It reminds me of a shaggy den. I like it."

I look around at the pelts hanging upon the walls between collages of birds' wings and Indian beadwork. A large woodcarving of an owl in oak sits on a shelf near the door like a pagan icon which, in a way, I suppose it is: my Seneca name loosely translated being "Nightwind" and my symbol the owl for He-Is-Wise-Who-Flies-Under-Cover-Of-Night. My crude furniture, unlike the delicate furniture resting upon spindly Queen Anne legs in the Georgian homes of Boston and Philadelphia, serves no purpose other than functional and comfortable.

"Yes," he says again, thoughtfully as if to reassure himself of his decision. "Yes, a den." He pulls a small breviary from an inside pocket and sits in the chair in front of the fireplace. He opens it and looks at me, a wry grin breaking across his face. "Should I offer a prayer of thanks for your return?"

"Don't bother," I answer. "He who would have had my soul would have kept it. May I have some water, please?"

"Of course," he says hurriedly. He rises and crosses to the bucket and dipper I keep on a small table next to a cupboard serving as my pantry tucked into a small alcove formed by a wall and the side of my fireplace. "I should have thought that it would be water you'd be needing not prayer," he adds wryly.

He fills the dipper and brings it to me. I drink thirstily and hand it back to him.

"More?"

I shake my head.

"No, thank you," I say, resting back against my blankets. "I think sleep. Will you stay?"

"Are you inviting me?" he gently asks.

"Yes I say tiredly. "You'll find fresh venison hanging in the lean-to at the rear of the cabin. Please remember to feed Esau as well."

"Is it sure you are in your mind?" he asked again. "'Tis not dangerous to your soul for me to remain here?"

"I do not think my Master will mind," I say. "He may look upon it as a challenge. But that's enough of your probing, Priest. You don't know me well enough to try for conversion."

He grins sheepishly. "'Twas worth a try. Sure, and I hope you'll be bearing me no hard feelings."

"No," I say, yawning. "Everyone is entitled to a little dishonesty—especially those with the heaviest crosses to bear. Will you wait while I rest?"

"Yes," he says. "And be sure that I'll be a-feeding your hound as well."

"You'd better," I say, closing my eyes. I feel the darkness waiting. "He's very partial to priests."

I do not catch his reply but welcome the embrace of the darkness like a warm coverlet.

I must have dreamed for when I awake hours later, thirsty and more tired than refreshed, I cannot remember the dream and after a drink I again fall asleep, feeling that something portentous has entered the cabin.

Chapter Eight

The sun rides high in the sky when I again awake, refreshed and anxious to leave my bed. O'Meara has thrown wide the door and windows to let in the fresh smells of the earth and trees and the sounds of the lake. A flight of geese flies by overhead, the noise of their passing making Esau whine and quiver with excitement. He looks anxiously at me, but I do not respond to the pleading in his eyes. I need a bit more time to rest before taking to the woods again.

A delightful smell of rich venison stew curls out of a pot hanging from the cauldron hooks anchored in the stone of the fireplace. Beneath the smell of gravy, I smell fresh coffee, and my mouth waters as my stomach rumbles with hunger.

"'Tis pleased I am that you are up," O'Meara says, beaming. He lays his breviary upon the table, rises, and crosses to my bed. He feels my forehead and nods with satisfaction. "No fever. I worried after that. How d'you feel?"

"A bit stiff," I admit, cautiously moving from beneath the blankets. "Especially my left side." His forehead wrinkles in concern.

"Can you feel this?" He pinches my arm hard. I

feel the pressure but no pain. I admit as much. He sighs.

"Ah, yes," he says. "'Tis as I feared. It's stroke I've been thinking you had. But, take heart: apparently it was not serious."

"Then perhaps we could have something to eat?" I ask, looking longingly at the simmering pot. He laughs.

"Well, perhaps a wee taste would hasten the healing," he admits, a twinkle lifting the tiredness from his eyes. "But, not a feast, not a feast, I'm telling you. 'Twould not be healthy to gorge your gullet so soon upon rising from a sick bed."

"Then," I say, gesturing towards the cupboard, "be sure to use the large plates."

He laughs and bustles around the cabin, setting the table. I reach for the wall and lever myself upright and limp to the doorway to stand in the sunshine. The world seems quiet with only a slight breath of the wind and the distant, cheerful chatter of the forest informing me it is still alive. New green grass peeks through the coarse brown of last year's grasses. I breath deeply and my eyes burned with a strange thankfulness. I look up and across the lake and wish thoughts to which I have no right. I sigh, and re-enter the cabin.

"There is something you can do for me." O'Meara says as he helps me to a chair.

"I thought we settled that," I say a bit crabbily. "I do not wish to appear ungrateful but . . ."

"Tell me about Simon Girty," he said, interrupting.

I stare at him, conscious of the quiet, of Esau's breathing. I look into his eyes, trying to read his soul, but the days have passed when I could do that with ease and living where I do, I do not receive many visitors upon whom I can practice. I look hard for the swift little change of light in his eyes, the sudden rise of red in his cheek, but he meets my stare, calmly masking reason behind his awareness of the obligation he has placed upon me. It is such a little thing he has asked: or is it?

"Why?"

"I wish to know the man," he says.

I shake my head.

"Very well. I understand," he says, and bows his head to give grace. "I'll leave you alone. I really must be getting back to my duties."

An uneasiness spreads through me as I try to move my legs beneath the table. They respond stiffly, and I know that I am not ready to be left alone, yet. I swallow my pride and carefully chose my words.

"No," I say. "You do not. I do you a bigger favor by not telling you. Such knowledge is dangerous."

"To whom?" he asks, spooning venison in his mouth. He chews quickly, his mouth open, sucking on air to cool the chunk of meat.

"To your soul," I say quietly.

"And you care for my soul?" he asks, swallowing and cooling his mouth with a draught of water.

I shrug and try to pick up my fork. It slips away and clatters upon the smooth planks of the table. A tiny smile curls his lips.

"Here," he says, sliding my plate across to him. "Let me help."

With deft strokes, he slices my meat into tiny chunks, then pushes the plate back to me. I pick up my spoon, holding it awkwardly in my fist like a baby. Frustration builds within me, but I am hungry and I push the spoon around on my plate until I pick up meat and gravy.

"Why don't you tell me? What do you have to lose?"

His eyes rise and hold mine, mesmerizing with their intentness like a snake with a bird. A familiar burning races along my veins. The years begin to slough off my shoulders, and dimly, as if from far away, I hear my voice begin . . . .

Chapter Nine

Three weeks after the ill-fated hunting trip, Simon found me setting fish traps in the Susquehanna. I ignored him, concentrating instead upon anchoring the willow basket cages in the gravel bottom. He watched silently from the bank for a few minutes then suddenly stripped and waded into the water to help. I looked at him in surprise: we had not spoken since our return from the hunting trip and massacre. Something had come between us, linking us together. Perhaps a baptism? I don't know. Something, and it disturbed me for I could find no logical reason for the strange feelings moving within me. An awakening, if you will.

"Thanks," I said roughly. "But I can manage." He laughed, his eyes crinkling with amusement. He ignored my protests and took a woven willow basket and anchored it firmly deep into the river bed.

"You've been troubled," he said while his fingers probed the gravel. "What is it? The settlers?"

"Yes," I said. "And the part we played in it."

"You mean," he said, a sly smile playing around his lips, "how you felt."

"Yes, " I said. Angrily, I slashed the water with a willow switch. "Yes! What need was there for their deaths? And the children!" I said disgustedly. "What manner of men have we become when we condone the slaughter of children? We were pagans offering sacrifices to Moloch!"

"Yes, I suppose that is one way to understand what happened," Simon said. He picked up another trap and moved a few yards downstream. He took a deep breath and went beneath the waters to place the trap. He emerged blowing like a whale.

"I suppose you have found a mystical justification for that slaughter?" I said scathingly. He shook his head, the smile still playing upon his lips.

"I do not have your education, Jonathon, but, then, neither do you have mine. I do not pretend to know philosophy. I can read and sum, but not like you. This I do know: more evil is done in the name of Good than is done in the name of Evil. Did you ever stop to think what those settlers had done?"

I shook my head. "I do not think the little wood they cut harmed anyone."

"No?" The smile slipped from his face, twin frown lines appearing across his forehead. His eyes began to burn with a hypnotic intensity. "How about the starvation of a whole people? Would you say the destruction of a people would be cause enough?"

"Exaggeration," I muttered, and moved away with another trap to set. He grabbed my shoulder with a broad, calloused hand and pulled me around. I winced from the force of his grip.

"Why do you think we had to go so far afield to find game? Those settlers drove it away. Clearing the forest will keep it from coming back. Even this river will soon be destroyed by them. When that happens, the Senecas will die a slow, painful death. The Senecas are hunters, not farmers. If they try to become farmers, then their spirit will die. Soon, the village will have to move, for it needs the game to survive. But even these savages know that there is only so much land to which they can move. After that, they will have to die. Do you know how hard it is to know your children will have to die?"

"But senseless slaughter...that cannot be excused!" I said hotly.

"Try judging the Senecas by their ways, not by yours," he quietly said. "To them, the only evil in the forest is brought there by the white man. I think they are probably right."

"Romantic disillusionment!" I said loftily. "You're too young.... "

"To know what I'm saying?" He laughed. "Maybe. Maybe." He turned to wade ashore, then stopped and looked over his shoulder. "But then I haven't seen as much of the world as you." I flushed at his jibe. He laughed and stepped from the river. He pulled up a handful of moss to dry himself, then paused, considering me still standing in the river.

"I have seen Philadelphia, and once Boston,

when Turner had to go pick up a shipment of trading goods. I have seen the rudeness and the deceit practiced in that world. Here," he swept his arm around him, "here, there is only honesty. Man's life depends upon being honest. I think that when man's life becomes too easy, he finds it less convenient to be truthful." He shrugged and pulled on his breeches and hunting shirt. He ran his thick, square fingers through his long, black hair, forcing it behind his ears to dry. "Tell me, truthfully, now: in which world were you happiest? This one or the one that you left behind?"

Indecision must have made itself apparent in my face, for he laughed mockingly and stepped lightly into the bushes behind him, merging instantly with the forest. I listened carefully but could not follow his passage.

"Drivel," I sniffed. "What argument can exemplify savagery, make murder honorable? Do you expect me to believe faulty logic?" I shouted to the trees. A mourning dove answered me. My legs began to shake from the cold of the rushing water. I bent to my task.

Chapter Ten

The rosy fingers of dawn had yet to appear over the tops of the trees when a hand gently shook me from sleep. I fought myself awake from the warm pile of skins serving as my pallet.

"What is it?" I asked alarmed. A low throaty chuckle answered me, and Simon's teeth gleamed in the darkness.

"Come," he whispered. "Before you wake the others." He turned and slipped through the hut's entrance.

"They're already awake," I muttered, catching the watchful whites of eyes gleaming from across the room. I slid from my pallet and followed him outside. I shivered in the early morning and gingerly stepped over the light frost dusting the grass beneath our feet. Rustlings in the forest told me dawn was not far off. My flesh pebbled; I shook, drawing in large gulps of cold air, feeling the pure and clean bite in my lungs.

"Well?" I asked crankily, remembering the warm pallet I had just left. "What do you want?"

"This, is to be the day of our birth. We must begin preparation," he said somberly.

How he had convinced the Senecas to adopt us

into their tribe, I do not know. The custom with prisoners had been to either kill them or to take them as slaves—usually into some family that had lost a father or son. But to adopt one as a warrior? I had never heard of that happening even among other tribes whenever we assembled during the time of the Council of the Six Nations. Often, I had observed Simon squatting on his haunches, earnestly speaking with younger braves about the land and hunting and how things had changed since the white men had moved into the Ohio River Valley. More than once, I marveled at his strength when packing deer from the forest and the willingness with which he helped the old people around the village.

Once, I recall, we came upon some unwed maidens washing in the Susquehanna. We sank down behind a thick stand of blackberry bushes and watched them sporting in the water: dusky, naked bodies wet and gleaming, ripe with youth, gracefully twisting through the water with the elegance of the otter. As we watched, I suddenly became aware of the purity of the moment and felt that I was in the presence of something mightier than either of us. The silence of the forest was broken only by their laughter which seemed to be not an alien, human sound but a part of the forest as natural as the birds singing in the early morning among broad-leaved poplars, densely foliated oaks, and maples hugged by wild grape vines. The sun painted dappled patterns on their bodies, making them a part of the wilderness music.

"This," Simon whispered hastily to me, "is what you were searching for all that time you spent among those books. This is what all those writers were trying to tell you."

I could not answer him for my body seemed to have merged with the forest, taut, humming a pristine melody in harmony with the music around us.

It was this, I would imagine later, that gave Simon the oratorical power to influence our captors to adopt him. As for me, well, they selected me to be his companion, a birth-brother, someone with whom Simon had something in common. Not a friend; no, not that, for Simon had no friends, had no need of friends. I was a familiar companion, nothing more.

We spent the morning in a sweathouse undergoing a systematic purging. We emerged from the hut to find two lines of braves armed with sticks forming a long path to the river—a gauntlet we were forced to run before we fell, battered and bruised, into the clean waters. Six maidens joined us to symbolically wash us, scrubbing out the white blood, renewing our veins with the blood of the Senecas. Naked and clean, they led us to the Long House where we stood among the braves before the council fire and were given our new names and taken into our new family. I was not surprised to find Rides-the-Moon clasping my forearm and calling me by my name: Nightwind, the owl my symbol for He-Is-Wise-Who-Flies-Under-Cover-Of-Night. But I could hardly contain my amazement when an elderly Delaware chief, the Six Nations Prophet, hobbled from the shadows, clasped Simon by his forearm, and called him The Chosen.

Quiet murmurings from the younger braves around us showed their pleasure at the Prophet's choice. A Seneca brave I recognized as Rides-the-Moon's cousin approached and laid forest green buckskins sat Simon's feet. Another approached and draped a finely-beaded belt with tomahawk and knife over the buckskins. A third slowly approached and after staring long and hard into Simon's clam gray eyes, hung a sewn bag made of parfleche dyed in a rainbow of brilliant colors—green, blue, purple, gold—around his neck. At that, the lodge erupted in joyous celebration. Drums beat long and hard, sending a wild fire through our veins, and the crier made his rounds through the village singing our new names. We were a part of the tribe, of the forest: I , the companion; Simon, the anointed one.

The Renegade by Randy Lee Eickhoff

Chapter Eleven

Chirruping crickets announce the fall of evening-tide as I wearily pause in my narration to refresh myself from the dipper in the bucket on a small stand by the door. I move to the doorway and lean against the jamb while drinking thirstily of the night, the coolness refreshing me. Overhead, a small flight of mallards coasts late into the small cove and talk contentedly to each other. A fish jumps out in the shoals. Rich, musky smells rise from the earth. The night forest begins to awaken: birds whistling tentative songs, a faint call of a wolf far off yet near enough makes Esau growl deeply in his massive chest only to whine anxiously as a timid doe, followed by a fawn, steps from the forest at the water's edge and bends graceful neck to drink. The faint outline of the full moon glows silver.

Earlier today, while O'Meara was meditating down by the lake, Keogh came to visit, bringing a case of brandy with him. His gray eyes glowed with pleasure as he stepped into the cabin and placed the wooden case on the table with a loud *thump!*.

"Well," he said, his lips spreading in a wide grin. "I see that you are still with us."

"Oh yes," I said. "And no thanks to that bloody

priest."

"And still as cranky," he said. "Good day, John Keogh. 'And how is the bright of the day with you,' you are supposed to say. But no greeting do I get from the likes of you, do I? No. Just a cranky old man ready to begin dribbling his porridge down from his withered lips."

"And I don't need a shanty pretension of an Irishman, either," I said. "I have enough of the real one living with me."

"And speaking of which," he said, sitting. "Have you learned anything further from him?"

"Learned?"

"Why he's here?" he said.

I shook my head and opened one of the brandy bottles, pouring a jot in two glasses, handing him one. "Not much. But I've been giving some thought to it."

"And?" he prompted, taking the glass and sipping with relish. I tasted the brandy: French, from apples, heady and smooth. I crossed to the door and looked out: O'Meara walked slowly along the shore, his hands clasped behind him, the hood of his cassock pulled up against the wind blowing briskly off the lake.

"Well, you are aware that James II issued the Declaration of Liberty of Conscience in 1687 that provided for religious toleration in England," I said, shrugging.

He gestured impatiently again. "Yes, yes. But

William of Orange came in 1688 and the Parliament barred Roman Catholics from the throne in '89."

"But the Toleration Act granted freedom of worship," I said, reminding him again. "I know, I know," I added, holding my hand up to stop his protestations. "Catholics are still regarded with suspicion despite the act." I frowned. "Especially with the Papal Bull *Unigenitus* that condemned the Jansenists in 1713. Hmm."

"And we had the riots against the Catholics in 1780 led by Lord Gordon," he said. "That pretty much limited tolerance of the Catholics. Which brings me to my question: What the bloody hell is he doing here? This is not a major outpost. Yes, we have enough of a force here to be a threat, but face it: we are mainly here to maintain the law in the territory. We are not meant to be a striking force.

"And," he said, warming to his task. "We have no large town or city nearby. Detroit is a long ways from here. So, why would a Catholic, a *Jesuit* Catholic at that, come here?"

"Missionary?" I suggested.

"I don't think so," he answered. "Those positions have pretty well been established. Or done away with," he muttered, sipping again of his brandy. "Remember: the Pope himself disbanded them. They exist in name only."

"Except in Russia," I said absently. "And a few

places like that."

"He's here after something," Keogh said, finishing his brandy and rising. "I sent a dispatch to Detroit asking for clarification. Maybe we'll have something back soon on that."

"Perhaps," I answered.

"So, you have nothing?"

"No. All he seems to do is question me about Simon Girty and the Nations."

Interest sparked in his eyes. "Oh? Nothing more? Just that?"

I nodded. "He seems to be taking an historical interest in what we did during the conflict. But, I don't think he's a historian. There is something behind his interest. I can't put my finger upon it, but there is some reason behind his interest."

"Keep listening and watching," he said, gathering his hat and crossing to the door. "He has an agenda; of that, I'm positive. But watch yourself as well. Just because he's a priest doesn't mean that he's adverse to treachery. Remember the Borgias."

"I'll be careful," I promised, then grinned. "But, what can an old man do?"

He laughed derisively. "If we had more old men like you, then we might have been able to keep the Colonies."

"You don't have any plans to renew that conflict, do you?" I ask.

He straightened and looked at me closely. The air sparked with sudden tension.

"Has he mentioned anything along those lines?"

"Then, you are planning something," I said, grinning.

"Well?"

"Speculation only," I answered. "But, perhaps that is why he is here?"

"But, why?" he stared moodily down at O'Meara, then heaved a sigh. "Ah, it's a will o' the wisp. I'll bring books next time, if the supply ship gets back from Detroit by then."

My reverie is broken as behind me, the Jesuit sighs and I hear the long skirts of his cassock rustle as he rises and crosses to the small pantry where he has stored a brandy bottle. I listen to the pop of the cork and smell the faint scent of apples as he pours two glasses before speaking.

"You realize what you are saying?" he asks quietly. For a moment, I'm at a loss, then remember our conversation and my story from the night before. I nod.

"You have an annoying habit of doing that," I say crossly.

"What?" His heavy eyebrows rise.

"Continuing conversations long finished. Oh, forget it. Yes, I do remember."

I cross slowly to the table to gather the second glass of brandy and carry it to the fire. I sit. Esau trails after me and grumpily flops at my feet with a heavy sigh, casting a last longing glance at the doorway before closing his eyes. I taste the brandy and rest my head against the back of my chair. O'Meara moves hesitantly around to sit facing me on a stool by the fire.

"Do not begin to make moral judgements, Priest, until you know the full story," I say, anticipating his question. He smiles wryly and sips from his drink.

"Sure, and you'll not be suggesting that Simon Girty was a prophet of some sorts!" His voice sounds its incredulity.

"Why not? Will one more make any difference to your church?" I sip thoughtfully from my glass as he remains silent, watching me. He swirls the brandy gently in his glass.

"I think Simon knew and understood the Indian world as well as any people of the Six Nations. They knew the white man as surely as they knew the animals of the forest. They knew something had to conserve objects as, being mere mortals, they could not. There was a force within Simon that gathered things to it. He not only walked through the forest, he *was* the forest, the trees, the grasses, the animals, the soil. But, he was not yet complete—he had more to learn.

"For three years, we were taught life as young Seneca braves. We learned the importance of the land and the forest. From the rivers, the Indian caught fish merely by throwing a spear at the flashing silver in the shallows or dipping a net beneath a low-hanging willow. In the forest could be found fat bears, deer, raccoon, wild turkey, and buffalo. By killing buffalo, deer, and bear, the Indian received not only food but clothing and bedding and skins for his cabin. Vegetables and corn could be had by simply scratching the ground in river bottoms and planting the seed after the waters had receded from the spring thaws. The land contained everything the Indian needed. If driven from it, he had nowhere else to go for each tribe had boundaries it dared not cross unless it wished a war with a neighboring tribe. And the Six Nations had strict laws forbidding that. Consequently, what each tribe had was reverenced. This, we were *very* carefully taught.

"During the day, we would hunt for bear and venison. At night around the council fires, we listened as the old men of the village told long stories about the history of the Senecas. We learned their customs and traditions—a surprising set of rigid rules governing morality stricter than your Ten Commandments—and suddenly I became aware that Simon was being groomed for future plans. Lessons were painstakingly taught over and over although he was a quick student and often arrived at the point of the lesson far ahead of the teacher. He absorbed the stories, the tales, the legends, the laws. I was tolerated indifferently simply because Simon wished it. It was almost as if I had been the subject of a decree made by Simon. But," I pause to take another sip of the brandy. Exhaustion begins to creep over me. "I do not know what might have happened if Fort Erie had not fallen to General John Forbes in 1758. The subsequent treaty with the Nations made it necessary for us to go back to the white man's world. Simon was loath to go and took to hiding in the forest until one day when The Prophet came to our village to speak to him."

"What did he say?" O'Meara asks anxiously, leaning forward on his stool, the brandy forgotten in his hand. I shake my head.

"I do not know," I say. He leans back, disappointment heavy on his face. "Immediately after, Simon stopped protesting. Within a week, preparations had been made for us to make the long journey east to Fort Erie. We were given a supply of jerky and parched corn and sent on our way." I yawn deeply and fumble as my fingers almost drop the glass of brandy. Esau raises his head and peers at me with sleepy eyes. I run my tongue around suddenly dry lips.

"It is best you get more rest," O'Meara says promptly, rising from his stool and firmly placing his glass upon the table. I do not argue with him but let him help me to my bed. Thankfully, I sink back on the pile of blankets. He carefully covers me with a Hudson Bay blanket, blows out the candles, and returns to his stool to read his breviary by the light from the fireplace.

Not a sound comes to disturb me—the soft dark

has hidden the whole day, and I lie comfortably content in the cocoon formed by the blankets as if I lie in the cocoon of the world and listen to the crickets singing and the soft, soothing sounds of the night, thinking of our last day in the Seneca village so many years before . . . .

I drew up suddenly as I came silently around a path, a brace of squirrels thrown over my shoulder. Simon and Speaks Thunder rested comfortably under an old oak in front of me, their bodies dappled by late summer heat. Bees buzzed lazily around them, flitting among wild roses at the edge of the small clearing. Speaks Thunder smiled gently and motioned at me to join them.

"I was just about to give another lesson," he said.

Simon grinned as I dropped the squirrels onto the bed of ferns beside him.

"I killed them," I said. "You get to clean them. Some must do the work."

"All right," he said, turning back to Speaks Thunder.

The old man's eyes sparkled as he considered us for a long moment, then began.

"A man and his wife lived with their five-year-old son in an ugly-looking lodge in the woods. One day the woman died while giving birth to another boy. This boy was bright and filled with life, but no larger than the palm of one's hand. The father did not believe that this boy would live so he wrapped him carefully and placed him in a hollow tree at the edge of the clearing where they had built their lodge. Then, he burned the body of the mother.

"Then, as he had done before, the man went hunting. He hunted every day while the five-year-old boy played around the lodge by himself. The boy became very lonely and after a time, he heard sobs coming from the hollow tree for the baby the father had placed there was lonely, too.

"The older boy looked in the hollow tree and discovered his brother and, aware that the baby was hungry, he made some soup from the intestines of a deer and the baby drank it all. Much stronger now, the baby crawled out of the tree and the two played together as brothers should. The older brother made a little coat out of a fawn skin and put it around the baby. He laughed because the baby looked like a chipmunk as he scampered around the clearing in the forest.

"When the father came home, he asked the boy what he had done with the deer intestines. 'Oh,' said the boy, 'I ate them because I was hungry.'

"Noticing a small track of very short steps around the fire, the father said, 'And whose tracks are these?' So the son told the truth about how he had found his little brother in the hollow tree and fed him some soup and gave him a coat he had made out of the fawn-skin.

"'Go and get him,' his father ordered.

"'He won't come,' the boy said. 'I think it is because he is very shy and afraid.'

"'We'll catch him. Ask him to hunt mice with you in the old stump behind the hollow tree,' the father said.

"Then, the father gathered a lot of mice and hid them in his clothes. He walked beyond the hollow tree and squatted down, covering himself and keeping very still so that he looked like a stump. After he had done this, the boy went to the tree and asked the young boy to come with him and help him hunt mice.

"The boy climbed out of the hollow tree and the two brothers rushed around the stump, trying to catch mice. The young boy laughed with excitement and said he had never had as much fun as he was having.

"Suddenly the stump turned into the father who caught the young boy in his arms. He ran with the boy to his lodge while the boy screamed and struggled. The father put a small club into the boy's hands and said, 'Use this to strike the tree.'

"The young boy struck the great hickory and the tree fell. Then, the young boy swung the club again and everything he hit was either crushed or killed and he became delighted with this power he suddenly had and stopped his crying.

"The young boy stayed with his older brother while their father went hunting. But before the father left, he warned them, saying, "Whatever you do, you must not go to the north while I'm away. Bad people live there and they could harm you."

"But after the father had left, the young boy looked at his brother and said, 'Oh, let's not listen to him. I am curious. Let us go to the north and see what is really there.'

"The older brother was just as curious and so they set off, walking until they came to wooded, marshy ground. Suddenly they heard many people calling, 'My father! My father!' But it really wasn't people, only frogs singing the frog song, '*Nohqwa! Nohqwa!*'

"'These people want to hurt our father!' the little boy yelled. He fixed a pile of red-hot stones and killed the frogs with the stones.

"When their father returned, he became very angry. 'You must not go again,' he said. 'And you must not go west because it is very dangerous for you to go there.'

"But the next day when the father had left, the little boy said that he wanted to go to the west and see what was there. So they traveled until they came to a tall pine tree that had a bed made from skins at the very top. 'What a strange place for a bed,' the little boy said to his brother. 'I'll climb up and look at it.'

"So he climbed the tree and when he had reached the top he discovered two naked, frightened children, a boy and a girl. He pinched the naked boy who cried out, 'Father! Father! A strange boy has come and scared me!'

"Suddenly the voice of Thunder came from the far west. It rumbled and grumbled, coming closer and closer, until it reached the bed in the treetop. Raising his club, the little boy struck Thunder and crushed his head so that Thunder fell dead to the ground. Then, he pinched the naked girl and she cried out, 'Mother! Mother! A strange boy torments me!'

"Instantly the voice of Mother Thunder sounded in the west and then she stood beside the tree. The powerful boy struck her on the head with his club and she fell down to lie dead with her husband. The boy looked at the two children and said, 'This Thunder boy would make a fine tobacco pouch for my father. I shall take him home with me.' And he struck the boy with his club and threw both of the children to the ground.

"The two brothers went home and the young one said, 'Oh, Father! I have brought you a splendid pouch.'

"'What have you done?' the father said when he saw the dead Thunder baby. 'These Thunders have never harmed us. They bring rain and do good for us, but now they will destroy us to revenge their children.'

"'Oh, we won't be harmed,' the young boy said.

'I've killed the while family.'

"So the father took the skin of the boy for a tobacco pouch, but said, 'You must never go north to the country where Stone Coat lives.'

"The next day, the older brother would not disobey his father for he had seen what would happen if he did. But his brother, the powerful one, went north by himself. When midday came, he heard the loud barking of Stone Coat's dog, which was as tall as a deer. Thinking that the dog's master must be nearby, the young boy jumped inside a chestnut tree to hide. But the dog did not stop barking and Stone Coat came up to look around.

"'Why are you barking?' he asked his dog. 'There is nobody here.' But the dog kept barking and staring at the tree and so Stone Coat struck the tree with his club and split it open.

"'What a strange little boy you are,' he said to the young boy as he came out of the inside of the tree. 'You're not big enough to fill a hole in my tooth.'

"'I didn't come to fill holes in your teeth,' the boy said crossly. 'I came to go home with you and see how you live.'

"'All right. If you are sure that is what you want, then come with me,' Stone Coat said. He began walking away with enormous steps. In his belt he carried two great bears, which seemed as small as squirrels. Every once in a while he looked far down and said to the boy running beside him, 'You're a funny little creature!'

"Stone Coat's lodge was very large and the young boy was filled with wonder at it. Stone Coat skinned the two bears and put one in front of the young boy. 'You eat this bear,' he said, 'or I'll eat both you and him together.'

"'If you don't eat yours before I eat mine, may I kill you?' the young boy asked.

"'Of course,' laughed Stone Coat.

"The little boy cut off pieces of meat, cleaned them as fast as he could, and stuffed them into his mouth. He ran out of the lodge to hide the meat, and kept running in and out until all the flesh of his bear had disappeared.

"'You haven't finished yours yet,' he said to Stone Coat. 'But now that I have won, I will kill you.'

"'Wait until I show you how to slide down hill,' Stone Coat said and took the young boy out to a long, slippery hillside which ended in a cave. Putting the boy in a wooden bowl, Stone Coat sent him down the hill at a great speed. But soon, the young boy ran back up the hill again.

"'Where did you leave the bowl?' asked Stone Coat.

"'Oh, I don't know,' the boy replied.

"'Well, let's see who can kick this log highest,' said Stone Coat.

"'You first,' said the boy.

The log was two feet thick and six feet long. Putting his foot under it, Stone Coat kicked the log up twice his height. Then, the boy, slipping his foot under the log, sent it whistling up through the air. It was gone a long time and when it came down, it landed on Stone Coat's head, crushing him to death.

"'Come here,' the boy said to the dog. The dog came, and the boy climbed up on his back and rode him home. 'Now my father will have a fine hunting dog,' he said.

"When the father saw the dog, he cried, 'What have you done? Stone Coat will kill us!'"

"'I have killed Stone Coat. He won't trouble us anymore,' replied the boy.

"'Well,' said the father. 'You must never go to the southwest to the gambling place.'

"But the next day about noon, the younger brother started walking southwest. He came to a beautiful opening in the woods, with a lean-to at the far end. Sitting under the lean-to was a man with a pair of dice he had made from wild-plumpits with designs on them and a head larger than a buffalo's. He played dice for the heads of all who came that way.

"Crowds of people were betting in groups of three. When they lost, as all did, the big-headed man put the three persons to one side. Then he played with three more and when they had lost, he put them aside as well and so on until he decided that he had enough and then he rose and cut off all their heads.

"As the boy approached, a number of people who had lost their bets and were waiting to be killed suddenly had great hope for they sensed that this child had great *orenda*—powerful medicine.

"The boy took his place, and the game began immediately. When the big-headed man threw the dice, the boy caused some to remain in the dish and others to go high so that the dice came to rest with different designs on them. But when the boy threw the dice, the dice turned into woodcocks, flew high, and came down as dice of the same design.

"The two played until the boy had won back all the people and the gambler lost his own big head. The boy instantly cut it off. The whole crowd shouted that the boy must be their chief, but he said, 'How could a little thing like me be a chief? Maybe my father would be willing to do that, but I will have to ask him.'

"The boy returned home with his story, but his father would not move to the land of gambling.

"'Now,' said the father, 'you must never go to the east where they play ball.'

"But the next day, the boy went east until he came to a great, level country of beautiful plains. There the Wolf and Bear clans were playing against the Eagle, the Turtle, and the Beaver clans.

"The boy took the side of the Wolf and the Bear. 'If you win,' they told him, 'you will own all this country.' They played, and the boy won. 'Now,' they said, 'you are the owner.'

"The powerful boy went home and told his father that he had won all the beautiful country of the east and that he wanted his father to come and be the chief of it. His father consented and moved with his two boys to the country of the east, and there they lived."

Speaks Thunder paused and looked from Simon to me, waiting. "Now," he said. "What have you learned?"

"Where we have come from," Simon said promptly.

Speaks Thunder nodded and looked at me. "And you? What have you learned?"

"The land is ours by right," I answered.

"And that right? How did it come about?" he asked.

"Through our power," I said. "The power we have from uniting the others as the boy united the North, the South, and the West."

"And how many had this power?" Speaks Thunder asked.

"Only one," Simon said.

"Yes," Speaks Thunder said. "Only one. But that one had to have his father with him in order to rule. Do you understand?" He looked at me and I smiled.

"Because the father is the one with the knowledge?" I asked.

Speaks Thunder nodded. He looked at Simon. "You must remember this. Remember who is your father."

A puzzled look came into Simon's eyes. "You are my father," he said doubtfully.

"A father is more than an old man," Speaks Thunder said. "He is also the man who can speak wisdom when wisdom is needed. Whether that wisdom is followed, is another question. Think on this."

He rose and walked slowly from the clearing while Simon sat, hunkered forward over his legs. At last, he looked up at me. "You? Is that what Speaks Thunder was saying?"

I grinned. "That is something you'll have to answer," I said.

He grabbed an acorn and threw it at me, but I rolled over to my feet and ran from him, dodging among the trees as he gave chase.

The day had been soft, but warm, giving promise of heat by late afternoon. Dust lay heavily upon the leaves of the trees beneath which Simon and I sprawled naked upon a bed of ferns covering the bank above the creek in which we had been swimming. The lazy current flowed south towards the Ohio. Sunlight sparkled, changing the surface of the water into a carpet of thousands of tiny crystals. Gray squirrels scampered among the hickory trees, gathering nuts for winter storage. A family of nuthatches twittered anxiously in one tree as a gray squirrel ran up and down the trunk. I admired the bronze of Simon's skin, his broad shoulders, long arms heavily muscled, then ruefully contemplated my own freckled skin turning pink from the sun's rays.

"You will be glad to go back," Simon said matter-of-factly, breaking the peace. The squirrels fled for the safety of the trees, their tiny feet scratching wildly at the dried leaves on the ground, the bark of the tree.

"Yes," I said. "I will."

"Why?" He rolled onto his stomach, propping his chin in the cups of his palms to stare at me, interest showing strongly in his eyes. I looked deeply into them, suspecting he meant to humor me, but found nothing but interest.

"All right," I said, levering myself up to sit cross-legged. "What do you wish to know?"

"Why do you want to leave this to return to the stench of the city? What is there except lies and knavery, swindlers and gullers, gamblers and whoremongers, all masquerading under the guise of respectability and blackguards flaunting their contempt of the law?"

"There is truth," I said, warming to my task of defense only to be interrupted.

"What 'truth?' Truth there wears coats of many

colors."

"Do you wish me to explain or not?" I asked. He nodded mockingly.

"Forgive me. I am not a gentleman. Nor do I have any pretensions to be."

"Never mind," I said, flopping onto my back. I plucked a fern blade and held it tight between my thumbs, blowing gently upon it. A high-pitched note emitted.

"All right," Simon said. "I apologize. Please tell me why you would rather go back than remain here." I threw the fern leaf away and rolled to stare at him.

"Why do you express this sudden interest? " I asked curiously. "Why do you want to return?"

"To learn," he said bluntly. "There is much I do not know about my own world. How can I expect to know this one?" He waved his arm to indicate the forest.

"Some people would be satisfied to know one world," I said. He gave me a strange look and rolled over onto his back, locking his fingers behind his head.

"And when the two worlds come together, what then?" he asked softly. He waited a minute for my answer, and when I remained silent, rolled again onto his stomach. "What then?" he repeated.

"Armageddon," I answered, knowing the word was unfamiliar to him. He smiled faintly.

"See? That's why it is best to know both

worlds," he said. "Now, you."

"I want," I said slowly, "what I have been missing. I want the dinners, the parties, the long evening talks, the books, the wine, the fine food. I want all that I do not have here."

He nodded, thoughtfully pursing his lips. Finally, he spoke. "You seek pleasure, then. But, maybe, maybe you look for too much pleasure? I hope not." He frowned, searching for words. "I hope also for your sake that you are not disappointed, but I think you will be. The society you wish to return to may be unwilling to do what you want."

"And what would that be?" I asked.

"Accept you," he said, leaping to his feet. "As you are." He turned, took two graceful steps, and dove into the water....

A low voice intrudes upon my half-dreams, a droning voice resembling a laden bee seeking entrance to his hive that makes me open my eyes. I roll my head and watch Father O'Meara kneeling in front of the fire, eyes closed, softly praying. I close my eyes again and drift off to sleep while listening to the dusty clicking of his rosary beads.

Chapter Twelve

The warm morning sun makes me drowsy as I lie in the heavy grass above the cove and watch the sea gulls whirling over the shoals, searching for tiny fish from the recent second hatch. The fish try to make their way to the deeper waters of the lake where, if they escape the larger fish lying in wait in the new and strange world, they will grow and learn for three of four years before returning to their birthplace to spawn and die. In the spawning season, bears and foxes wait near shallow stream beds. The bears scoop the fish from the water and fling them to the bank. The foxes dash from hiding and steal what the bears have caught.

Today, I see no bears and no foxes; just seagulls wheeling and twisting while high up a lone eagle soars in ever widening gyres, looking for larger prey. Beside me, Esau snuffles and jerks in his sleep as he dreams whatever happy dreams a dog dreams. Distantly, I hear a beaver tail slap the water and the dreamy whistle of a cardinal followed by a bluejay's angry chatter.

Last night had been a bad night: I awoke with a burning pain lancing through my chest and down my left arm. The priest arose and gave me a tablespoon of brandy and a small glass of water into, which he had mixed some herbs. In a short while, the pain abated, and I managed to catch my breath. Afterwards, I slept soundly until mid-morning when I moved outside to enjoy the sun's warmth.

I do not think there will be many more days like this as I heard locusts the other night which could mean a short summer and fall.

Near noon, the priest brings lunch down to me. We haven't spoken about Simon for a few days. He is patient, though, spending his time in quiet contemplation with short walks in the woods and taking care of me while waiting for the time when I am ready to resume my narration. I feel somewhat reluctant to do so for my story seems almost a confession. I am also a bit suspicious for I do not know why he wishes to know and why he has received dispensation to remain with me for I know (although I pretend ignorance) that the Society of Jesus was disbanded many years ago by the Pope. However, if he wishes to appear a Jesuit, then I am willing to let him: the charade does not harm me and can mean only another rosary for him as a "secret sin."

After lunch, he goes for a walk along the shore. I watch him as he rounds the point of land forming one arm of the cove. He moves slowly, head bowed as if he carries a tremendous load upon his shoulders. Esau lays beside me, watching me, whining softly.

"All right, boy," I say, affectionately rubbing

him behind his ears. "Let's give it a try." He leaps to his feet and bounds away only to stop and stare to see if I follow. I lever myself painfully to my feet and begin a slow, hesitant walk back to the cabin. By the time I reach the cabin door, the stiffness has disappeared. I gather my shot bag and powder horn, take down my rifle from over the fireplace, and leave the cabin, following Esau across the meadow and into the trees.

The woods are cool and dark and deep, and Esau courses the ground back-and-forth in front of me, searching for spoor. I hope he wouldn't find anything for we don't need any meat as a haunch of venison still hangs in the shed behind the cabin. Suddenly, a rabbit leaps up in front of him and streaks off through the woods. Esau pauses and turns half-apoligetic to me. I laugh and wave him on.

"Go! Get him!" I yell, and he gives a happy bark and races off in hot pursuit through the woods. I walk on until I come to a tiny glade with a small, sweetwater spring bubbling merrily through an old stump and sit down to rest with my back against a birch. Everywhere around the glade I see soft, fresh greenery. Around the spring grow heavy ferns, the rocks thickly coated with lichens and moss. Little brown and yellow birds— wrens and finches—flit among the trees and bushes; orioles sing melancholy notes while robins and flickers chase each other from tree to tree, trying to establish territorial rights. Gray squirrels scurry over the leaves, leaping daringly from branch to branch. I feel warm and secure and close my eyes in contentment.

I must have slept deeply, for when I awaken, it is late afternoon. Esau stretches out at my feet, separating me from O'Meara at the other end of the glade. The birds and squirrels are gone, and I realize that it must have been the sudden coldness and quiet that has awakened me.

O'Meara smiles and closes his breviary and puts it away and folds his arms across his belly. He smiles gently and asks, "Now, was it a pleasant nap you were having? You seemed so peaceful I didn't wish to wake you. And, then," he adds, eyes twinkling, "there was the matter of your big dog. He wouldn't let me near you. Sure, and wouldn't you be thinking that he'd be getting used to me by now. Why do you suppose that isn't so?"

"He has his reasons," I say, and yawn. "At least, he lets you into the cabin. And you feed him."

"Yes," he says. "He tolerates me. But 'tis no gratitude he shows."

"Of course, there is," I say. "He hasn't killed you. Yet."

O'Meara looks uncomfortable at that and elects to change the subject.

"This is a beautiful spot," he says, looking around the glade. "Is it often you come here?"

"No," I answer. I reach down to scratch Esau's ears. He grunts with contentment. "Just for special times."

"And what special time is this?"

I don't answer but continue to fondle Esau's ears.

"Sorry," he says after a long moment. "Didn't mean to pry."

"Of course, you did," I say. "It's your nature to pry. That's what you're here for—to pry. You can't help being you."

He smiles, uncertain if he should take offense or not, and plucks at the fabric of his cossack. I see that I had made him unsure of himself, of his relationship with me, and that is how I want him to be. Uncertainty will make him reluctant to press any obligations he might feel I owe him. He clears his throat, looking apologetically at me.

"Perhaps we'd better be getting back to the cabin," he says. "It's late; getting on to evening-tide."

"No hurry," I say. "The cabin's not far off. We can take a shortcut through the woods." I point off to the right. "Of course," I add, looking at his cassock, "that might be a little difficult as we'd have to skirt a bramble patch. But even going back the other way, the cabin is not far."

"That is good to hear," he says doubtfully, uneasily glancing around the clearing at the lengthening shadows made by the drawing dusk. We sit in silence for a long time, he nervously shifts at the secret sounds of the forest, I enjoy the beginning of the change from day to night, the sleeping of one world, the awakening of another. Unlike him, I do not fear the night for I know the spirits that walk in its darkness: the owl, the nighthawk, the lynx and panther. I think about his religion and briefly about turning the moment into a jest by reminding him of his vows and offices, but I desist: that will be too cruel for I will be reminding him of his hypocrisy for paying unwilling reverence to the old superstitions that are a part of his heritage. He looks so pitiful that I immediately regret my earlier thoughts and decide to give him another snippet about Simon as penance for almost taking advantage of his weaknesses.

"This," I say casually, waving my hands around to include all the clearing, "reminds me of the last night Simon and I spent on the trail from the Senecas to Fort Erie."

"Really?" He straightens, eagerly leaning forward, eyes sharp with interest. With great difficulty, I keep from laughing at his exuberance and wonder again about his reason for seeking information about Simon. I pick a clump of ferns, crushing them, and hold them close to my nose, inhaling their rich, pungent odor. The years fly back, and I again feel the singing of youthful blood in my veins . . .

It was again the fall of 1759, the close of a day promising a cold night and crisp morning. But, with youthful disdain, Simon and I lit a small fire to cook our simple supper and rolled in our blankets, butt end to the fire, our hearts beating with wary excitement in anticipation of what the morning would bring when we arrived at the gates of Fort Erie.

"What do you think we might expect?" he asked, after a long minute of listening to the crickets.

"In truth, I have no idea," I said. "Questions surely from the military leader and the odd questions from the curious, but that will soon disappear, I should expect. The good people will have more to concern them than continuous curiosity. The idle who can afford curiosity do not last long out here. Of course," I frowned, "there will be some who will mistrust us and hate us, but we shall have to deal with that when the time arrives."

He was silent for another long moment, then said. "And what will you do?"

"Back to Philadelphia, I suppose." I said. "I have, *had*," I corrected myself, "a position there." I suddenly felt a strange misgiving as if something uncomfortable had been suggested to me as I gave voice to thoughts I had not considered.

"A school teacher?" The words sounded plain and dull coming from his lips. A brief pang of doubt crossed my mind, but I set it firmly aside and tried to interject enthusiasm into my reply. I felt the emptiness, however, as soon as I made it.

"Yes," I said, the feeling growing stronger. "Very little else that I can do other than teach. I do not have the capital to go into trade nor the amount to apprentice myself off to a lawyer. I'm afraid it must be the classroom. And you?"

"I do not know," he said quietly. "I have even less than you to recommend me—only a strong back and willing hands."

His hesitancy surprised me; for once he seemed unsure of himself. During the long course of the night, he tossed and turned as if trying to cast off fearful bonds, and I wondered what secret god or goddess had his spirit in thrall.

At last, he gave up his search for Morpheus and rose to prowl the edges of the clearing, waiting impatiently for morning light. Finally, he squatted on his heels before the dying embers of our fire and silently stared into it, the red light burning his cheek a burnished bronze. His eyes showed melancholy in their gray depths as he seemed to accept with resignation what he saw in the dancing, dying flames.

Chapter Thirteen

I was partly right: the military leader sent for us as soon as it became known in the fort that we had been captives of the Indians for three years. We were met with suspicion, however, by others in the fort and treated to cruel jokes. Simon, being younger than I, especially fell prey to the young bordermen, wastrels lazing about the fort, who often lay in wait for him and took savage delight in pummeling him. At first, I was bewildered by this turn of events, then discovered the reason why after speaking in complaint to one of the officers.

Apparently, we were not the first prisoners the fort had seen. Others, most notably two women, Marie LeRoy and Barbara Leininger, had made a deposition describing their treatment at the hands of the Indians, outlining in lurid detail the tortures of an Englishwoman after Lieutenant Colonel John Armstrong's senseless attack on the Deleware town of Kittanning that ended in the slaughter of forty or more Indians, mostly women and children, the warriors being out with the French at that time. The Indians retaliated by bringing this English woman back to the burned town of Kittanning where they began her torture by scalping her and sticking burning splinters of wood into her naked flesh after the men had raped her in the middle of the village. The women who had not been slain cut off her ears and fingers, forcing them into her mouth so that she had to swallow them. After eight hours of this torture, a French officer took pity on her and put her out of her misery with a bullet in her brain. The Indians then chopped her in two and left her for the dogs to devour.

When told about this after he gave his deposition to the military commander, Simon laughed and said he did not believe a word of it. He had been a captive at the same time, and the only white tortured to death had been his stepfather, John Turner. It was, he said, warming to his task, the type of tale two white women might have told to escape the particulars of their captivity in which they may have enjoyed a lusty relationship with the savage, crying "rape" later after being freed by the whites since the delicate subject of rape was considered one too painful to be explored with a woman who may have suffered such indignities.

Simon's charge, although an example of extraordinary insight, did not set well with the military commander nor with the soldiers present to witness our depositions since that was not what they wanted to hear. Like most of the people on the frontier at that time, they preferred to believe the worst about the Indians. It gave their lives a sense of meaning, a justification for their existence there, the seizing of the lands, the rape of the forest.

Within hours of our dismissal, the story of our callousness had spread throughout the fort, told, I am sure, by satisfied, wagging tongues with a love for scandal.

Meanwhile, we learned that Simon's mother, Mary, his stepbrother, John Turner, Jr. and his brothers Thomas James, and George, had also all been released by the Indians and were living in a cabin near the fort. Ignorant of the story beginning to make the rounds, we made our way to the cabin, Simon insisting I follow until we had determined our respective courses of action.

Mary was extremely happy to see us as were his brothers, although I fancied her eyes lingered more on me than on her son. We ate well that evening and exchanged stories long into the night until at last, exhausted from the excitement, we tumbled into the loft to sleep. The Girty brothers planned a hunting expedition the next day, but I demurred, explaining that I had letters to write to acquaintances in Philadelphia, making them aware of my continued existence and my pressing need for employment.

Sunlight streaming in through a chink in the logs awakened me. I yawned and stretched, revealing in the smooth feel of the blankets beneath me and the warmth of the loft. Suddenly, I felt eyes watching me and spun to face the ladder leading to the loft. I groped for my tomahawk and knife then froze as I recognized Mary in the dim light.

"Good morning," she said. Long black hair gleamed in ringlets across her wide shoulders. Heavy breasts threatened to leap from the tight confinement of her bodice. Her almond-shaped eyes gleamed hypnotically. Her tongue flickered over full, red lips. "I didn't mean to startle you." I shakily laughed and lay aside my weapons.

"The fault of the woods," I said. "I am afraid I haven't been out of them long enough to enjoy civilized pleasantries."

"Yes," she said, looking at my buckskins lying on the floor between us. "I can tell." Her hands slowly went to her neck and began to unbutton her dress. A strange thickness filled my throat as her breasts leaped free and her dress fell in soft folds to the floor around her feet. She smiled lazily and stepped forward, her naked body gleaming in the loft's dim light.

For two months, I waited to hear from those in Philadelphia to whom I had sent letters of inquiry. My days swiftly slipped into a routine: lazy mornings spent in bed with Mary, the odd work around cabin, then a leisurely walk into the fort to the sutler's to check on the coach mail. I began to wonder if I would ever hear from them. Coupled with the dark looks and sneers that followed me around the fort and the lack of an answer to my letters, a burning resentment began to smolder within my breast for I began to feel deliberately slighted for having been a captive of the Senecas for so many years. I became truculent in my dealings with the people of the fort, garrulous when addressed, argumentative when reproached on my behavior.

Only once, though, had I come to blows and that when a drunken border ruffian accosted me on the sutler's porch, sneeringly addressing me as "squaw man." I tried to push by him only to be brought up short when his calloused hand reached out to grab my buckskins. I glanced around the circle of men, at their smiles and winks. A fine gray haze fell over my eyes. I seized him by his collar and hunting belt, raised him high overhead, and slammed him across the hitching rail at the foot of the porch. He broke through the timber, his ribs cracking like matchsticks, and fell senseless into the dust. No one stopped me when I stepped down from the porch and walked away.

For Simon Girty, however, it was a different story. For some reason, the sight of this broad-shouldered youth brought detractors in packs like wolves snapping at his heels. At least once a week, he would limp home, cut and bleeding from a beating he had received at the hands of the Christian men of the fort.

One day as I left the sutler's to follow the

wooded path through the woods to the cabin, I heard the shouts and yells that signified yet another attack on Simon Girty. I followed the yells to the back of the stables to find Simon pinned against a tie-post by four men while a fifth swung heavy blows to Simon's stomach and face. A small crowd had gathered to watch the fun. Incensed, I stepped forward, burying my moccasin foot in the assailant's groin. He screamed, grabbed himself, and fell to the ground, vomiting rum onto the packed earth at Simon's feet. I reached for one of the men pinning Simon's arms only to be brought up short by a steel band wrapping itself around my throat and the sharp edge of a hunting knife biting my cheek.

"We've been waitin' for you!" a voice hissed in my ear. I smelled rotting flesh from his breath and nearly gagged. "Waitin' for both of you! Injun lovers! We're goin' to make catamites outta you for your redskinnies!" I smelled raw onions and the odor of burned leaves clinging to the buckskins of my captor. Small black dots began to dance in my vision.

"Let them go," a voice said quietly. The shouts abruptly ceased, the men looking apprehensively over my shoulder. Their hold loosened on Simon. With a violent wrench, he freed himself. His lips were swollen to twice their size. One eye was nearly closed.

"Thank you," he said quietly, looking over my shoulder.

"I do not like repeating myself, Wetzel," the

voice said, rising with inflection. A cold dread swept over me as I realized who held me: Lewis Wetzel, the insane borderman whose rabid hatred of Indians had made him an outcast among all but the hardiest bordermen. Few could match his cunning, his legendary strength, his viciousness. In the city, he would have been locked in a madhouse. Here, he was a hero.

"Wetzel!" the voice snapped warningly. "I *will* shoot!" Slowly, he pulled the knife from my cheek. I stepped away and turned shakily to face my attacker and savior for I had felt the pressure behind the blade and knew Wetzel had meant to use the knife in the manner he had explained.

Wetzel was tall—nearly as tall as I, but half-again as broad. His face was seamed and hard with a touch of madness about the eyes. A long, black rifle stood at the corner of the stable behind him. His belt held a tomahawk and a sheath for the huge knife, a butcher knife, he held in his hand. His long black hair was drawn into a heavy bun at the nape of his neck. Although he had recently bathed, I could smell old blood on him, a smell that no soap and water would ever be able to cover.

Our savior stood a head shorter than Wetzel but his wide shoulders made him seem as formidable as Wetzel. His face was broad with cool gray eyes and shoulder-length brown hair. He held his rifle steady, the bore centered upon Wetzel's mid-section.

"I shall remember this!" Wetzel hissed. He grabbed his rifle and stalked away. The others scrambled after him, nearly tripping him up in their eagerness to remain close upon his heels like faithful dogs.

"Well," our savior said, lowering the butt of his rifle to the ground. He leaned on it considering us.

"I greatly appreciate your help," I said. "I'm afraid that man meant us mischief."

"Reckon so," he said laconically. "The Indians don't call him 'Deathwind' for no reason a-tall." He stuck out his hand. "But it's best to put it out of mind. Remember him, though. I'm afraid you're not done with him yet. Name's Kenton. Simon Butler Kenton." I shook his hand.

"Jonathon Francis Huntington," I said. "I hope someday to repay you for your kindness." Kenton nodded absently, eyes carefully studying Simon who smiled faintly and stepped forward.

"Simon Girty," he said extending his hand. Kenton hesitated, then took it.

"Aye," he said coolly. "Reckon I've heard of you. With the Senecas, weren't you?" Simon nodded, a ghost of a smile tracing around his lips. He continued his careful study of Kenton, eyes holding Kenton's with a burning intensity. "What I don't understand is why you come back?"

Simon remained silent, folding his arms across

his breast. Slowly, Kenton nodded as some secret message passed between them.

"Ay-huh. I can see that now." He turned, his gray eyes carefully studying me for a long moment. "And you must be Nightwind, then. The Companion?" I nodded. He shook his head and shouldered his rifle. "Well, glad to have been of help." He hesitated, then shook his head. "I really should mind my own business, but this once I'm going to break my own rule. I'd think about leaving here if I were you. Shake the dust from your heels and find some place where no one knows you. Best for all concerned if you'd do that. Save yourself some grief, it would. Next time, I woun't be around. If you catch my meaning?" he added significantly. He nodded with his telling, eyes hard and urgent.

"We'll remember your words," Simon said. "And your kindness." Suddenly, a strange light beamed from his eyes, hard, brilliant, mesmerizing. "One day, you will be repaid when your hour is the blackest, and you will be thankful for the friend you made today, although you now are having second thoughts about the enemy your generosity earned you in Lew Wetzel."

His words rang with prophetic clarity although I believe Kenton thought them to be little more than a young man's braggadocio. He nodded at each of us, re-shouldered his rifle, and stepped off down the path with a light spring to his walk.

The Renegade by Randy Lee Eickhoff

"A strange way to thank someone for saving you from a savage beating," I said to Simon as we watched Kenton until he disappeared among the trees. He gave a short bark of laughter and turned glowing eyes upon me.

"You cannot understand," he said. Slowly, the glow disappeared as he moodily stared into the forest darkness. "No one will be able to understand," he said softly, enigmatically

"You know," I said irritably. "I'm getting rather tired of this 'you cannot understand' nonsense. I understand more than you realize."

"Perhaps," he said, and turned and walked away, leaving me standing angry and frustrated behind the stables.

I fall silent, feeling O'Meara's eyes straining through the darkness of the clearing towards me. He waits for me to continue, fidgeting impatiently as the minutes lengthened. Finally, he speaks.

"Are you all right? Why did you stop?" I listen to the rustle of his cassock as he awkwardly climbs to his feet and begins to feel his way uncertainly across the clearing towards me. Esau growls, and he stops. I sense his fear and laugh silently as I rise to meet him.

"Let us go back to the cabin," I say, touching him on the arm. He starts then grasps my arm to peer closely into my face.

"You startled me!" he says. He releases my arm and takes a step backward. "You were quiet so long I thought something had happened to you." Warmth spreads through me as I hear the concern in his voice, and I feel a moment's guilt at the worry I caused him.

" It's late," I answer gently by way of apology. "We had better return to the cabin. Take my arm, and I shall lead you back." Obediently, he follows my bidding and carefully steps after me, stumbling over roots and stones, remaining quiet until we break clear from the forest and the cabin looms darkly on the knoll against the star-lit sky in front of us.

"Why did you stop?" he asks again, dropping my arm and moving a step away.

"Do not seek to know too much too fast," I say in warning. "The understanding must come from within you. If," I add, "it ever does. Frankly, I do not have much hope for that ever happening for you are a man satisfied with what he is, too secure in your self, to see with clarity. Your own beliefs blind you."

"Must I," he asks quietly, "cast off my religion to understand?"

"No," I say slowly. "But you must accept time. And that," I say flashing him a grin, "is something of which we have a dearth."

"Then, perhaps," he slyly prods, "you had better tell me now."

"I had better not tell you at all," I countered, my

voice sounding sharper than I intend. "Have you forgotten my earlier warning?"

He remains silent as we climb the short path to the cabin. Behind us, a nightingale sings his lonely song and is answered by the wild laugh of a loon from the lake. A wind begins to moan through the trees, and I suddenly shiver as I recognize the sound.

I cast a quick glance back towards the woods before I close the door to the cabin firmly and bar it against the night. For a brief moment, a phantom moves against the shadows of the forest and my heart lurches within my chest.

I step quickly into the cabin and shut and bar the door. O'Meara looks up questioningly but I ignore him and cross to the bottle of brandy and pour a glass, drinking it against the ancient memories that still frighten me after all these years.

"What is it?" he asks.

"Nothing," I answer.

"Something, I think," he counters.

I laugh. "I prefer the reality of brandy to the metaphysical speculation of your rosary beads, Priest."

"But is it as comforting?"

"Infinitely," I say.

"I wonder," he says, turning away.

A flash of irritation sweeps through me. "Enough!" I snap. "I am getting tired of these enigmatic droppings of yours like bird shit. You are no Aristotle to talk in speculative wanderings. Explain yourself. Be clear. Be logical. Even a priest has to be logical at times. Or, are you too caught up in mystery to recognize logic any more, Priest?"

"I wonder if contemplation alone will help you to escape your anguish," he says gently. "Or doubt."

"I was right," I sigh. I finish the brandy and pour another. "You cannot avoid metaphysical speculations."

"You are afraid," he says.

I bristle. "Afraid? Of what?"

"Of what you love most," he says.

"And that is?"

"What is behind these walls."

"And I suppose you are going to deliver me from those fears?"

"Then, you do not deny they exist," he says, a spark of triumph beginning to shine in his eyes.

"I admit or deny nothing," I answer. "It is simply a question. You are going to deliver me from these fears, real or imaginary?"

"Oh, deliverance is easy," he says. "It is the way to the deliverance that is hard."

"And why is that?"

"Because you must listen to the silence within you," he says seriously. "The silence, the humility, the detachment, the purity of heart and the indifference."

"Nonsense," I answer. I cross and settle in my chair beside the fire and gesture at the brandy. He crosses and pours a glass and takes it to his stool in front of the hearth and settles with a sigh, sipping.

"Tell me: Why have you never married?" he asks.

The question jars me and murky shadows begin to unfold within my memory. I swallow brandy hastily to drive them back into their crypt.

"Do you enjoy the contemplative life you lead here?"

"It is the only life that I can live," I answer. "Or have you forgotten?"

"No," he smiles faintly. "I haven't forgotten. But I do wonder about the absence of woman that so many men find necessary."

"I am old," I begin, but he interrupts.

"Not that old."

I fall silent, staring into the fire, retreating into my thoughts. How do I explain to him in a way he can understand why I have married the silence of the forest, taken the whole sweet, dark warmth of the world for my wife? How do I explain so he will understand how out of the heart of that same dark and secret warmth I have heard the secret that is the root of all the secrets whispered by all lovers in their beds?

I cannot. I have an obligation to preserve that stillness, that silence, the poverty, the, what? The virginal point of pure nothingness. The tree that produced the fruit for Adam and Eve and all the lovers of the world. Ah, *nulla silva talem profert*.

"You cannot answer?" he asks slyly.

"No, I can answer," I reply. "But you cannot understand." He stiffens in protest, but I continue. "Your own shadow limits your understanding." He glances involuntarily at the obscure outline of himself upon the stones of the fireplace. I laugh. "No, not that shadow; the illusory one of your false self. But enough of this. I am tired. Tomorrow we shall try again to make you understand."

"But . . . "

"Be prudent, Priest," I warn, placing my glass on the table beside me. I rise. Esau raises a sleepy head and looks questioningly at me. I shake my head and he drops his head back onto his massive paws. "Remember your obedience. Think of me as your abbot and this as your monastery. Yes, I like that," I say with relish. "Rattle your beads, now, while I visit a more familiar goddess."

I turn and cross to my bed. I hear the tiny click of the first bead of his rosary and smile contentedly: there is a bit of comfort in listening to the soft muttering of his evening prayers; the same satisfaction I take in listening to the soft flutter of butterfly wings.

I roll onto my side away from the firelight and watch the shadows dancing on the wall. I sleep.

Chapter Fourteen

Indian summer today and the lazy warmth of the sun lures me outside the cabin where I loll, my back against the tall, gray stone, the heat of the stone slowly seeping through my muscles. The wind on the north side of my cabin has a tiny bite to it. On the south side, I feel no wind, only the false summer day. Only the leaves of the trees—the yellow leaves of the poplars, brown or white, and black oak, the red and purple of the maples, the green of pines and hemlock—and the smoky taste of the day tell of fall and the close-coming winter and not summer. A hundred chores await me, but I ignore the urgency of the season and enjoy the moment. So few of them are left that I steal whatever moments I can against the finality of infinite emptiness. It is the time of year I enjoy most when the animals and forest prepare themselves for a long rest, confident of the eternal return in the spring.

Yesterday, John Keogh brought a crate of books with him that had recently arrived on the supply sloop from Detroit. With great eagerness, I tore apart the crate and discovered several old friends—Spenser's *The Faerie Queene,* Shakespeare, Greene, Jonson, Swift— and a few whose acquaintances I eagerly await to make—Boswell, Chateaubriand, Coleridge—and two I am determined to give O'Meara: Denis Diderot's *Pensees philosophiques* and *Lettre sur les aveugles* for I know that although he will not like them, he will feel obligated to read them on the off-chance that I will later question him about them. I chuckle at the idea of O'Meara forcing his way through Diderot's tracts.

"So," he said, straightening after placing the books on my table. "How have you been keeping?"

"It's been a while since you've been over here," I said crankily. "One of these days you'll come and I'll be dust."

"I doubt that," he laughed. "You'll be around long after the rest of us are buried. How many post commanders have you outlasted?"

"Six," I said. "But that means nothing. Most of them were transferred and one other was killed in the rising of the Nations ten years ago."

"Yes," he said, laughing. He handed a bottle of brandy to me. French, I noticed. I raised an eyebrow, studying him. He smiled.

"I stole it from the commander's pantry," he confessed. "It was part of a shipment we confiscated bound for Quebec. Came up through the Colonies."

"A lot of things come up through the Colonies," I grunted. I placed it carefully in a cupboard. "Will you be staying for dinner?"

He shook his head regretfully. "No, I'm due for

a patrol. But, I'll be back at the end of the week with some supplies for you." He looked over at O'Meara. "The commandant would like to see you, though, Father O'Meara."

O'Meara's eyebrows raised in surprise. "Me? Are you sure?"

"Oh, yes. That's why I was able to come over today. I'm supposed to bring you back with me."

"What on earth . . . " he began. Keogh shrugged.

"Who knows? Shall we depart?"

"Yes, yes. Of course. Let me get my bag." He scurried to his corner and took his small leather shoulderbag from its hook, checked its contents, then looped it around his shoulder and pronounced himself ready.

"Go on," Keogh said. "I'll catch up to you. Take the path around by the water. I'd like a moment with Jonathon."

I waited until O'Meara bustled out past the rock, heading down toward the rocky beach, then looked at Keogh. "What is it?"

He frowned. "What have you learned about him?"

"O'Meara?" He nodded. "Not much. As I told you before: he seems to be interested in my past."

"Why?"

I shrugged. "Who knows? Maybe he's a student of history."

"No, I don't think so."

"Do you have any ideas?"

"No, but we have to be careful."

"Why? Because he's a priest?"

"No, that has nothing to do with it, although I must confess that I'm a bit uneasy as to why a priest would stay here on the island instead of heading over to Detroit or one of the missions up north in the back country. There's something not quite right about his presence here," he said.

"Why does the commandant want to see him?" I asked.

"That's just it," he said. "He's going to make him the Post Chaplain."

"What?"

"Yes," he nodded. "That's what I thought. Frankly, we are all a bit surprised about this, given the Privy Council's position on Catholics. Pressure is coming from somewhere for this appointment. And that's what bothers me. Why here? What is there about St. Joseph's Island that we need to have a Catholic priest here?"

"Don't you have Catholics at the fort?" I asked.

"Of course," he said. "That's not the question. We have periodic visits from Detroit, you know. Why do we suddenly need to have one stationed here?"

I shrugged. "I have no idea."

"Watch him for me, please," he said.

"Meanwhile, I'll see what I can discover through the dispatches."

He left and I watched as he caught up with O'Meara and the two of them disappeared along the path that ran along the shore. I wondered about his words.

I have become quite fond of the good Father and dependent upon him. In truth, I am not sure that I would now be able to get along without him. But how long will he be able to stay? How long? Many weeks have passed since I last visited with O'Meara about Simon. The good Jesuit has become moody, restlessly awaiting the time when I am again disposed to pick up my narrative. I am extremely cruel, I know, for deliberately holding back the story, but . . . .. I am afraid, I am afraid. Poets—including that over-regarded Gray!—liken deaths to a long sleep: but who will explain the dreams to me who has experienced their reality and knows the lies of Death? I know my own limitations and those limitations become more day by day. It is not death I fear, but the path to that death. I have no desire to spend the last hours helpless, wallowing in my own dung and urine. To save myself from that, I need a companion to care for me.

And so, I stretch out the story that he seems so desirous of, dropping little tantalizing bits from time to time, enough to keep him interested, not enough to satisfy him. In a way, this, too, has become a game that we play: I must choose carefully, balancing tantalizing tidbits against the certainty of the moment.

I am not sure why this story of Simon and myself has become so important to O'Meara. I know that it is important enough to keep him here with me when he could be elsewhere. Perhaps it is because he is a good man, one of those rare creatures who actually believes in his offices. But nothing is more suspicious, in a man who seems holy, than an impatient desire to reform other men. So, I sit, I watch, I listen.

A tiny dot of white shows against the blue-gray of the lake as the supply sloop swings south and away from the island on its return trip to Detroit. It will probably be the last we'll see of it until spring for all signs promise an early winter—even Esau's coat is thicker than before and, although he lies panting heavily in the sun now, he will be glad of its warmth in a week or two.

A thrush perches on the lintel above the door and sings a happy song to me, but I didn't bring any crusts of bread out-of-doors with me and cannot give him the treat for which he begs. Just as well, I imagine, for the sea gulls would rob him of it before he can escape to the woods. They have become very bold of late, dancing saucily around my feet, even into the cabin itself. They are a source of constant irritation to Esau who more than once has been startled from sound sleep by the raucous, triumphant call of one who has found a morsel left on the floor for Esau. But, I am reluctant to shoot them for their flesh is no good—it does not even make a decent broth when steeped for hours in thyme and rosemary and wild onion—and I find a certain content and contemplative solace in the balletic movements of their flight.

Father O'Meara has returned from the fort more at ease than when he had left. The twin frown lines he had carried between his eyes upon his departure have smoothed away, and he appears relaxed and as happy as a Jesuit can become. I pretend surprise at his news that the post commander has consented to his bishop's request that he be appointed the post chaplain and given him leave to stay and care for me.

I pretend to be mad at this insinuation concerning my ability to care for myself, but I think he sees through my ruse for his face wreathed in smiles halfway through my grumbling, and he interrupted to inform me that he had decided to go into the woods to gather some nuts. He collected a pail and disappeared around the corner of the cabin while I tried to draw breath to continue my ranting. Esau raised his head and looked with concern at me. I laughed. "Well, old boy, what do you think of this sad state of affairs? A skirted penitentiary and the Companion of the Devil under one roof! And a long winter ahead! Spring should show some interesting developments. One of us is bound to recant! I wonder if he was a Pelagianist?"

The Renegade by Randy Lee Eickhoff

Esau's tail thumps uncertainly against my leg. Suddenly, I remember where he is off to. "Nuts!" I exclaim. "Nuts for the winter? Wear me down by a spartan diet? Well, Esau, I'm on to him! I'm on to him!"

I sighed, squinting at the sky. "Well, there's nothing for it but to go hunting!"

Esau's ears prick at the last. He leaps to his feet, stretches, yawns massive jaws, vigorously shakes himself, then grumbles deep within his chest. I laugh, lever myself up with the aid of the stone against my back, and hobble into the cabin for my rifle, powder horn, and shot bag.

"Deer, boy!" I say to Esau upon returning outside. "No rabbits today! Venison!" He whines, slobbering in his eagerness to be off. I wave my arm towards the forest. He bounds away, great paws barely touching the grass as they reach out and rapidly pull distance behind. A tune bubbles up from within me, and I purse my lips to give it air. I cross the clearing behind my cabin, my heart light, my step firm, and I am twenty again with *The Wild Tralee Women* pouring from my lips, remembering when I first heard the air: with Simon on the day we left Fort Erie for Fort Pitt. And I remember as well, O'Meara's questioning about women. And, unwillingly, I remember the woman who could have been a part of my life. . . .

Chapter Fifteen

We found life at Fort Pitt to be little better than that we had led at Fort Erie. Yet, Simon and I, accompanied by Thomas and James and young George, determined it could not be worse than our present predicament. We had been lucky with Simon Kenton's intervention but could not rely upon that help being forever forthcoming. We waited until Lew Wetzel left the fort, taking care that none knew our plans, for we feared we would be attacked once we were away from the fort and the reluctant protection afforded us by the soldiers who, for the most part, relegated us to a spare rung up from the savages on society's ladder.

At last, Wetzel left, alone as usual, on another of his Indian hunts. We left the next day, creeping away early in dawn's false light, leaving a tearful Mary behind with a promise to send for her once we had safely reached Fort Pitt. Thus, to all eyes, it would appear that the five of us had left on an extended hunting trip. We made the trip to Fort Pitt in all haste for we did not want to be surprised along the trail. Even though we were five and Wetzel only one, we had heard enough about his dark, butchering ways, and knew that an encounter with him would leave some of us dead.

Shortly after our arrival, I learned Mary did not long mourn my absence, electing to share her bed within two days of our fond farewell with a handsome young soldier recently arrived from Virginia. For well over a week after discovering this, I moped around the fort, causing the Girtys—with the exception of Simon who watched my antics with an amused eye—great puzzlement. But I was young and impressionable enough then to believe in love and the *de rigour* posturing expected of men when summarily dismissed by their ladies.

Her memory, however, quickly dimmed when I discovered a young, red-haired Irish lass with wild, flowing locks and flashing green eyes, working off passage money as a scullery maid in one of Pitt's taverns.

Metzar's tavern stood on the front of a bluff down river from Fort Pitt with its main doors looking into the road, a long, one-story log building, an evilly-run place with a low ceiling and crude benches and tables cut from oak, splintered nailed and carelessly lashed together with strips of rawhide. The smell of unwashed bodies filled the room, the figures moving murkily behind a dense cloud of smoke. The floor was spotted with old bloodstains.

"'Lo, boys," Metzar said, turning a scraggly-bearded face towards us as we entered the low-studded door. "What's your pleasure?"

"Rum," Jim Girty said.

"Brandy," I answered.

Metzar laughed. "Brandy? Well, well. Boys," he said to the room, "I reckon we have a gentleman here."

The men laughed as he turned back to me, squinting through the smoke.

"Boy, you'll drink panther juice or rum, take your pick," he said gruffly.

"Water," I said quietly.

A loud laugh broke free from the room, jeering, mocking. Metzar opened his mouth to speak, then quickly closed it as Simon leaned over to him.

"I'll have a glass of water, too," he said quietly.

Metzar stared into his eyes for a moment, then his face went ashen and he pulled back from the counter serving as a bar. He licked his lips, then shifted back to me.

"Sorry. No offense meant," he said.

"Oh?" I answered. "Are you sure?"

A slim, white arm curled around in front of me, plopping a tankard of water in front of me. Another appeared magically in front of Simon. I turned to look into the dancing green eyes of a lovely red-haired girl.

"Sure, and wouldn't it be better if more drank water instead of the watered rum in this place?" she said.

"Keep your lip, woman, or I'll knock it from

you," Metzar growled, flushing at her words.

"I don't think so," I answered.

"And . . . ."

"Make mine water, too," Jim growled, shoving the tankard of rum back at him.

Metzar silently dipped a tankard into a wooden bucket and placed it in front of Jim. He moved off down the bar, casting dirty looks over his shoulder at us. I nodded towards him.

"Your husband?" I asked.

"God, no!" she said emphatically. "I owe him passage, that's all."

"I'm Jonathon Francis Huntington," I said. "And this is Simon Girty. And his brother Jim."

"Well, now, ain't you the handsome ones?" she said archly, but her eyes stayed with mine. A quiet chuckle came from Simon.

"We'll meet you back at the cabin," he said, nudging Jim. They left, but I was scarcely aware of their going.

"I don't believe I heard your name," I said quietly.

She laughed again. "Sure, and it is a gentleman that Metzar was fooling with. And isn't it because I never gave it to you? It's Deirdre O'Kelly from Cork."

I looked into her eyes, feeling myself pulled within their emerald depths. The mutterings and thumpings of the tavern seemed to disappear as a soft, rosy glow traveled up the white column of her neck. She grinned and my lips stretched into an answering smile.

"Well, now, do you suppose that I might visit you for a walk after you are finished with your work?" I asked.

She arched her head, her eyes looking, considering. Then, she nodded.

"It will be late," she cautioned.

"Doesn't matter," I said. "It's a full moon tonight."

"A highwayman's moon," she answered. "What will you steal?"

"A kiss, if I'm lucky," I added.

"Aren't you the saucy one!" she laughed, moving away, rubbing down the counter with a rag. "But, we'll see. We'll see."

And we did. I remember her skin, soft and translucent, her breasts pert and rosy-nippled, her legs long and shapely, joining at a magnificent, red and curly beard full and thick.

Loneliness attracts, and we spent many a night consoling each other, eventually parting friends when a young man who had followed her from Ireland (a highwayman, I believe, who wisely slipped away before the Redcoats could catch him) repaid her passage money to the tavern owner and married her.

Strangely enough, work was easy for us to find

at Fort Pitt for the burly, brawling post was rapidly growing from a lusty outpost to a more sedate station. More elaborate homes than the rough cabins of Fort Erie began to emerge from the frontier settlement although the gentility and elaborate architecture of Philadelphia was still far into the future. In such a transitional stage, one can easily become lost, his past forgotten by tactful consent of all unless something happens to warrant its discovery. The Girtys quickly took advantage of this, becoming reliable interpreters for the English and Pennsylvania traders who, now that the French had been driven from the Ohio Valley, had made Fort Pitt a major trading center for expeditions north and west.

Except for Thomas, that is, who plotted out a small farm and settled down to the dual life of farmer and trader. He did not become, as Girty detractors later claimed, "an Indian of the worst stamp in everything but complexion and costume" for he had been a captive of the Indians less than forty days from the taking of Fort Granville to the destruction of Kittanning. He had little opportunity and little desire to learn Indian ways and, being the oldest of all, undertook the responsibility of providing a home for his younger brothers. But, he was too late for James and George who had already acquired the habits and manners of the wild, free life of the woods, preferring the familiar company of the Indians to that of the settlers. As for Simon, well,

Simon was a different story altogether. He tried to follow in Thomas's footsteps, but he was ill-suited for the plow, his hands molded more to fit the haft of a bow or the stock of a rifle rather than the smooth, curved neck of a plow. Still, he tried, finally giving up in disgust to join James and George as an interpreter, although making a special point to stay away from Indian camps.

I was puzzled by this odd behavior but did not give it much thought at the time, having severe problems of my own as my letters to Philadelphia still remained unanswered. After three weeks of restless waiting following the departure of my red-haired Irish lass, I tired of paying compulsory calls upon the proper ladies who laid a barren afternoon tea in mock imitation of their Eastern cousins as the token celebrity of the fort (my manners and education making me more socially agreeable than either of the Girtys) and listening to the sighs and twitterings and gazing into moon-struck eyes from matrons who knew and probably had experienced more terrible stories than the watery versions I related concerning my own captivity. I determined to go to Philadelphia and seek my own fortune among the people I still remembered as being the elite of society.

I arrived in Philadelphia in mid-August in the middle of a bright, sunny day and immediately made my way over the cobblestoned streets to the home of Benjamin Franklin, neatly tucked next to his printshop and post office. With great eagerness, I thrice lifted the heavy ornate knocker and let it fall. I imagined his face changing from cherubic inquisitivity to joyful greeting. "Well! Bless me! If it isn't young Jonathon Francis Huntington! Come in, my boy! Come in!" Flinging wide the door, he would pull me into the entry then tuck his arm through mine and propel me down the long hallway to the back anteroom.

When I heard the door click open, I eagerly turned and faced not Benjamin but his wife, dour Deborah, who observed me with sour distaste as I made polite greetings and expressed my wish to be commended to her husband.

"He's not at home," she replied, pursed mouth primly puckered in prudish disapproval.

"I am most distressed to hear that, Mistress Franklin," I said soothingly. "By chance, would you be able to tell me when he is expected to return?"

"No," she abruptly said, and made to close the door. She hesitated, then added with a bit of malice in her voice: "He spends his time playing with the winds and storms, and if not making a fool of himself amidst the foul weather, he can be found wasting his time in idleness at the Philosopher's Hall with other wastrels!"

I started to voice my thanks only to find myself addressing the door slammed shut with the vigor of a woman half her age to punctuate her exclamation. I turned my steps towards the Philosopher's Hall three blocks distant across the street from the Commons. The sun felt warm upon my shoulders, making me drowsy which, coupled with my musings upon Mistress Franklin's behavior, was enough to distract my attention from my path. I failed to note the young lady laden with packages exiting from a dressmaker's shop. I had a brief glimpse of startled eyes and red lips pursed in an exclamation of surprise before we collided. I tried to sidestep at the last moment to avoid her, but, in the confusion, our limbs became entangled and she landed upon me. Her eyes were inches away from mine: green with flecks of hazel in their depths.

"I'm...I'm terribly sorry!" I stammered in apology. Hands quickly lifted her from me.

"What's going on here?" a loud voice demanded.

"He's drunk!" someone exclaimed.

"I am not!" I hotly denied, but my words floated unheeded into the air above the crowd quickly gathering around us.

"What do you expect from the likes of him? Look: no lace, no ribbons, a woodsie! . . . "

"What's he doing here! . . . "

"What happened? . . . "

"A bumpkin, a drunken lout attacked Anne Leggett! . . . "

"On the street! . . . "

"In broad daylight . . . "

"Take him to the magistrate . . . "

"Major Leggett will not like this . . . "

"Take him . . ."

Their voices merged into a senseless babble. I took a deep breath and turned to face the young lady now safely tucked between two bulky dowagers whose ample hips formed an impregnable bunker between us.

"I most sincerely beg your pardon," I said, offering as correct a bow as the increasing press of citizenry would allow. "I hope my reverie did not cause you any harm. I am most contrite for any embarrassment I may have caused you."

She looked at me wonderingly, unafraid, the blush still high in her cheeks, but with a sense of curiosity in her air as well as she absorbed my rough exterior and compared it to the courtliness of my speech. The two dowagers eyed me suspiciously, stern expressions unforgiving and formidable with warning for me to keep my distance.

A hand roughly grabbed my arm. Angrily, I shook it off and spun to face my would-be restrainer. A rather burly man with two suety chins looked back through porcine eyes. He wore Parson black with a bunch of lace at his chin and cuffs. His lips pulled down in from annoyance and again he reached for me, hesitating uncertainly when I spoke.

"Sir," I flared icily, "please be good enough to keep your hands to yourself or I shall be forced to extract satisfaction."

"A challenge!" someone in the crowd said loudly. A sudden hush fell over them, and they backed away to give the portly man and myself distance. Annoyed, he started to stretch forward his hand, glanced into my eyes, and paused as his eyes uneasily considered the respect shown us by the crowd. I slapped his hand away contemptuously. His mouth dropped open in astonishment then closed again into a thin line. His face suffused darkly with blood as the unhealthy blush of humiliation filled his features. He glanced back and forth between the crowd and myself, but no one came to his aid. Someone sniggered, and anger flashed from his eyes. He took a deep breath and relief swept over his features as someone shouted, "Make way!"

Slowly, the crowd divided to make a path for a tall, angular man wearing a scarlet coat over breeches of brown doeskin. Lace moved elegantly at his cuffs. A powdered wig curled around high cheekbones. In his hand, he carried a silver-banded riding crop. He halted in front of me, cold blue eyes contemptuously considering then dismissing me. He addressed the burly man.

"What is the meaning of this?" he asked. "Why is my sister the center of this gathering?"

The burly man gave me a look of triumph.

"This . . . creature, has insulted her, Major Leggett," he spitfully said, words dripping with venom. Leggett turned eyes like ice upon me.

The Renegade by Randy Lee Eickhoff

"Well?" he demanded. "Explain yourself, sir."

"It was an accident," I began, but broke off when the young lady interrupted.

"Really, Henry," she said. "It was just an accident. I wasn't watching."

"Nor," I added, "was I. We collided . . ."

" . . . and he pulled her to the ground!" the burly man interjected with relish. Leggett's face darkened with rage.

"That is a lie!" I snapped, then recoiled as he swung the riding crop against my face. The crowd gasped and growled with sudden satisfaction at the blood welling from the cut across my cheek. An answering growl surged forth from my chest. A coldness settled briefly in my stomach only to ripple through my limbs, swelling the muscles along my back. A roaring like a strong wind moving heavily through the trees began in my ears. A mist fell before my eyes.

"Damn you!" he said thickly, raising the crop to strike me again. He gagged as my fingers clutched around his throat. I bore him backward in a rush across the street. His heels caught on a cobblestone, tripping him up. He grunted in pain as I landed heavily on top of him. I rammed my knee into his groin, and suddenly my knife was in my hand, pricking him hard beneath his chin. The crowd slipped into shocked silence.

"Do not move!" The words escaped from my lips in a hiss alien to my ears. He lay still, eyes black

131

dots of hatred. My hand seemed a hundred feet away from me, a separate appendage with a life of its own. I smiled down at the hatred in his eyes, trying to soothe it, feeling the words of apology beginning to form again in the back of my throat. Suddenly, fear replaced the hatred in his eyes. I looked down at my hand as it slowly moved across his neck, pulling the knife after it as a thin paintbrush drawing a fine line of blood. Fascinated, I watched the line grow larger and larger. I was powerless to stop it. I didn't want to stop it, but it stopped on its own. Then, I felt a hand upon my wrist and heard my name being whispered loudly in my ear.

"John! John!"

I blinked the mist from my eyes; the roaring ceased. I turned my head and gazed into the anxious eyes of Benjamin Franklin.

"For God's sakes, John!" he said, giving my arm another assertive shake. "Let him up!"

Slowly, I rose from my knees, the knife held low in my hand. Wisely, Leggett lay still, blood running in a tiny rivulet down his throat, soaking into the lace. I stepped away; he raised a hand to his throat and drew a deep, shuddering breath.

"I'll kill you for that!" he said hoarsely. Franklin jabbed him in the chest with his cane.

"I would say, sir, that you are quite lucky to have escaped with your life." His voice rang out with authority. "You were told by both parties that what happened was an accident. Both suffered embarrassment, and due apologies were made. Your temper, sir, is unmitigated. *Your* apology has yet to be made!"

"I'll see him in hell first!" he mumbled thickly. He lurched to his feet and drew a handkerchief from his sleeve to press against his wound. He threw me a withering glare and shakily walked away. The crowd slowly dispersed in silence and disappointment, their blood lust unassuaged.

I turned to the young lady and bowed. "I deeply regret this incident, madam. The blame is mine. I hope nothing more shall come of it, but I fear I have angered you brother."

She smiled shakily and took the packages Benjamin handed her with a murmured thanks. She turned to go, then hesitated.

"I am afraid, sir, that my brother has also a long memory," she said lowly. A faint blush touched her high cheeks, and I became aware of her beauty and stood tongue-struck as she nodded at Benjamin and hastened away. I watched until she rounded the corner at the end of the block.

"Perhaps," I said softly, "I had better know his name."

"Major Henry Leggett," Benjamin said with distaste.

"Major?"

"An honorarium, I believe," he said. "He recently arrived from the West Indies." He lowered his voice and conspiratorially tapped the side of his nose with his forefinger. "He made his money in the slave trade. He claims to be a-waiting orders from the Crown, but I have my doubts about that."

"And his sister?" I asked casually.

His eyes twinkled behind his glasses. A small smile secretly tugged at the corners of his lips.

"I wondered when you would ask that question." He shook his head and laughed as my face reddened. "A most lovely creature, but her brother keeps her firmly in hand. No suitors there, for who would be willing to put up with him as an in-law? Forget it, Jonathon," he said regretfully. "She's not for you. Now, come! I'll buy you lunch, and you can tell me the extraordinary story of your capture!"

He laced his arm through mine. Together, we marched briskly to The Coach and Crown, a small tavern that was a favorite of Benjamin's (due in part, I am sure, to the landlady's generous bosom). I tried to keep my thoughts organized while I related my story to him, but my mind seemed reluctant to give up the memory of soft green eyes with flecks of hazel and full, red lips.

Chapter Sixteen

The tussle with Leggett proved to be my undoing. Doors once gladly open for me now remained firmly shut. No one wanted *les rénégate* near the easily influenced young. Whenever I walked the streets, children scattered at my approach. Curious stares followed me on my rounds, but I could find no work despite Benjamin's efforts. My capture and time spent with the Senecas coupled with the Leggett incident had stained my reputation.

At first, the rejections left me somewhat amused, but as interviews became fewer and fewer, I became bitter at the treatment I received. I became argumentative, aggressive, and soon all began to avoid me; even the members of the Philosophical Society who normally relish argument turned hastily away at my approach.

At last, I found a small position as tutor to a young lady. The job paid poorly but included a small room in the attic and one meal a day with the cook in the kitchen. The father, Pieter Voorhees, was a miser, who paid his bills grudgingly only after the second notice, and was adamant about what his daughter was to be taught.

The Renegade   by   Randy Lee Eickhoff

"Women," he announced solemnly whenever the occasion arose, "have no mind for politics or coinage and as for philosophy and art, why they are fortunate to have men about who can explain such things to them."

I found his daughter at first to be shy and withdrawn, seemingly paying scant lip service to her lessons on the days I set aside for oral tutelage then promptly forgetting them. For a few weeks, I thought the daughter to be feebleminded, but soon realized my error when I introduced a copy of Blake's poetry into her curriculum. She blossomed overnight from childhood into the splendor of a mature, fully grown, mysterious woman. There was no magic in this; just the realization of what she was: woman.

Even now, I find her locked into my memory: thin, small-breasted like plums, almost ascetic, with golden curls falling down her pale, swan's neck, blue eyes eagerly searching mine for approval as memorized passages spill from her lips. I recall the fall days under the cottonwoods along the creek at the back of the large frame house and beneath the willow in front where we surreptitiously declined the Latin verbs forbidden by her father. She absorbed knowledge like a sponge, and had it not been for that, she would have been a fleeting memory only: formless, colorless, a gray shade against which to compare other memories. But the more knowledge she gained, the less interested I became until finally I began to wait impatiently until the day's lesson was over, and I could once again escape to the muffled whisperings of the forest, probing deeper and deeper into its mysteries, thrilling to the slightest breeze, my heart lurching at the call of the grouse or chatter of a squirrel.

I blame myself for what happened for had I not been content with the *elixir vitae* of the forest, I would have noticed her growing unhappiness and maintained our relationship on a more platonic level. Unfortunately, I did not and forgot her vulnerability and the eagerness with which she greeted my entrance into the library.

One day in early spring, I was lying upon my stomach, idly watching the lazy movements of rainbow trout in a pool in the middle of the forest, when I heard a slight rustle as of silk brushing against leaves. I rolled quickly to my knees, ready to spring away from danger, then halted when she stepped from behind a large oak tree to confront me.

At first, I was very angry for we were quite some distance from her home and she had come alone. But my anger quickly fled when she suddenly burst in tears and threw her arms around my neck, proclaiming her love. I was quite taken aback with the intensity of her display and said nothing until her sobs died to hiccoughs.

"Child," I said (although I was, if I remember

clearly, only a few years older than she), "I am deeply touched, but this I cannot allow to happen. I am your tutor and to betray that trust your father placed in me would mean our ruination. I would be a dishonored man and, as such, would never be able to make you happy."

"Oh, Jonathon," she wailed. "Please. We can leave here and go to . . . to Virginia. Or . . . anywhere."

"I'm afraid," I began, but she stopped my words with an awkward kiss, pressing herself frantically to me. With some effort, I pulled free, holding her at arm's length.

"No," I said quietly. "Now, listen to me. You cannot do this to yourself. You know what people think of me. You would be ruined if people suggested that we were alone in the forest now!"

"Jonathon," she said.

"No," I said firmly.

A bright-red blush showed high on her cheeks and she turned her head away. I touched her hand to assure her that I felt privileged to have been the focus of her love, but she drew away from me, asking in a small voice if I would see her home. Relieved to have the situation resolved, I rose and led her from the forest, taking her arm only to help her over deadfalls and across mossy rocks. When we emerged at the rear of the house, she left me without a word and darted inside, slamming the door behind her.

I walked thoughtfully to the stream at the end of

the property and sat, leaning my back against a burr oak. I knew I had very little time left at the Voorhees for my presence would be a continued embarrassment to her. Perhaps I could return to Boston and find a position at John Harvard's college. The thought did not have much appeal to me, but I did not have many options open.

Maybe, I mused, I should find another Moravian Mission. A chill atmosphere descended over me at that moment, and a loud voice shook me from my reverie. I rose to face Voorhees and Major Leggett accompanied by a slim youth with heavy-lidded eyes and the bloated face of a dissipater. All three looked grim, although Leggett's eyes held a malignant gleam.

`"Sir!" Voorhees shouted. "Explain yourself!"

"In regards to what?" I asked mildly. He spluttered for a moment at my calmness, glanced at his companions, took heart from their stern looks of disapproval, and turned again to the attack.

"In the woods, sir," he said stiffly. "With my daughter. You took liberties."

"Is that what she says?" I asked coolly. He hesitated, and I knew she had not, yet he had started the lie and now had to follow through with it. His lips thinned out into tight lines.

"Yes," he said defiantly. Tiny beads of perspiration suddenly appeared on his brow. His voice sounded tight, constricted. But I could feel no pity for him, only contempt.

"You," I said deliberately, "are a liar." He flushed to the edge of his powdered wig, an unhealthy blush, deep purple. He tried to meet my stare but failed, his eyes slinking away from mine of their own volition. I waited a long moment for him to express his denial and to take affront, but it was not forthcoming.

"Be good enough to make settlement while I pack," I said curtly. "It will only take a few minutes for me to gather my belongings."

I turned away only to find the young man blocking my path.

"You, sir," he said, "are a cad."

"And you, sir, are an imbecile. Be good enough to stand from my path."

He exchanged a quick look with Leggett and took a wider stance, stubbornly refusing to move.

"Coward," he said, raising a glove to slap my face. The blow never landed. My fist drove him backwards to the ground. I ignored him and turned to Leggett.

"This," I said lowly, "is your doing, Leggett. Do not try to deny it. I'll no longer be juggled with!"

He took a cautious step backward from my anger. His eyes grew wide, watchful.

"What," he asked, "do you propose?"

"A settlement between us," I answered.

"I do not," he said, "play a fool's game."

"But, you are a fool," I said, baring my teeth. "And a conspirator. I daresay a coward as well, for now, you have introduced this young man into your dark schemes."

"This," he said, indicating the young man struggling to his feet, "is Miss Voorhees's fiancé, Andrew Mallon, the son of Sir Charles Edward Mallon of His Majesty's Court. I do not believe I have introduced him into your affairs. You seem to have managed that very well upon your own with your misbehavior concerning Miss Voorhees."

"For that," the young man said through clenched teeth, "you will answer. By God! Pistols! Twenty paces! Name your seconds!"

"I have no need of them," I said icily. He looked taken aback as confusion clouded his eyes.

"No seconds?" His lips pursed open and shut like a fish.

"I have no intention of fighting a duel over something as insignificant as this," I said scornfully.

"As insignificant as honor?" Leggett interjected.

"There is no honor here," I answered. "Just the posturing of a pimply-faced adolescent trying to be a man under the tutelage of one who's forgotten what the term means." I nodded at Voorhees. "Be kind enough to have my separation ready upon my return."

Mallon stared open-mouthed as I pushed my way past him. Leggett's eyes glittered with anger, and I had to force myself not to turn and watch him as I walked to the house. I had seen those eyes once before, on the faces of the savages before they began Turner's torture.

Chapter Seventeen

Snow fell two days ago: huge, thick flakes a lovely, downy blanket, but it did not last. By afternoon, a late seasonal chinook raised the temperature dramatically, changing snow to rain. The rain and the wind did their work and melted the snow, leaving behind a chill atmosphere of uncertainty in which nature seemed undecided, hung in the balance between autumn and winter. Rotten branches cracked and complaining crows cawed and croaked in uncertain flocks before grudgingly heading south over Lake Huron as the temperature suddenly threatened to dip once again below freezing.

The next morning, the sun suddenly shone through the forest, casting golden highlights against the rich green of hemlocks and pines, and a sweet pang shot through me. I took down my rifle and shot bag and powder horn and whistled up Esau. Together, we eagerly plunged towards the forest in silent rejoicing of the fall reprieve.

A sudden burst of energy filled my frame and, finding no lack of game, I shot what I wanted: a rabbit, two squirrels, a late-rising ptarmigan, finding at last a spring buck that I dropped in a small clearing a scant thirty feet from the lake shore. I could have shot more, but there was no reason to: the meat would have spoiled long before we could use it.

I dressed the buck and left him hanging high in a tree to keep the animals away from him—especially wolverine for I had seen the tracks of one—and returned to the cabin to get O'Meara to help me bring it in.

Upon my return, I found where my soldier friend had obviously visited and left several tiny cheeses flavored with caraway and poppy seeds by way of greeting. I walked down to the shore and found O'Meara fishing and reluctant to help me fetch the young buck for he claimed it was Friday and fish more needful for supper. He gave way, however, when I reminded him that Friday was only one day in seven which logically made the other six of more importance, considering a diet of air would be suicidal.

Surprisingly, I did not receive the argument I expected. He meekly put aside his pole and followed me back along the trail to where I had left the buck.

That night, after the buck had been hung in the storeroom to age, and I had eaten the ptarmigan (O'Meara contenting himself with a couple of crappie he pulled from the lake), I sat outside my door to watch the sunset, reveling in the quiet and hush.

An enchanted light hung over the forest and danced glittering steps over the surface of the lake. The sky was clear, and I watched waiting for the stars to slowly emerge. For a brief moment, I felt immortal as if I were face-to-face with the architect of the universe. My beating heart slowed as if it had finally, after all these years, found a home.

Perhaps, I thought, there is some festival above this world with music from the stars in their celestial cycle.

A splash from the lake drew my attention, and I watched as an Indian paddled a canoe with a raven painted on the prow towards my country. The contented feeling slipped away from me, leaving me sad and lonely.

Esau whined and nudged aside my arm to lay his head upon my lap. I twined my fingers in the thick fur on top of his massive head and gently tugged it. He grunted with pleasure. A mourning dove began to sing off in the distance. O'Meara came out and sat on the other side of the door. For a long moment, he said nothing, seemingly content with the dancing lights on the lake.

At last, he spoke. "This is truly one of the miracles of God. Cannot you feel it?"

I did not answer for I did not wish to argue, being content to sit quietly in the twilight and listen to the mourning dove. A shadow flitted over us, and I raised my face to watch my guardian glide silently overhead. From afar, I thought I heard someone call my name, but it was only the owl. I rose and entered the cabin. Immediately, I felt a strange breath and knew we were no longer alone. I stood for a moment listening to the silence, then picked up a brandy bottle and two glasses and returned back outside.

O'Meara have me a quizzical look as I resettled myself against the cabin wall. I passed him a glass of brandy and poured one for myself.

"At first," I began, "I thought Simon Girty to be my salvation."

I paused to take a sip of brandy and felt the quickening pulse of the forest and the soft whispers that seemed to say: it is time; it is time.

Chapter Eighteen

I do not remember if I thought the Voorhees incident to be finished or not, but if I did, then I badly erred in my judgment. Looks of loathing and disgust greeted me when I walked the streets of Philadelphia. Even in the cheapest taverns where I was forced to take my meals, I more often than not ate alone at a table and received the reluctant attention of serving wenches who placed before me the poorest cuts of meat, the stalest bread, and soups culled from the dregs of the pots. More than once, I was rudely jostled by passers-by who waited to see if I would take offense before moving on with a coarse laugh of contempt when I chose to ignore them.

I was totally alone during this trial for my friend Benjamin Franklin was away in Boston on business, and I knew better than to attempt an acquaintance with Deborah who regarded all of Benjamin's friends *no compos mentis*. Without his support, Philadelphia society doors remained firmly closed.

In desperation, I finally put my sound mathematical background to work at the gaming tables and managed to eke out a more than comfortable living. Few of those who visited the gaming tables were capable of computing odds or remembering cards, and I found it relatively easy to separate fools from their money. But the necessity of survival that forced me into gambling also caused irreparable damage to my reputation. I found myself existing in a limbo between two worlds: shunned by the patricians for earning my livelihood with cards and dice (though they were not reluctant to join me at the tables), shunned by the plebeians for my alleged misbehavior with Miss Voorhees and reported cowardice. No one, however, would refuse me at a gaming table for all welcomed my participation in games of chance with relish and a certain abandon in their wild determination to humiliate me. This, however, worked to my advantage as long as I was prudent with my play.

One night, I was enjoying an exceptional run of luck at dice in the Blackoakes, a foul, evilly-run tavern owned by a man named Morton. Several men had come and gone from my table, leaving behind piles of gold coins that had rapidly grown to a small mountain in front of me. At last, I was alone, the other players having lost enough to blunt their wildness with common sense. Suddenly, Mallon and Leggett stood in front of the table before me. With a languid wave of his hand, Mallon indicated the pile of gold.

"You seem to be winning, sir," he said. His lip curled at the corners as he glanced meaningfully at his companion and others who, sensing a conflict, drifted to the table. His cockiness reminded me that he had reinvented the truth of our last meeting and convinced himself and others that he had set me fleeing at heels.

"A bit," I coolly said. "Would you care to try your luck?" He shrugged and pulled out a chair.

"Maybe." A reckless gleam suddenly shone from his eyes. "One throw." He waved again at the gold. "For it all."

A gasp went up around the room for the stakes would amount to a considerable sum, enough to keep most men in comfort for two or three years. But more than that, the onlookers recognized that it was a challenge to me.

"Very well," I said, moving the cup of dice to the center of the table. "Do you have that much money with you?" His face tightened in anger, and he glanced at Leggett who made a small, almost imperceptible nod.

"My word is good enough. The word of a gentleman," he said haughtily.

"I have seen many 'gentlemen' for whom I would hesitate to give a halfpence," I answered. "My money is visible: make yours as well."

"My father . . . " he began, but I interrupted.

"I am not gambling against your father," I said. "I am gambling against you."

"I will guarantee the debt since a gentleman's word is not good enough for you," Leggett said.

"Would mine be good enough for you?" I asked.

He smiled faintly. "I thought not. But, since your voucher is present . . . . "

I nudged the cup of dice closer to him. He lifted it and with a contemptuous twist of his wrist, upended the dice upon the table. A triumphant shout went up from the crowd: he had rolled five-five-five-four. I needed four fives or three sixes to beat him. With a mocking gesture, he pushed the cup across the table to me. The crowd's excitement pressed hard against me, and I knew they waited eagerly for my final humiliation: the moment when I would throw and lose. A cold fury descended upon me. I gathered the dice and dropped them into the cup, shook them twice, and rolled them from the cup. Heads eagerly craned over the table; avid eyes quickly counted. A long drawn breath nearly emptied the room of air as the blood drained from Mallon's face, leaving it pinched and drawn. Six-six-six-three.

"I shall call tomorrow for your wager, sir," I said, rising from my chair. I swept the gold coins from the crude table into a leather bag. "Would two o'clock be convenient?"

Hatred glitterd from his eyes as he rose to face me.

"I'll pay you, never!" he hissed.

The room quickly dropped into silence as everyone watched for my reaction. A roaring filled my ears and a fog slowly rolled up around us, thick and cloying. I heard a faint chuckle that slowly grew into a roar of laughter as the crowd sensed my predicament: I had no way of collecting if he refused to pay for to press the matter in court was an impossibility. I had won, but I had lost.

"A gentleman does not traffic with barbarians," he said loftily. I glanced past him to the satisfied smile on Leggett's face and recognized the trap carefully set for me. But, suddenly, I didn't care.

"Then, you should have nothing to worry about, sir, for a gentleman does not retract his word. As," I added, "I am sure your father has repeatedly told you, knowing the value he places on honor."

He flushed as a light laugh ran around the room. All there knew the judge to be quite willing to alter judgment for a slight fee.

"Nor does a cheat warrant the word!" he said thickly. My hand caught him across the cheek, a stinging blow driving him back a step. The crowd fell quiet as if a razor had sliced through the laughter.

"This time, you have gone too far," I said. "The glade. At six."

"Pistols?" he asked, blinking hard to drive the water from his eyes.

"Yes." I turned to go, but his voice stopped me.

"And your seconds?' Slowly, I faced him. He took an involuntary step backwards but came up against Leggett who stopped him.

"I have no need for seconds. I have no intention of losing," I said contemptuously. I turned on my heel and left, the crowd parting to form a wide aisle to the door.

I stepped outside the tavern, closing the door behind me. Excited voices began jabbering like anxious crows in a cornfield, and I knew odds were being set and wagers made. I drew deep gulps of air, trying to clear my mind, but only tasted the foul odor of the tavern and surroundings. Loathing swept over me, and I strode rapidly away from the tavern, heading for my rooms. A window flew open high overhead and a voice shouted, "*Garde loo!*" I hastily stepped out of the way as the contents of a chamber pot splashed into the middle of the street. Rats scampered down the street, dodging into alleys to escape my approach. Dogs snarled and fought over a scrap of bone on a corner.

A pang shot through me, and I lowered my head and hurried to my lodging. I slammed the door behind me and poured a glass of wine and carried it to the casement window to wait in loneliness for the sun.

Chapter Nineteen

A foul-smelling fog crept down from the city to glade just inside the edge of the forest along the Schuylkill River. I shivered in my greatcoat as the fog wrapped clammy tendrils around my neck, leaving my skin feeling cold and damp. Mallon stood a few paces away, looking haggard, his eyes sunken hollows smudged with black. Leggett, dressed in somber gray, stood beside him. Two other gentlemen I did not know stood between us, soberly watching the referee, a Richard Wadkins, as he carefully finished loading a brace of dueling pistols. He frowned as he stepped forward to allow me my choice.

"This is highly irregular. Have you no one to second you?" he asked.

"In Philadelphia?" I said, putting an edge to my words. "I am afraid friendship is a commodity too easily sold to the highest bidder. No, sir, I do not."

I lifted a pistol from its niche in the box. My hand closed comfortably around the curved grip. The balance surprised me. Someone had leaded the butt to compensate for the long barrel. I nodded. "This will do."

Wadkins bowed and crossed to Mallon. The

young man took the remaining pistol and turned burning eyes in my direction. Wadkins stepped back and cleared his throat.

"It is my duty, gentlemen, to ask if either of you wishes to make an apology and withdraw from the field," he gravely intoned. Both of us silently shook our heads. "Then, if I may so suggest, it would be quite appropriate at this time to begin. The challenge is for pistols at twenty paces. You may cock your pistols before I begin counting, but you may not turn to fire until after the tenth step. If either of you should turn prior to reaching that position, I shall be forced to kill him. Is that understood?" We nodded. "Then let us begin. Please take your positions."

I turned and faced an oak stand at the end of the glade. Mallon's back softly touched mine. The hammer of his pistol grated back.

"I am sorry for you," I said softly. "You are only the dupe for Leggett's anger. You may stop this foolishness if you want. I do not wish to kill you."

For a moment, I sensed his hesitation, then heard his hard, brittle laugh as Wadkins began a toneless chant, counting off our paces one-by-one. At nine, I heard a loud report and the whistle of a ball as it narrowly missed my ear. I flinched and glanced quickly over my shoulder. A white-faced Mallon looked, despairing, from me to the pistol in his hand. A fine stream of white smoke curled from its barrel around his arm dissipating into the gray air.

"My God, sir!" Wadkins exclaimed in shock. "Do you realize what you have forced me to do?"

I knew from the desperation in his voice that Wadkins was remembering Mallon's lineage, and the duty he was now sworn to perform. I laughed loudly. There would not have been the slightest hesitation on his part to perform that same duty had I turned and fired before the count.

"Mr. Wadkins!" I called, fighting to keep my voice steady from the anger bubbling inside. "Be kind enough to finish your count, please."

Dead silence followed my words broken only by the sudden call of a mourning dove and a faint whisper among the heavy grass behind me. Then, Wadkins, resigned, but firm, announced: "Ten!"

I took the step and slowly turned. Mallon looked wary, eyes flickering desperately back and forth from the referee to his seconds to me. Slowly, I raised my pistol and sighted along the barrel. Mallon's legs began to shake. His tongue slipped out to wet his lips. The front of his trousers suddenly appeared damp. I lowered the pistol.

"You owe me a shot. Remember that," I said tonelessly.

"For God's sakes! Do you know what you have done?" Wadkins said.

"I think so," I said stonily. "For the rest of his

life, he will wait for my shot, knowing that it could come at any time, hoping for it during times of great sadness, dreading its coming during the times when he is happiest. And," I added, "he will have to live with the memory of his cowardly act as it will haunt him among gentlemen wherever they gather. I hope, sir, you have a very miserable life!"

I lowered the hammer of the pistol and contemptuously tossed it on the ground between us. A wave of relief washed over Mallon's face as he realized I was not going to fire. The bitterness, I knew, would come later when he became pointedly ignored by those whose friendship he had once enjoyed.

Leggett's lips curled back into a wolfish snarl. "There will be a death here, yet!" he shouted, and started to raise his pistol in my direction before suddenly freezing as Simon Girty, followed by his brother James, stepped forward from the stand of oak, rifles held pointedly at their hips.

"Jonathon," Simon said, nodding at me before turning his attention to Leggett. "Hope we're not intruding in your affair of honor."

"I don't think you are," I said. "Mr. Wadkins?"

Wadkins stepped between us. He bowed formally to me before speaking.

"I apologize, sir, for the gross misbehavior on the parts of Messrs. Mellon and Leggett. Never have I been so ashamed of the actions of two individuals who have represented themselves so long as gentlemen. These incidents," he continued, turning to face them, "shall not be forgotten. On that, you have my word."

He strode quickly to a carriage waiting at the opposite end of the glade and climb into it, directing the black to take him back to Philadelphia.

"Well, what do you want to do with them?" Simon asked me.

I looked at them, considering. Leggett's eyes blazed hatred back, Mallon seemed ready to burst into tears. A weariness slid over my shoulders.

"Let them go. If you kill them like this, there could be trouble." I said.

"Be trouble, too, if you let them go, I'm thinking. Best to kill them and be done with it," he objected.

"This isn't the woods. Here, things are done differently. There are laws, customs, traditions," I said, my voice trailing off lamely.

"Civilization?" He smiled as he said the word then shook his head. "Are you sure? This one," he pointed at Leggett, "was going to kill you. This other one tried to kill you. Seems to me there isn't much difference between the way people behave here and the way people behave out there. Except in the woods you have an idea what to expect from certain people. They don't hide behind their manners and clothes."

"Maybe," I answered. "But it can't be helped.

Right now, people think of them as honorable men. It'll take a little time before the truth makes its rounds." Simon gave me a mocking look and shook his head.

"Scat," he said, contemptuously waving his hand at Mallon and Leggett. He turned back to me. "I believe you are being very foolish," he said somberly. "You would be much better off killing them. Allowing an enemy to live keeps you constantly looking over your shoulder." I ignored his chiding.

"What brings you to Philadelphia?" I asked. I watched carefully as Mallon and Leggett walked to their horses tethered at the side of the glade. They untied them and mounted and turned to canter away.

"You," Simon said. "Leastways, to visit you before returning to Fort Pitt. We brought a load of lumber up to the mill, and now we're heading back. Can't be too soon, I'm thinking." He watched carefully, monitoring the progress of Leggett and Mallon. Deep lines had appeared around the edges of his lips. His cheekbones were hard planes over hollows, but more importantly, there seemed to be a restlessness of the spirit about him, a tension I had not noticed before.

"Best, too, if you'd come with us. No good'll come of this now that you've let them go."

"Leave Philadelphia?" My voice must have sounded shocked for he threw a quick glance at me.

"Why not? What's to keep you? All this brotherly love I've been seeing?"

158

He gestured with disdain at Mallon and Leggett. I shrugged.

"Maybe the situation will improve now that the truth is out," I said unconvincingly.

"Truth is a will o' the wisp," he answered. "Depends solely upon who's telling it, and who's your friend. Some people have a way of seeing things differently. From what I've seen back here, truth is in short supply." His eyes narrowed. "Look out!" he shouted, and threw himself flat upon the ground. Automatically, I dropped beside him as a ball whistled overhead followed by a report from down the trail. He grunted and rose to a knee, quickly sighting down his long, black rifle. He fired, and a long scream answered. I lifted my head to watch Mallon fall to the ground, hands trying to clutch at the sudden pain in his back. Leggett cast a swift glance at Mallon then dropped his whip over his horse's rump, leaning over its neck. He quickly galloped away.

I slowly rose to my feet and brushed the sand from my trousers. I knew whatever chance I had had for acceptance in Philadelphia had disappeared with Simon's shot. Leggett would see to that: the evidence to support his claim for a cowardly kill on my part lay down the trail with a bullet in his back.

"Maybe," I said to Simon, "I'll take you up on your offer."

He silently stretched forth his hand. I took it.

The Renegade   by   Randy Lee Eickhoff

Chapter Twenty

As it turned out, Simon and his brother had spent little time in Fort Pitt. Simon had tried to settle on a small farm in Bedford County, but soldiers and missionaries alike demanded his time and that of his brothers, George and James, as interpreters. I, too, found more than enough work, sometimes guiding missionaries into the woods, but more often than not, working as a translator at the fort for the English troops. Simon took an interest in public affairs and even voted in the first election in Bedford County that included the whole of western Pennsylvania in 1771. He began to make many friends among the settlers and became a man of influence among them.

I, however, used my talents differently, finding among the wives those starved for a cultural life. I began to widen my sphere of influence within the garrison. Between the two of us, Simon and I soon became quite well off, and a steady stream of visitors found its way up the path leading to the small cabin we shared as offices on the bluff above the fort.

James spent most of his time beyond the Ohio among the Shawnee with the Reverend David Jones from Freehold, New Jersey, helping the worthy gentleman to establish a mission on Paint Creek, a tributary of the Scioto. George became a trader while Thomas moved into Pittsburgh and established a small business as a permanent tinker.

I believe we were happy, although I remember very little of those years other than fleeting glimpses that slip, like autumn leaves, past the edges of thought to fall upon the barren ground of memory lost. I remember a few wintery evenings snugly wrapped in the tender arms of faithless wives and hopeful maidens, a few parties, but the rest is an insignificant blur. I began to spend less and less time in the woods as Simon and I found a mutually acceptable division of labor: his taking to the woods while I kept close to the garrison.

In 1773, Westmoreland County was formed out of the western portion of Bedford. Hannastown, thirty miles east of Pittsburgh, was named county seat. That summer, Lord Dunmore, governor of Virginia, visited the western county and, finding the fertile ground and rolling hills to his liking, entered into a bitter rivalry with Pennsylvania for jurisdiction over the county along a highly disputed boundary line that enclosed the Girty farm on the Virginia side.

I believe it was in August of that year when Simon returned from guiding a trading expedition to the Deleware villages and voiced his concern regarding the dispute. I remember the day although the month is vague other than being in the fall for I had just received a barrel of freshly-made applejack from a grateful client. Somehow, the smell of apples combined with the smoky crispness of fall—the russets and golds of the oak and maple leaves, flights of geese swinging south, crisp mornings with a thin skiff of ice over the water barrel—stays with me.

"I worry," he said, frowning over the cup of applejack I had poured for him. "We must soon declare ourselves for either Virginia or Pennsylvania."

"Which will you select?" I asked. He smiled.

"Virginia. But, that will cause us problems if Pennsylvania presses her issue," he said.

"Why not Pennsylvania?" I asked.

"Virginia is stronger," Simon explained. "And, the farm lies closer to Stanton in Virginia than to Hannastown."

"Is that the full reason," I murmured, idly sipping at the applejack. Simon's eyes flashed for a moment, then relaxed. He quickly laughed.

"No, and, you know why," he said.

I did. The number of settlers in the west had risen dramatically over the years in the fertile Ohio Valley, causing several minor conflicts between the settlers and the Shawnee and Mingoes. If a rift developed between Pennsylvania and Virginia, chances of an alliance between them during a war against the Indians would be slim indeed.

"Do you think there'll be trouble?" I asked. He nodded grimly.

"Yes, I do. Negotiations between Pennsylvania and Virginia representatives are not going well at all. Whoever loses will also lose a substantial amount of revenue," he replied.

"That's not what I meant," I said.

"I know," he answered calmly, and I knew he had no intention of speculating further. As to whether or not this was a complex conspiracy of Simon's to help the Indians, I hesitate to guess for what transpired over the next few years left Simon an enigma, a murky picture of such complexities that reason had little chance to emerge.

To further complicate matters, Major Henry Leggett was assigned to Fort Pitt as adjutant and promptly let it be known that he took a dim view of anyone trafficking with the Girty and Huntington concern. If Simon had ever considered joining the Pennsylvania crowd, Leggett's unofficial position concerning us firmly detered him from making that selection. He declared himself for Virginia, and at the October session of the court of Westmoreland County at Hannastown, a bill for a misdemeanor was found against him. A process was issued for his arrest, but Simon wisely stayed within Virginia's legal boundaries during the dispute. Although we did not know it then, this was precisely what Leggett wanted.

The Renegade   by   Randy Lee Eickhoff

In January of 1774, Lord Dunmore selected Dr. John Connolly of Pittsburgh as his agent in the boundary dispute. Dr. Connolly called on the people to meet on the twenty-fifth of that month to support his formal announcement of Lord Dunmore's intention to annex the lands in question.

Heavy snow fell on the eve of the twenty-fourth, but by morning, the gray clouds had cleared, leaving behind a crystalline world covered with a downy blanket. Out of curiosity (and a sudden restlessness that had left me pacing the floor the night before), I suddenly decided to hear what Dr. Connolly had to say and rode to the meeting at Hannastown. I arrived just in time to watch Dr. Connolly, a short man who, with his thatch of red hair, reminded me of a bantam rooster, stand upon a chair in the tavern to read a prepared statement.

"His Excellency, John, Earl of Dunmore, Governor-in-Chief and Captain-General of the Colony and Dominion of Virginia, and Vice-Admiral of the same, has been pleased to nominate and appoint me captain-commandant of the militia of Pittsburgh and its dependencies, with instruction to assure His Majesty's subjects, settled on the western waters, that, having the greatest regard for their prosperity and interest, and convinced, from their repeated memorials of the grievances of which they complain, that he proposes moving the the House of Burgesses and necessity of

165

erecting a new county, to include Pittsburgh, for the redress of your complaint, and to take every other step that may tend to afford you that justice which you solicit."

He paused to look out over his audience. Several people stirred uneasily, murmuring lowly to each other, fearing to meet his eyes. Suddenly, a loud voice spoke from the back of the room.

"Treason!"

The room fell quiet, and a narrow aisle opened, leading to the speaker, a short, stocky man in powdered wig and bottle-green coat. His lace was stiffly starched, draping over the backs of his hands at the cuffs. He advanced a step into the room and calmly met Dr. Connolly's eyes. Dr. Connolly blushed.

"Treason, sir?" he said, his lips twisting wryly around the word. "Nay, that is not so. My duties and sympathies lie with the King. I but do my Lord's bidding."

"And, I say, that is treason," the man stoically repeated. "I charge you with intent to incite to unlawful rebellion and arrest you in the name of the King."

"And, who might you be, sir?" Dr. Connolly asked, flushing darkly.

"I am Arthur St. Clair, Justice of the Peace of the County of Westmoreland."

"A charge that is illogical as treason can only be against the state, not one of its colonies," I murmured,

166

unable to help myself. Slowly, he turned to stare at me from beneath lowered lids.

"Who...are...you?" he asked, spacing his words out in the quiet.

"Jonathon Francis Huntington," a voice said mockingly. I looked behind him to where Major Leggett leaned negligently against the rough-hewned timbers of the tavern wall. A squad of soldiers stood respectfully beside him. "A scoundrel, a liar, and a cheat. I suspect him to be in legion with Dr. Connolly."

"Do you so charge him?" St. Clair asked. Leggett's eyes gleamed with satisfaction, with triumph.

"I do," he said firmly, his voice ringing with false conviction.

"Then arrest them both and hold them for trial," St. Clair snapped and, turning on his heel, marched from the tavern.

Leggett motioned to the soldiers. A burly sergeant stepped forward and clasped irons around my wrists.

"Where is your friend now, Huntington?" Leggett murmured as the sergent led me past. He gave a malicious chuckle, and my heart sank as I followed the sergeant from the tavern to the jail, fully aware of what I could expect in the way of Leggett's sense of justice.

I thought fleetingly of Simon and glanced around at the curious faces watching as we passed, wondering if one of them might carry a message to him about my arrest. I noticed Jimmy Burnes and thought I could read sympathy in his eyes. Hoping that the guard would not dare shoot into the crowd, I suddenly darted to his side, grabbing the lapels of his coat.

"Here, now!" the sergeant shouted. "What are you up to? Don't shoot, you idiot!"

A loud curse exploded and a crash of steel against steel rang out as he struck up a soldier's musket.

"Jimmy," I said desperately in a low voice. "Get word to Simon about this. He'll know what to do."

His eyes grew wide and flicked from me to the soldiers behind. My heart sank at his words.

"Help you? I wouldn't help a man like you for a section of bottom land and the horses to work it with." He spat on my chest then added in a low voice, "I can't, Mr. Huntington. I'm sorry, but I have a wife and six children. Who'll mind them if I follow you to jail?"

I released his lapels and stepped back. "Sorry, Jimmy," I murmured. "I can't tell you what to do. You'll have to decide that."

Pain exploded in my frame like hot iron as the butt of a musket slammed into my back above my kidneys, knocking me forward onto my knees.

"Attempting to incite a riot, too," Leggett said with relish. "Attempting to escape lawful arrest. Oh, yes, Huntington. This will do splendidly."

Rough hands swiftly bound my arms behind my back, savagely bending them back until my shoulders creaked in their sockets. Someone jerked me erect, propelling me towards the jail. I thought in despair of what Leggett had in mind for me.

Chapter Twenty-one

I did not have long to wait. The sergeant marched us to the jail and pushed us inside in a cell on the first floor behind a stone fireplace. Fresh straw lay scattered about the floor. The narrow bunks crowded into a corner had extra blankets upon them that appeared reasonably clean.

"At least," Dr. Connolly observed wryly, "we shall be warm while we wait for Lord Dunmore to release us."

He started to extend his hand to mine than froze as the sergeant returned and opened the cell door.

"What is it?" he asked.

"Him," the sergeant answered, pointing at me. "They want him."

"For what?" I asked. He shrugged and motioned me out.

Obediently, I stepped into the corridor while the sergeant relocked the cell door behind me.

"Do not worry, my friend! I shall be certain Lord Dunmore hears of this!" Dr. Connolly called as the sergeant led me down the corridor to the steps at the rear.

"Won't do you any good," the sergeant said

softly for my ears alone. "He won't be able to find you. Sorry, lad."

"Sorry? What is there to be sorry about?" I asked, alarmed by the regret in his voice.

He shook his head and opened a door at the foot of the stairs. His face looked grim, tightly-knotted muscles moving at the corners of his jaws. I stepped through the door. Leggett sat casually on the edge of a rude table, tapping a riding crop against one polished boot.

"You really cannot believe how pleased I am to have you here," he said without preamble. I sensed movement behind me and tried to turn, but unseen hands suddenly seized me. I struggled but could not free myself. Leggett laughed and stood away from the table.

"Yes," he said. "Very, *very* happy."

Without warning, he swung the riding crop across my face. "I will enjoy this." The toe of his boot crashed twice into my groin, and I fell, vomiting, to the floor as blows began to rain on my head, my shoulders, my back.

The toe of a boot landed in my ribs as a prelude to a bucket of foul water being dumped over my head. I gasped in pain and doubled up on the rotting straw serving a two-fold purpose as floor covering over earth and my bed. The boot crashed again into my ribs followed by a harsh voice demanding I rise.

"Get up!"

Slowly, I rose, forcing myself up with my back against the wall of my cell. I squinted in the dim light at the bewhiskered face of Groad, my jailer, a demented devil disposed to the use of whips and limber canes when the fancy came over him—which was often in my case. I did not know how long I had been in that cell for my window had been boarded shut from the outside the day of my internment. A lone lantern continuously lit rested on the jailer's table and provided the sole light for the interior of the cells. My clothes were in tatters; my scalp moved from a massive infestation of lice and fleas; my face felt mottled and bruised, tender lumps greeting my fingers whenever I gingerly passed them over my features; a terrible hacking cough threatened to tear my lungs from my battered chest whenever I moved too quickly. Yet, within me burned a small coal of hate that I fed daily hour-by-hour by remembering who had placed me here and who had yet to arrange for my trial. The hatred fed me when my belly growled with hunger, warmed me when the cold shook my bones like ague, kept my spirit strong when philosophical argument called for surrender.

Groad laughed and lashed out at me with a cane. I barely had time to raise my arm to take the blow. He struck again, feinting at my ribs then dusting them when I refused to lower my guard.

"And 'ow were yer sleep, yer 'onor?" he growled mockingly, lashing out again with the cane. "Did ye like yer breakfast in bed? Should I draw yer water?" I refused to answer. A flicker of irritation passed over his face. "Not to yer likin', I take it? It could git wuss, could git wuss. Wot say ye to that?"

A familiar coldness settled in the pit of my stomach; a burning raced through my veins. I cleared my throat, knowing discretion prohibited an answer, but knowing I was going to answer all the same.

"I do not need handouts from your table, you piece of trash!"

His face swelled with anger. In rage, he lifted his cane high overhead to strike me. I moved away from the wall, rolling under his arm as it swooped down, striking him in the mid-section with my shoulder. I raised my head to butt his chin with my crown, then swiftly lifted my knee into his groin. He gagged and fell face forward upon his knees, vomiting his breakfast onto the straw. I seized his cane and lashed it across the face of his helper. He dropped the ring of keys he held and shrank back into a corner of my cell, howling with pain. I picked up the keys and stepped out of my cell, locking it behind me.

I leaned against the wall opposite the cell door and drew deep breaths, struggling to control the hammering of my heart. A wave of dizziness washed over me. I turned and stumbled down the corridor leading to the outside. As I reached for the handle, it swung away from me, opening to the outside. I took a firm grip on the cane, determined to fight despite the odds. Simon stepped through the door and stopped, staring in shock at me. Behind him stood the Redcoats of Lord Dunmore's men and Dr. Connolly who took one look at me and breathed, "My God!"

"Welcome to hell," I said, swallowing heavily against the emotion that threatened to choke me. Dr. Connolly reached and gently took the cane from my hand.

"Jonathon," Simon said with a strange clicking in his throat. Tears unashamedly flowed from my eyes as he tightly clasped me about the shoulders.

Chapter Twenty-two

I blink, bringing myself back from the agonizing memory of the past, focusing on the flickering fire in front of me. I sense rather than remember the glass of brandy on a table at my side and raise it to my lips. The liver spots on the back of my hand startle me for a moment for I am still on the edges of the past, seeing myself as a young man. Esau senses my uneasiness and lifts his head from my slippered foot and rests it with a whimper upon my knee.

"Are you all right?" Father O'Meara asks anxiously . "Would you care for a drink of water? Another brandy?"

I shake my head. The wind howls outside, driving hard flakes of snow against the shuttered windows, the shake shingles on the the roof. Strange that I do not remember the storm.

"The memory was too close," I say. "Too close not to be real. Do you understand?"

"Yes," he answers quickly, but I can see that he really does not. Priests and monks always try to hide behind the transparent veil of their faith but fail. A tiny muscle twitches in their temples or jaws when they are lying. This comes, I believe, from so many years trying to convince themselves that the mysticism of their belief is reality that they become Janus-faced. I feel his thoughts running away with him, I concentrate on the embers of the fire, trying to read his mind, his thoughts, before they flee south for the winter like the geese, But although the night is so old it is about to become young again, I feel old and tired; too tired to concentrate on anything but the embers and the fire. I give up and lean back in my chair.

"Perhaps another brandy," I say resignedly. Obediently, he rises and brings the brandy bottle to refill my glass.

"The storm sounds terrible," he says, conversationally. I look away from the fire. The muscle at the corner of his jaw again begins to twitch. I smile secretly to myself. He is trying very hard to control his disappointment, masking his eagerness to hear the rest of the story behind concern for me. A bit of a hypocrite, to be sure, but the harmless sort who is, for all practical purpose, a sorities. Yet, I feel a certain uneasiness in condoning this for when a man lies, he murders some part of the world. It does not matter how small the lie; a death is a death that diminishes man. Yet, there are times when I, too ....

"Are you feeling better?"

The concern disjoints my thoughts, and I turn, sighing with relief from them for they are silly thoughts that do more damage than good. Men outside the forest are only men and cannot help being liars. Waxing philosophical about common behavior leads only to mundane mendacity.

"Yes, much better," I answer. I sip a little of the brandy. The wind blows harder, making the shutters chatter.

"The storm grows fiercer," he says. He looks worried as he walks to the window and gently places his hand against the shutters as if to bless them. "I have never felt such a storm! It is almost as if the world was in convulsions."

I do not answer but carefully watch him at the window. Presently, he turns and, with a shaky, self-conscious laugh, returns to his place beside the fire. "What do you do in such times when you are alone?"

"I think," I say. "Or read." I do not tell him that I write for I sense that he would want to read what I have written.

"But . . . don't such storms drive you mad when you are alone?"

"I am seldom alone," I say. "I have Esau."

His head rises at his name. He looks closely at the priest, a hesitant growl rising in his throat.

"And," I say playfully, "I think of the storm as a lover, wild in her embrace."

"Oh." His face reddens, and he looks away from me. "I, er, better think of something else."

"Demons?" I suggest mildly, dropping my hand

to soothe Esau. "Bold creatures roaring forth from the infernal pit? Moloch? Belial? Baal?"

Esau leaps to his feet and shakes himself. He begins to pace anxiously back and forth in front of the fire. Slobber drips from his massive jaws.

"Stop it!" O'Meara says sharply. He nervously fingers the black rosary beads at his waist.

"It is only a storm," I gently remind him. "Only a storm. There will be many more before this winter is over."

"I know. I know. I am sorry." He looks away, biting his lip. I feel badly for teasing him. I forget sometimes that some become frightened in storms. It is too much to ask one's faith to sustain him from fears older than his God. I know those fears only too well. Sometimes, they crowd in upon my thoughts despite all I can do to press them out. At those times, the cabin becomes a tomb and the storm living mortar holding me prisoner, torturing me hourly with shrieks and moans of the undead. But then I remember why I am here, and the fear turns to anger and the storm a vengeful spirit fanning the flames of that anger, and I merge my spirit into the storm and become one with it.

But this I cannot tell him for it would only upset him more, and he would feel the need to pray for me. I do not need the rattle of black rosary beads calling forth dusty imprecations against the purity of the storm's violence. I resign myself, close my eyes, and begin again my story of Simon and I and our work in the Ohio River valley with the Nations against the certainty of his prayers.

Chapter Twenty-three

The storm had blown over when I awoke, taking with it last night's anxiety and fears. I quietly cross to the cabin door and carefully open it. The eternal green of the pines and hemlocks peep through their heavy coats of snow. Large drifts make an undulating blanket from my cabin door down the knoll to the lake's edge. A hawk's quiet *"kree"* sounds faintly in the distance. Esau whines at my feet. I breathe deeply and feel the comfort of the numbing air in my lungs embrace me and wrap me in a cocoon safe from the evils of night. I shiver with content and close the door, turning to find O'Meara somberly regarding me from his cot against the far wall.

"Good morning," I say, briskly rubbing my hands together. "I hope you've awakened with an appetite for I am famished! How about some buckwheat cakes and maple syrup? Coffee won't take long for the coals are fair banked."

I scurry to the side table to set out the large, stone bowl and buckwheat flour. I feel O'Meara's eyes still upon me as I lift down the coffee grinder and sack of beans and begin to ready the pot. He grunts, and the cot creaks on its rawhide straps as he sits up and swings his feet to the floor. A familiar clicking sounds faintly as his fingers seek the hidden mysteries of his morning rosary.

"Won't be much doing today except clearing a path to the outhouse," I say, holding a one-sided conversation during his prayers. He does not answer, but I know he hears me for once-in-a-while he hesitates in clicking his beads. "And, someone will have to make it down to the lake to check the fish traps."

He sighs and yawns. "By somebody, I expect you mean me," he says. "Now, why do you suppose I would be thinking that?"

"Because you can't cook buckwheat cakes and your coffee tasted like mud," I answer. "And, it's your turn. I checked yesterday before the storm," I add. I lie, but I know he won't remember or, if he does remember, will pretend he does not. He sighs deeply and pushes himself erect. I hear his quick bubbling as he splashes cold water upon his face and scrubs his hands across his cheeks, the click of his brush around his shaving mug, the draw of his razor over the night bristles on his chin.

"Breakfast will be ready by the time you return," I say, more to hurry him on than to remind him of his duty. He grumbles but buttons himself into a heavy bearskin coat that hangs to his knees, stamps his feet into a pair of fur-lined boots, and slams out the door.

I laugh, delighted with my lie and my place in

the warm cabin. I pull a haunch of venison, the remains of last night's supper, onto the cutting board and carve several thin slices from it and layer them on the bottom of a heavy, cast-iron Dutch oven. Between the layers, I spread a mash made of finely ground acorns and hickory nuts, and wild honey, sprinkle the top with ground cinnamon, and place it on a grill over the coals in the fireplace. I pour the batter out on a iron plate and slide it into the oven built into the side of the chimney and gently pump air from the billows over the coals. I rock back on my heels, content with the smell of the woodsmoke, the heat on my face, the small fire flickering around the coals.

Images begin to gracefully dance and shift among the flames. Then suddenly a forgotten piece of wood catches then flares up. Graceful dancers turn to the monsters of bad memory. The wood burns in my head, unraveling thought. I lick my lips against sudden dryness, powerless to wrench my gaze from the writhing torture of the flames. My heart pounds wildly, threatening to shatter the bones in my chest. A long forgotten scream breaks again from my lips. Darkness falls, and I pitch forward, inescapably drawn into the flames. A familiar voice victoriously cries, "*Vae victis! Vae Victis!*"" Then, dimly, as from a distance, I hear my name and nothing more.

Chapter Twenty-four

During the darkness, I hear Esau repeatedly rise from his corner, and growl threateningly as he paces back and forth beside my bed. He snuffles suspiciously at the feet of shadowy figures erratically moving in and out of my vision, voices murmuring unintelligible words. Spoons force my lips apart, and tasteless liquids slide down my throat. Rosary beads click repeatedly from afar. I try to shout for them to stop their senseless rattling, but only silence speaks from my throat, the words remaining frozen in my mind. Slowly, forms begin to take shape in the darkness. I watch warily, commanding my muscles to remain in readiness to flee, knowing instinctively they are unable to respond. One of the forms moves through the darkness towards me; a woman with fiery cheeks, her face radiant.

"Have you been waiting?" she asks. "I am sorry to have been so long."

"It doesn't matter," I answer. The words surprise me; they had not been there moments before.

"It is good of you to say that," she responds and smiles. "Take my hand."

"Why?" I ask. My hand, trembling, lifts of its own will.

"Do you remember . . ." she begins, then stops, frowning.

"What is it?" I ask, suddenly alarmed. She shakes her head and does not answer. Slowly, she begins to draw away from me. Her form softens at the edges, then slowly begins to swirl and merge into the mist behind her. I cry out, "Come back! Come back!"

"Jonathon! Jonathon!" shouts a deep voice nearby. The darkness begins to lift, and I find myself back in my cabin. Esau whines and pushes his muzzle against my shoulder.

"Thank God!" O'Meara says. I turn towards him. He looks haggard and drawn, lines etched deeply into his face.

"Maybe," I croak, stop, and painfully swallow, then try again. "Maybe it would have been better if you would have left me there."

He smiles and shakes his head. He bends, and I hear water splashing in a pan, then a rag being wrung out. He straightens and lays the rag upon my forehead. It feels cold, but nice.

"You are not ready, yet," he gently says. "In time. In time."

"Ready for what?" I ask.

He raises my head and holds a glass to my lips. I swallow and taste cold water laced with a little brandy. He ignores my question.

"What happened after Girty removed you from

your cell?" he asks. "Was it still winter?"

"No," I answer. "Spring was almost over."

"Tell me about it," he says softly.

Irritated, I start to refuse then I catch his eyes and read the secrets lurking deep within them. I feel an insane urge to laugh for there are greater secrets than those he thinks he holds.

"Tell me," he says again, his voice soothing, commanding.

I force myself to relax and allow myself to be lulled by the hypnotic suggestion of his eyes. A tiny voice questions me: "What madness are you doing?" But I do not listen to the voice for I know now the reason that he has been sent to me.

"Tell me," he repeats. For a brief moment, I feel sadness for what he has lost through his zeal and ignorance. Then, the feeling passes as I feel my age and recognize the need for him sent to me. How much time is left? It doesn't matter: there will be enough. I begin.

Chapter Twenty-five

Summer nights and quiet moving water and the endless cathedral stillness of the forest. I moved through the dappled shadows of the trees, leaf mold collecting around my moccasins, following the river downstream, the water, clear above a gray-green bed, quiet now, but I knew the strength was there that could turn it to white and angry foam as it smashed against the rocks of the narrow canyons and deep cuts of the mountains where it would roar like Boanerges. Here, I thought, where Simon had brought me to heal, the river was broad—forty yards at least—and shallow—two-and-a-half or three feet deep. Clean gray granite chips filled the bed, and bits of quartz and flint striking fire from the bed from the flickering stars and weeping moon, silver maple leaves bobbing like clots of blood in the water. Another splashed in the shallows ahead of me. Graceful willows wept long arms over deep pools to shade the brown trout lying in their depths. Furry hawk-moths flew soundlessly in front of me, and frogs ceased their croaking at my approach only to begin again as I crept past.

Six months had passed—the Planting moon was long over—since Simon had brought me, my spirit shattered and spent, to the Seneca village and left me with Rides-the-Moon to heal. I remember very little of the time, and for that I am grateful. I was left alone much of the time save for the daughter of Rides-the-Moon who led me twice a week to the sweat lodge beside the frozen river where she scrubbed me clean and then patiently rubbed fragrant oil into my skin.

Sometimes, Rides-the-Moon would sit with me in front of the lodge fire and softly chant stories from the past, interweaving the myth of the warrior with the reality of the forest, while I slowly became aware of what was around me. I knew spring had arrived when I found the early ferns and monk's hood by the river and a clutch of mallard eggs. Yellow butterflies covered a clearing, like a carpet, and when I stepped into the clearing, the air became luminous with their startled flight. I moved through them, inhaling deeply the sudden smells of life that surrounded me and knew that I, too, was alive.

A branch snapped. I paused in the dark, waiting for him to emerge. I do not have to see him to know he is there. From first light, I knew he was watching me, following me as I moved through the day. I stepped beside a large oak and slid down its length to squat upon my heels, my back feeling the rough bark beneath my leather hunting shirt. A footstep sounded lightly in the glade behind me.

"Don't you think this has gone on long enough?"

I asked conversationally. "The night is getting older."

A quiet laugh met my words, and a dark figure soundlessly dropped beside me. His teeth flashed whitely in the dark of his face. I smelled the wood smoke upon his clothes: his long, black hair gleamed in the white starlight.

"I was beginning to wonder," he said. "Been following you a fair spell."

"Yes," I said, adding, "since morning."

He chuckled again after a short pause and lay back to stare at the stars through the leaves of the oak. The moon began to show: a hunter's moon, casting a pale fire on the silent waters of the river.

"Well," he said. "Either you are better, or I'm getting old."

"You'll never get old," I said. A sudden breeze blew quickly over the waters, pebbling my flesh. An owl called once from nearby. Suddenly, the woods burned in my head, and I saw with startling clarity the truthfulness of my statement for he had become the wind and the river and the trees and the owl and the moon, the birth of babies and the death of all men, and all moved in unity with him. A lump formed in my throat, and I rested against the oak, not trusting myself to speak further. My heart felt as if it would burst with affection for this woodsman who had taken such pains with me. I wanted to touch his hand and express my gratitude to him but held back, content to sit quietly in the dark beside him, watching the hunter's moon play upon the waters.

Finally, Simon broke the silence, startling me. "Will you follow me?" he asked without turning his head.

"Where?"

"To do my work," he quietly answered. "It is time."

"Yes, I will follow you," I said.

An owl hooted closer this time. He smiled and reached to touch the back of my hand. My flesh prickled from the contact.

"Good," he said. "We leave tomorrow for Kittanning for the Council of the Nations. Do you remember? Everything began there. Be ready by first light."

He touched my foot and rose and melted away into the darkness of the trees. When the sounds of his going passed, I crept forward on hands and knees and stretched out on the spot where he had lain. The grass was soft and warm, and I felt safe and comforted lying there alone with the night.

Chapter Twenty-six

Simon began his work as one of Lord Dunmore's emissaries under John Connolly at Fort Pitt, soon to become known as Fort Dunmore. Yet, I sensed this was only a means for an end known only to Simon. In the past, he had bitterly opposed settlers moving into the virgin wilderness and raping her with axes and plows, yet at times, he seemed willing to help the various land companies trying to force westward colonization. Some had even surveyed claims in lands that were sworn to members of the Nations by treaties passed years before.

Simon had been engaged to help strengthen Virginia's claims in the new territory around Fort Pitt. I dutifully followed, providing support whenever it was needed which was not often: Simon's brawny arm was usually enough to dissuade all but the most hot-tempered dissidents from the error of their ways.

Once in Hannastown, during a particularly bitter election, he stepped in front of a surly voter aiming a blow at the head of a woman who had made an uncomplimentary statement about one of the candidates and promptly broke the man's jaw with one well-aimed punch. After a while, the mere mention of his name and, I modestly add, his companion were enough to keep a sort of surly order around the polls.

For over a year, the boundary warfare continued as Pennsylvanians stubbornly resisted the attempts of the Virginians to expand north and west. Simon did his best to promote this ill-feeling, but other events disrupted the dispute when angry Shawnee and Mingo Indians began to attack and murder white families along the Ohio River. Dunmore seized the opportunity to organize a militia to drive the Indians farther westward and protect the settlers. Dunmore had planned a brilliant coup for he had no intention of disbanding his militia once he had resolved the Indian problem. Of course, no one but a few were aware of that: John Connolly, Simon Girty, and myself.

Simon found me busily packing a rucksack in my quarters at the fort the evening before we were to take the field with Dunmore's men. He glanced into the open rucksack resting on top of my cot, then settled himself in the room's lone chair.

"Take an extra blanket," he cautioned. "For the night may prove chill ere we return, I'm thinking."

"I shall," I said. I rolled needle and thread into a flap of soft buckskin and dropped it into the rucksack. I glanced at him: thin frown lines appeared faintly between his eyes. I sat on the bed, facing him.

"What's wrong?" I asked. He shook his head. A crooked smile appeared upon his lips.

The Renegade   by   Randy Lee Eickhoff

"Beginning a life with the gypsies and tinkers? But, then, you've always known me, haven't you?"

I nodded. "Yes. It is not hard when you become close to someone. I have often thought to write a monograph upon the subject. What is the problem?"

He frowned, his heavy eyebrows diabolically curling down over his eyes. "This whole march of Dunmore's. It's wrong. No good will come of it."

"Why don't you tell him?" I asked. "Better yet, why not tell him why the Nations have taken up arms?"

He shook his head, laced his fingers behind his neck, and leaned back in the chair until it creaked in protest.

"Dunmore hears only what he wants to hear," he mused. "Like all the whites. He does not think like us."

I noted the collective noun, and, although I felt pleased to be included in his thoughts as his peer, a vague uneasiness gnawed at the back of my mind. I quickly and firmly forced it away, focusing on Simon's words. I knew to what he referred: the extermination of our native brothers, the militia and settlers creating an unholy epiphany with the dates of their inhuman slaughter.

The Shawnee had slowly been pushed to the west, forcing the once urban dwellers to become wanderers. The iron plow quickly ate their hunting grounds. Lately, they had found a refuge as neighbors of the Wyandots and the Senecas and Delawares, but still, the settlers slowly whittled them down and my old nemesis Leggett publically proclaimed them vermin and, as the King's representative, paid out a shilling bounty for their scalplocks.

Settlers from Virginia found this not only beneficial for eliminating claims to the lands they wanted but profitable as well. Hunting Indians for bounty helped the settlers over thin times by providing them with money to buy the supplies for their families. The peaceful Indian, the mission Indian, the squaws and the children, all were easy prey. Once the hair had been separated from its wearer, no one could tell if male or female or even child had once worn it. Such was the fate of the family of Logan, a Mingo chief, the one for whom Dunmore had raised his militia.

For years, Logan had tried to live in peace with the white settlers who repaid his kindness with murder. Finally, Logan became mad and set out on a bloody trail of murderous revenge. I felt badly about the betrayal of Logan for he had been one of the Indians at our adoption ceremony, and anger at the post chaplain who continually used his name as a synonym for Satan while pronouncing the same blessings Herod gave his soldiers for the slaying of Jewish babies on the post melitia before their raids upon the Indian villages. I had fond recollections of the Logan who once played with the children in front of his lodge and patiently taught them the blessings of the forest.

"What will happen if Dunmore finds Logan?" I asked.

"He will destroy him," Girty answered bluntly. "One way or the other, Dunmore will destroy Logan."

"Is there no chance for a peaceful settlement?" I asked. He shrugged his shoulders.

"Maybe. But only after a great loss, I fear. Logan still loses even if he settles peacefully with Dunmore. Right now, Dunmore pretty much has things his own way. And," he emphatically added, "the people want him to kill the Indians. It's better that way for the settlers: the death of an Indian is one less obstacle to overcome to their land titles."

"And for us?"

He sighed and rose, stretching his arms to the ceiling, arching his back until it cracked.

"We'll do what we can," he said quietly. "Try and lessen the loss wherever possible. But we are dealing with stubborn men here, and there is great danger in that. Stubborn men are foolish men who do not see their foolishness. There's not much else we can do for the moment."

He walked to the door then paused. "This may well be one of the greatest injustices man will commit against man." He started to say something else, then changed his mind and, bidding me good night, left.

I crossed to the latch and set it for the night. I thought about the army Dunmore had raised and the men he had chosen to lead them: George Rogers Clarke, Colonel Cresap, Simon Kenton, John Gibson, and William Crawford. And Lewis Wetzel who loomed dark and dangerous over all. I shivered for remembering his name forced me to remember the man and the terrible things that had happened in the places in the forest where he visited.

That night, I dreamed of Simon, spread-eagled between two birches, and Wetzel, maniacally laughing, repeatedly thrusting a lance into Simon's side while I watched helplessly from an oak where I was bound tightly with green rawhide straps. I awoke near dawn, wet and shaking, my mouth dry with fear, my head aching, the blankets of my bed wrapped tightly around me like a winding sheet, fearing the meaning of the dream.

Chapter Twenty-seven

A cold and gray morning greeted us with that promise of winter August sometimes brings. High overhead, a vulture flew in widening gyres as we marched out of Fort Dunmore to the piping of fifes and the rattling of drums. It did not seem a very auspicious omen.

Our plans called for us to march down the Ohio River to meet Colonel Andrew Lewis at the mouth of the Great Kanawha. Lewis had taken half of Dunmore's three thousand men, and, I discovered to my relief, Lew Wetzel as his lead scout. I offered a silent prayer of thanks to whatever gods listened for that blessing.

Dunmore was anxious to get this adventure out of the way for he had a round of parties to attend in Williamsburg in celebration of the coming Christmas. He would have cut a heroic figure with a victory of this sort, but his haste proved costly for him. Dunmore's plans were for Lewis to march westward, following the route of the Great Kanawha while Dunmore led his men down the Ohio, pincering the Indians between them.

Simon and I were the flank scouts and took advantage of Dunmore's ignorance of the area to bring back reports of massive Indian movement west of the

Ohio. As Simon expected, Dunmore eagerly turned away from his planned route and led his half of the army through the forest away from Lewis. Later, I discovered what had happened to Lewis from a drummer boy.

When Lewis arrived where the Great Kanawha empties into the Ohio, he moved out onto Point Pleasant, a V-shaped piece of land jutting out to the southwest. The Kanawha ran along its lower shore while the Ohio bounded the upper. His men encamped there, confident of Dunmore's arrival the next day. Lewis did not know that Logan, who somehow had escaped Wetzel's discovery, had been moving parallel to his left flank.

When the attack came in the early morning, Lewis and his men had just begun their cookfires. Logan, his Mingoes supported by the Shawnee under Cornstalk and Blackhoof and the Senecas led by Rides-the-Moon, tried to surround the camp. An alert sentry, however, spoiled that part of their plan. The Virginia riflemen quickly spread out among the trees, desperate to keep the Indians from completing the circle and cutting off any chance of retreat.

Lewis's brother, Colonel Charles Lewis, in command of the right flank, fell in the first charge, but Colonels Field and Fleming quickly moved squads of riflemen up to keep the attackers from plowing through the gap in the line. Slowly, the Indians drove the

Virginians back along the spur towards the point where the rivers converged. This proved to be a blessing for the Virginians, however, for the rivers provided a natural barrier against further flanking attacks. Despite Cornstalk's constant urging of his warriors to, "Be strong! Be strong!" no advance could be made.

When night fell, the warriors carried away their dead and wounded. Roughly a quarter of their force, almost two hundred thirty men, had been lost. The Virginians lost half their officers and fifty-two enlisted men. But they acted quickly under cover of night to build a large redoubt out of driftwood and fallen timbers to make their position impregnable. Sadly, Cornstalk and Logan broke off the attack.

Meanwhile, Dunmore had grown restless with the lack of contact with the Indians and started questioning us closely whenever we brought in our "reports." We were not surprised, for we had not come across much evidence to support our claim of having stumbled across a large force. We had found a young buck hunting and dispatched him with a message for the Indians living along the Ohio to move away from the river north along the track we originally planned to follow. Our "detour" would allow them to escape behind us.

The fifth day out, a light drizzle found Simon and me hunkered beneath the low-swinging branches of an old oak. Roots jutted out from its trunk like low altars. Around us lay leaves colored deep russets and browns. Dunmore and his men waited impatiently a mile to the southeast of us. Simon pulled a piece of pemmican from his pack and divided it with his knife, handing a piece to me.

"What do you think?" he asked, chewing methodically on the cured meat. I stuffed the pemmican in my mouth, rolling it into a ball in my cheek to soften it.

"I think we've stretched this out about as far as we dare,"I said. "I didn't like the look in Dunmore's eyes last night after we delivered the report. I think he's getting suspicious."

Simon grunted, swallowing the pemmican in installments before he spoke.

"Either that," he agreed, "or restless. That could be good, though. It might make him reckless."

"Or wondering if he should change his chief of scouts," I countered. "I think we'd better lead him around towards Point Pleasant now. We could make it a sense of urgency. He'd swing the column south hoping to catch the Indians between Lewis and us. When we get close, we can fire off a couple of shots and claim a sentry saw us and lead them back north. By then, our provisions will be running out and Dunmore will have to return to the fort."

He nodded thoughtfully, staring into the forest in front of us, carefully examining the plan for any problems.

"Might work," he said slowly. "We'll have to be careful. Clarke came in last night. He'll cause us problems: he's a friend of Wetzel."

"That's another problem we'll have when we join with Lewis. Wetzel has no love for either of us. We can keep ahead of Clarke by sending him to the southwest on our flank."

"All right," he said, and stood in one fluid movement. He checked the priming of his rifle and carefully wrapped a piece of smoked deerskin around it to keep the powder dry. "We'd better run back. Might make things a bit more convincing if we appear a mite rushed."

We headed back towards Dunmore at a dog trot, carefully staying away from the game trails for we did not wish to encounter a stray Shawnee or Seneca who might not recognize us. But the woods were not thick at his point, and we had little trouble with the undergrowth.

Dunmore waited impatiently just inside the flap of his tent as we trotted through the camp towards him. "Well?" he snapped as we halted. "Did you find them?" His eyes flashed darkly like green pools in the deep forest. He slapped a gauntlet against his thigh. "I do hope you will not disappoint me. Again."

The last word carried a hint of finality to it. I cast an involuntary look at Simon: he showed no concern, his dark eyes meeting Dunmore's without flinching. His broad chest rose and fell perceptively from our run but not, I knew, from weariness.

"They've swung southeast, your Lordship," he said. "The whole lot of them. I reckon the trail to be not more than two days old."

"South*east?*" Dunmore said skeptically. "Are you sure? To now, they've been heading on a straight westerly point. Why would they change?"

I sensed the faint stirrings of suspicion in his voice, saw the rise of color in his powdered cheeks. I started to answer to support Simon's story, but a smooth tenor voice broke in.

"Begging your Lordship's pardon, but that follows what I came in with."

I turned to face a red-haired man, slim like an alder, dressed in forest-green-dyed buckskins.

"And what do you surmise about this, Mr. Clarke?" Dunmore asked. Clarke gave us each a cool look then directed his attention towards Dunmore.

"As Girty said: they've swung. Towards the Ohio. That's plain to see."

Simon and I exchanged quick glances. He made an almost imperceptible movement with his head. Unknown to the two of us, we had been paralleling the movement of a large band to the north of us in Clarke's scouting area. That explained why we had not crossed their trail. But when and where had they swung south?

To do so would have forced them across our track.

"They've got big plans, looks like," Simon said slowly. "You follow them long?" Clarke nodded.

"About a day. From the north. They've got direction. And, there's a lot of them. Most a hundred. Maybe more. Something funny, too. Tracks show Shawnee and Seneca along with the Mingoes. Might even be a Huron or two."

"Lewis!" Dunmore said suddenly. "By God! Those filthy savages are after him!"

"Way it looks to me," Clarke said. "*If* Colonel Lewis has made it to Point Pleasant."

"If he hasn't by now, then he's run into an even larger band," Dunmore grimly said. "Bugler! Sound the call!"

The notes of "March 'o the Clans" began to pipe simultaneously with "To Arms."

"We might get lucky and catch them between us, your Lordship," Simon said.

"Yes," Dunmore said moodily, "There is that possibility. But, I fear the worst. Too much time has been lost! Too much time!"

He strode towards his horse as the strikers began to rapidly pull down the tent.

"As straight a march line as you can lay, Mr. Girty! And, set your flankers shallow. 'Tis speed we want now, man! Speed!"

Simon looked at Clarke and smiled faintly.

"Well, you heard him. Take the southwest flank and stay within a quarter mile. Jonathon and I will take the point. I do not think we'll have to worry much about the north but set young Travers out anyway. Can't do any harm."

Clarke nodded and briskly moved away to follow Simon's instructions. Simon gave me a slight grin.

"Lucky," I murmured least a striker overhear me. "We were very lucky Clarke could corroborate our story. Things were about to get a bit sticky."

"Luck?" He laughed. "Is that what you call it?"

"What else?" I asked. He shrugged and strode away. I stared after him for a moment, my thoughts in a daze. Then, I slowly moved after him. Luck, I told myself. It had to be luck. But a part of me began to wonder.

Chapter Twenty-eight

We never made it to Point Pleasant. About a day away from the mouth of the Kanawha, we stumbled over a day-old large trail leading west away from the Ohio. From the tracks and broken bushes, it was evident the band included several badly-wounded Indians. Dead leaves, oak, maple, and sycamore, had been pushed aside by several travois dragging wounded.

"Injured?" Dunmore said after Simon explained. "Battle injuries from Lewis's contingent?" Simon shrugged his shoulders and spread his hands.

"Likely," he reluctantly said. "He's the only other force out here that we know about." Dunmore frowned and walked a few paces along the trail.

"Then, we can assume that we're too late to do Lewis any good," he said softly. "Would you agree, Mr. Girty?" Simon silently nodded, his eyes intent upon Dunmore. "And, these Indians are badly injured, you say?"

"Looks like it," Simon said dryly. "I'd say that they probably came off the worst for wear against Lewis. Course, we don't know how badly Lewis came out of it, either."

"Yes," Dunmore said, and thoughtfully stared down the trail. A woodpecker hammered in the silence and startled a squirrel who angrily chattered back. "But, either way, our continuing on to the Kanawha and Ohio will serve no practical purpose. On the other hand," he gestured down the trail, "we could, with a forced march, come upon these Indians by early morn and put a stop to their maraudering. Yes." He gnawed his lip for a moment then decisively clapped his hands together and turned to face us. "We'll do it! Follow the trail, if you will, Mr. Girty, with all possible haste."

"But, sir, Colonel Lewis!" Clarke protested, only to be cut short by Dunmore's icy stare.

"Colonel Lewis is a soldier!" he snapped. "As such, I am sure he will understand our pursuit of the enemy. It is our duty, sir, to protect the citizens of Virginia's frontier, and, by God, sir, I intend to fulfill my obligations! I hope I have made myself perfectly clear upon that point!"

Clarke mumbled he allowed that he had whereupon Dunmore fixed him with an icy glare for a moment before turning back to Simon and myself.

"Do you," he said to Simon, "or you," indicating me, "have any questions as well?"

"No, your Lordship," Simon said. "We'll take you where you want to go. You might want to send a detachment back to Colonel Lewis, though, to inform him where we're headed."

The Renegade by Randy Lee Eickhoff

"Impossible!" Dunmore said. "We may need every man ourselves. A runner should be able to handle that quite well, I should think," Dunmore added. He paused to look at Clarke. "And, since you are so concerned about the welfare of Colonel Lewis, sir, you may be that runner." Clarke stiffened at Dunmore's words. His face whitened with fury. To ask a scout to do a runner's work was a grave insult. To order it was tantamount to a demotion in the ranks.

"I am a scout, sir," Clarke said, barely controlling his anger. Dunmore impatiently turned away from him and strode quickly back to his horse. He spoke over his shoulder.

"For the moment, you are a runner. Tell Colonel Lewis to place his wounded in a small vanguard and leave a squad with them for protection and follow us with all due haste. It is imperative that he join with us as quickly as possible for a joint punitive operation against the savages. Do you understand?"

"And if Colonel Lewis is dead?" Clarke asked quietly. Twin spots of red appeared high on his cheeks.

"Then tell him nothing," Dunmore said, swinging into his saddle. His horse snorted and danced a bit, but he quickly brought it under control with a firm hand upon the rein. "But do not bother me with the details until this is over! For the moment, I have a date to fulfill with destiny! Mr. Girty! If you please!"

Simon jerked his head at me, and together we

moved out on a lope along the Indians' trail. Before we disappeared from view, I looked back and saw Clarke still standing where we had left him: glaring murderously at Lord Dunmore who pointedly ingnored him, staring after us *quasi vestigias nostras insistere.* Then, he disappeared behind a stand of trees, and Simon and I were alone in the forest. High above our heads, ravens flew in tight circles, following our progress like guardian angels. Or messengers. But for whom? I wondered.

For three hours, we trotted along the trail, making good time through the woods, veering slightly towards the northwest. Suddenly, Simon drew up beneath an ash tree and squatted on his heels to study the trail in front of him. I dropped beside him. The trail divided a short distance in front of us. A small group had broken off from the larger band and headed towards the southwest.

"You notice anything?" he asked, eyes darting from side-to-side. I turned my attention to the front. Ahead of us a bluejay squawked indignantly at a gray squirrel creeping along a branch of a walnut tree. Robins hopped upon the ground beneath a mayberry bush, searching for worms. A hummingbird flitted in and out of a screen of wild grape vines crawling up an elm. A bee buzzed us once, then headed away into the forest.

"The trail," he said, lifting his chin. "Why have

they not tried to hide it?"

"An ambush?" I asked, then shook my head. "Maybe further on but not here. The signs aren't right."

"Or maybe, they're too badly hurt to make an ambush," he said slowly.

"You're right." He pondered the trail for a moment, then chuckled deep in his throat. "You know where they're headed? Old Chilicothe, the Shawnee headquarters. There are missionaries at Chillicothe. Priests." He threw his head back, laughing. "I don't think Dunmore is going to get the battle he wants. Not, that is, if the Indians manage to reach the Shawnee village ahead of him."

I considered the trail again: it ran straight in front of us, veering only to avoid trees or brush too thick for a man to crash through. A sense of urgency hung over the trail, fear that still cloyed the nostrils like overripe apples. And death. I could sense that as well.

"Whoever leads this band must be very clever," I said "And, Colonel Lewis must not have been massacred for if he had, there would not be a trail such as this. There would be no reason for such a hurry. They could not know of our presence. Yes," I continued, musing, "he must be very clever. I wonder who it is?"

"Cornstalk. Or Logan. But I would wager it to be Cornstalk. Logan has too much hate within him to head for a village where missionaries live. That would be surrender. No, I think the smaller band is being led by Logan while Cornstalk leads the others to the missionaries. He would be the one to sue for peace," he said.

"Yes," I said, remembering Cornstalk from the days when I lived as a slave in the lodge of Rides-the-Moon. "But will he be able to make it to Chillicothe before Dunmore catches him with the wounded slowing him down? Or," I gestured towards the trail leading to the southwest, "will we give him Logan? Who shall we sacrifice?"

"Why sacrifice anyone?" Simon asked."All we have to do is slow Lord Dunmore down to give Cornstalk the chance to reach sanctuary at Chillicothe."

"How are you going to do that?" I demanded. I pointed at the trail. "You heard Dunmore's order. There's no way that we can pretend to have lost that. Even Dunmore could follow that trail. We can't even disguise it."

"True," Simon said. "But we can give him more decisions to make by creating other trails."

"And if he chooses the wrong trail? As chief scout you will be held responsible," I added.

"Maybe," he said smiling. "But he will only ask my advice after he has wasted time trying to decide upon his own. I, of course, will hesitate before giving him the correct trail. We have only to keep up the deception until nightfall. Dunmore will not be able to march then."

"And will we have time to do that?" I asked.
"Dunmore moves swiftly behind us."

"We have our first choice already made," Simon
said indicating the trail to the southwest. "I'll wait for
him here while you follow the main trail for a few miles
and make another. I'll tell Dunmore that you're
following the small trail in an attempt to discover their
whereabouts."

"I somehow thought it would be me," I said. He
laughed and leaned back against the ash.

"We all have our dates with destiny," he said,
solemnly mimicking Dunmore.

"Make sure you find my trail. I wouldn't want
my effort to be wasted," I said, rising to my feet.

"Join us at nightfall," he called softly as I moved
down the trail. I waved and walked as quickly as I
could. The day felt warm upon my back and soon a fine
sheen of perspiration covered me. My muscles felt
loose and relaxed. A dove called mournfully to me as I
passed, and once I frightened a deer that crashed
through the brush away from me. A sense of peace
worked within me as I moved through the forest. A
sweet, sulphurous smell from the old leaves rose from
the forest floor to greet me as an old friend. I felt I
knew well the places I passed: the trees stood as
familiar acquaintances and their solitude became my
solitude.

The Renegade   by   Randy Lee Eickhoff

Chapter Twenty-nine

Simon's plan worked so well that the column never made it to the last false trail I had cut before night overtook them. Dunmore had seemed disappointed when I reported in with nothing of significance. (I lied and told him I had lost the trail in a creek—a story that seemed to affirm his opinion of me as an incompetent.) But Simon had been well pleased with the work I had done. Our ruse had given the warriors almost a day's lead over the column. Dunmore had no chance of catching them before they reached Chillicothe. Of course, he did not know their destination; we carefully kept that information from him. The only other one who might have had an inkling to the warriors' plan—Clarke—was far to our rear. We only had to pace the column's march to match that of the warriors in front of us for the next sixty miles or so. We had gained them the breathing room they needed; more than they needed, as it turned out, for Dunmore had become so perplexed by the "trails" and choices left to him that we made little distance the next day as he paused several times to reflect back upon the previous day's proceedings.

The day held a bite of cold to it against which

fires in the lodges had been lit when we finally arrived at Chillicothe. The heavy air kept the smoke close to the ground, making the village appear covered by fog. Unfriendly eyes watched our approach as we emerged from the bleak autumn forest with pipes and fifes wailing and wound our way through the village towards the Council House in the center. A tall, thin, Jesuit monk robed in black waited for us in front of the Council House. Flames of hatred spewed forth from his zealot's eyes at our approach. I think his name was Claude something or other—Charmolue, I believe, French, I do remember—who did not make us welcome.

"Father, I am surprised to see you here among these heathens," Lord Dunmore said, stepping from his stirrups. His words were smooth, noncommital, but I could hear the dislike for the priest behind them.

"And, among which heathens would you expect to find me?" Charmolue answered in almost flawless English. His eyes contemptuously flitted over the militia behind us. "Those whom you lead?" Dunmore turned a dull red.

"Now, see here, Father," he spluttered, but Charmolue did not allow him time to protest.

"I am not fond of you," Charmolue said through thin lips. "You are not wanted here."

"We have never met," Dunmore said stiffly.

"We do not need to," Charmolue said. "You are

English. That is enough. I do not want you in my village."

"*Your* village?" Simon interjected angrily. "By what right do you claim this village?"

The priest shifted eyes burning like hot coals to flare against the gray ice in Simon's own.

"Their souls belong to God," Charmolue said, his voice quivering with rage. Spittle bubbled at the corners of his lips. "I, as God's representative, brought them out of the darkness to the true light. From the primitive savages of *that*," he gestured at the forest behind us, "to the beauty and civil harmony that now awaits them in heaven. Because of this, I have earned them. Each and every one of them is mine. Mine!"

"Yet, in the twinkling of an eye, they can be destroyed. Where once they would have resisted, would have fought for life, now they will complaisantly and eagerly greet their deaths. You have not saved their souls; you have enslaved their will," I said accusingly.

"Heresy," he hissed, the word an adder's strike. He turned to Dunmore. "Be gone! Leave us!"

"You leave," Simon growled, his eyes pinpoints of fury. "You black-garbed devil! What God did you bring to replace the one they already had. The Master of Life who continually struggles against his evil brother Stony Coat? Where is the force of *orenda*, that which fills the world and endows men with spiritual power and gives them the ability to do great deeds? What have you done? Black friar! Meddlesome fool! How dare you bring evil here? Do you count their souls, using your black beads as a ledger? I could kill you for what you have done." He raised his rifle, but Dunmore quickly stepped forward to knock it down.

"That will be enough!" he snapped. "You!" He motioned at me. "Take him from here and stay with him until I send for you." He turned back to the priest as I caught Simon by the arm and pulled him towards the forest.

"You take much upon yourself, sir!" he said. Angry words leaped to Charmolue's lips only to fall silent before Dunmore's next words. "And, by God, sir, if you persist in this, I may well let Girty have you! Whether or not we are to fight here depends upon whether the savages are willing to listen to reason. You have one day in which to convince them!" He turned and mounted his horse. He paused and again addressed the priest. "One day. I would advise you to consult their leaders and do your utmost to convince them they have little recourse but to agree to my terms. If not," he looked meaningfully around the village. "If not, then a lot of innocent deaths will be upon your soul." He spurred away, leaving the priest alone with his anger.

I pulled Simon to the outskirts of the village and into the trees. He jerked his arm free and stalked into the forest's depths. I followed at a discreet distance. At last, he came to a quiet pool surrounded by blackberry bushes in a small clearing. He fell beside it and thrust his face into the waters of the pool to cool it then rolled onto his back to gaze through the naked limbs of the trees at the leaden sky, flinging his arms out to make a cruciform. I sat beside an old, gnarly oak and listened the quiet of the forest around me.

"There is no hope in the white man's God," he said. "Too much evil has already been committed in His name. The bounties, the destruction of the forest . . ."

He fell silent. Slowly, the movement of the forest returned: the tiny rustle of mice under the dead leaves, tentative chirps of birds, the rustlings of larger animals behind bushes. Finally, he rolled his head to look at me. He tried to smile.

"The day has become burdensome, and I grieve for my people. Even the sun must be soothed from its full radiance. Speak comfort to me."

"What would you have me say?"

He laughed and rubbed the palms of his hands over his face.

"Ah! A question! Always your answer. But when will you supply answers to your questions? All right. Why do you follow me?"

"I owe you a service," I replied. I shrugged. "And, you asked."

"No other reason?"

I sighed, and laid my rifle across my knees.

"I feel we belong together," I said slowly. "I feel

. . ." Vague images began to swirl and form hazy pictures in my mind: the strange circumstances surrounding the death of his stepfather, the early massacre in the forest, the strange meeting with Kenton.

"Yes," he prompted.

"Nothing," I said, unfocusing from the past. "Compelled, maybe."

"Do you remember the time we were together in the Seneca village?" he asked suddenly. Taken by surprise, I answered I did. "And when we were brought into the tribe? What happened that day?" I nodded. He smiled and rose to his feet. "Think upon that," he said. "Perhaps you'll find your answer there. Now, I am calm. Let us return to Lord Dunmore and that . . . that priest."

I rose and followed him from the clearing back to the village. I pondered over his words and wondered if for the first time he was beginning to have self-doubts. Then, I laughed at my fears: *Et fili non prae metu pater.*

A squirrel chattered angrily as we passed too close to his winter's cache. Dimly, I registered the hammering of a woodpecker, a single, solitary whistle of a quail, the long, plaintive cry of a mourning dove, and, suddenly, silence.

Alarmed, I halted, raising my rifle to readiness. Ahead of me, Simon, too, stopped, warily cocking his head to one side, listening to the sharp stillness. Then, I heard it: a soft, gentle sighing, rising and falling as if the woods were breathing, followed by a low moaning that made my arms gooseflesh.

"What is it?" I whispered. He smiled, lowering his rifle.

"Do not be alarmed. There is not danger," he said.

"How do you know?" I asked.

"Because he is singing a song of mourning to come," he answered.

"He?"

"My father," he answered, a hint of impatience in his voice. "Can't you hear him?"

I shook my head in answer. The annoyance disappeared from his face to be replaced with a look of great sadness. "I am sorry. But, be patient: the time is not far off when you will understand all."

He turned and slowly walked away. I hesitated, listening to the moaning of the forest, trying to conjure a breeze in the stillness of the air. At last, I surrendered and, holding my rifle in readiness against the unknown, followed Simon back to the village, remembering Matthew's words: *Vox clamantis in deserto*, but equally rejecting them.

"Nonsense," I said to myself, recognizing the suggestion of the words. "You are ignoring logic. Man makes his gods when he wishes."

Suddenly, I felt frightened.

The Renegade   by   Randy Lee Eickhoff

Chapter Thirty

"My God! Do you know what you're saying?" explodes O'Meara, recoiling away from me. His eyes flash a mixture of anger and betrayal with a flicker of fear at the core. "This is blasphemy! The sin of Lucifer!" He crosses himself reflexively upon mentioning the fallen angel.

Esau grumbles in protest as I slide my slippered foot from beneath his head. I rise from my chair and place another log upon the fire. Outside, the wind howls. The winter storm has been with us for two days. Even Keogh has not been able to visit us from the fort. I bring back the brandy bottle and pour my distraught priest a healthy dram. He drinks quickly, then places the glass upon the table and again crosses himself.

"*Omnipotens Domine, Verborum Dei Patris, Christe Jesu, Deus et Dominus universae creaturae...*" he intones. I pour him another drink.

"It is a bit late for that, don't you think?" I ask loudly over his recitation of the *Ritual romanum*. "I have lived with these devils for too many years to see them as little more than old friends. Most of them, that is." I amend, involuntarily shivering against memory. "And, some I do not want to remember so please stop this nonsense."

"Exorcizo te, immundissime spiritus, omnis incursio adversarii, omne phantasma, omnis legio..." he bellows, ignoring my entreaty.

A gray fog fills my vision. Dimly through the sudden roaring in my ears, I hear Esau growling. Thick saliva fills my mouth. Suddenly, the years fall away like scales from my eyes, and I see again the burning fires, the naked, twisting, oily bodies of the savages, Simon, myself, and hear the throbbing drums. A scream explodes from deep within me.

"Stop it!"

The air suddenly seems sucked out of the room, leaving behind a vacuum. Silence falls. A log cracks on the fire. Esau howls. Air flows back into my lungs with a rush, and I fall, gasping, into my chair. I feel a glass being forced into my hand, then raised to my lips, and taste the familiar bite of brandy.

"Forgive me, 'Tis a terrible thing I have done to you. I do not know what got into me," O'Meara says shakily.

"Excessive religious fervor," I mutter weakly. The glass again nudges my lips; I sip dutifully. I raise my hand and shakily sketch a cross in the air over the brandy. *"In nomin Patri, et Fili, et Spiritus sancto..."*

"No," he interrupts. He shakes his head and pulls the glass from my lips. "'Tis no joking matter. Do not be trying to make it one. The good Lord may not be taking it as such."

"Perhaps he should. He has played a monstrous one upon us," I suggest.

"Man, Jonathon, made his own destiny," he murmurs. "You cannot be asking God to take responsibility for our sins."

"Why not? We are forced to take responsibility for His."

He sighs and places the cup of brandy upon the table and returns to his chair. He fingers the black beads of his rosary for a moment then folds his hands and places them in his lap.

"It is a privilege to suffer for that is God's way of showing that He forgives us," he explains, carefully enunciating each word as an elder will to a child. I bristle: I am old but far from my dotage. I swallow to contain my anger.

"But," I deliberately say, "whoever can possibly forgive God?"

"Cannot you be thinking of forgiveness. Jonathon? 'Tis His to which I am referring. You have a great need of it, I'm after thinking."

"No." I push myself erect. "No, that I will not do," I say, adding ruefully, "nor would there be much use in doing so." He opens his mouth to speak, but I wave him to silence. "I am not in the mood, Father O'Meara. I warned you about this, but you insisted. Do you wish to hear the rest or have you heard enough to satisfy yourself?"

He hesitates, hands straying again to the rosary at his belt. Finally, he sighs and reaches his glass from his seat. "'Tis a duty; 'tis a duty. Pour me another jar, if you be so disposed, and be on with your story."

A large gust of wind strikes the cabin, rattling the shutters and shooting down the chimney, cusing the fire to flare. He looks startled, then nervously laughs.

"An old wives' superstition, that one. Sure, and I'll not be holding back for a bit of wind. A foul day, a foul day. Tell your story, tell your story."

I pour his glass full and lean back in my chair. I stare deeply into the burning coals and let the memories creep like grave worms into my mind, searching, sorting. Then, I begin.

Chapter Thirty-one

We were awakened the next morning by Lord Dunmore's runner. We gathered our rifles and followed him to Dunmore's tent where Dunmore paced anxiously back and forth, casting worried looks in the direction of the Council House.

"Girty? I am most afraid that scoundrel of a priest means us mischief. He went into that building a half-hour past and has not re-appeared. He was to deliver my words to the council. I fear the priest feels more obligation to *le bon patrie* than to *Dieu*," he said with intensity immediately upon noting our approach.

"What do you want us to do?" Simon asked calmly. Lord Dunmore's eyebrows shot upward in surprise.

"Can't you stop him? In there? I thought . . ." He lamely let his words trickle away, embarrassed by the thought a white man could be friends with savages. For priests, it was an obligation, but for others it was a question of character. Simon smiled faintly and leaned his rifle against Dunmore's tent. He unbuckled the belt that held his long knife. I followed suit.

"Yes," he said, upon straightening. "That I can do." He gave me a significant glance, and we walked together through the village to the Council House and entered. We stood for a moment to let our eyes adjust to the gloom for the windows had been covered with heavy shutters signifying the council meeting, the interior lighted by torches deeply anchored into primitive wall sconces. An odor of sweat and grease and burning tar and pine greeted us. I noticed the tribal emblems of the Iroquois: the Mohawks, Oneidas, Onondagas, Cayugas, Tuscaroras, and Senecas. Opposite them sat the Mingoes, Shawnees, a few Delewares, and, I blinked in surprise, Hurons, the bitter enemies of the Iroquois. I recognized Cornplanter of the Shawnees and Red Jacket from the Seneca. Thayendanegea, a Mohawk also known as Joseph Brant, the new self-proclaimed prophet Handsome Lake, and Wingemund.

Peré Claude Charmolue whirled from his place beside Cornstalk in the center of the Long House to face us upon our entrance.

"Get out!" he ordered. Arrogance rode heavily upon his brow. "You have no place here!"

A figure stirred in the shadows near the wall, and Cornplanter stepped forward.

"I greet our brothers Nightwind and The Chosen," he said. Upon the mention of Simon's name, the other Indians in the lodge rose respectfully, offering soft words of greeting. Confusion clouded Charmolue's face. He stood uncertainly for a moment, staring at

Simon, then grudgingly stepped aside and made to sit at the wall.

"No!" Simon said abruptly. "This is no place for you, Blackfriar. It is a meeting for the Six Nations." The priest flushed and stood glaring at Simon.

"I have as much right here as do you and your friend, Girty!" he hissed.

"You have no rights," Simon calmly said. "You attempt to mislead these people by placing fear in their minds as you have in the minds of others in other villages. You convince them to give up their weapons and take up the plow, but when the grasshoppers come and eat their crops, they starve because they have driven the game away by clearing the land for their crops. You give them only crackers to eat in place of the food that they cannot grow. Or, you promise them cake if they will but give some of their land to the church."

"And you, Girty, what would you give them?"

"Stones," Simon answered. He turned from the puzzlement in the priest's face to Cornstalk. "Since when do the Nations allow outsiders into their tribal council? Is he a slave? If so, his place is at the door. If not, then he does not belong here!" Cornstalk slowly nodded.

"It is as you say," he answered. He motioned to Charmolue. "You must go."

"But what about him? And him?" Charmolue

226

exclaimed, jabbing forked fingers like an ancient curse at us. Wingemund rose and stoically motioned at the door as had Cornstalk.

"Our Seneca brothers are welcome in the Council of the Nations," he said.

Understanding slowly filled Charmolue's face. His lips twisted in a bitter smile as he looked with loathing at us.

"So. To whom do you give your obedience, Girty?" he asked scornfully.

"To myself. As a man," Simon answered. "To the Master of Life as His son."

Savage satisfaction gleamed from Charmolue's face at Simon's deliberate avoidance of the question for in Simon's silence he had the answer he wanted. A brave touched the priest's arm. He turned and stumbled from the Long House.

Simon gripped Cornplanter's arms, affectionately saying, "It is good to sit in council again with you, my friend." Cornplanter grunted with pleasure and returned Simon's grip.

"It is good to see The Chosen again," he said.

"And He-Who-Follows, Nightwind," another said, rising to greet me.

"Rides-the-Moon!" I exclaimed with delight. His broad face broke into a smile as we gripped each other's forearms. I was surprised to see how much older he had become: a touch of gray in his hair, wrinkles deeper, mouth thinner, a fresh scar over one shoulder. But I could still feel youth in his grip and see affection in his face. "It has been far too long. I have greatly missed you."

"Will you be long with us?" he asked. I threw a quick look at Simon and shook my head.

"I do not know," I answered regretfully. He nodded, trying to keep the disappointment from showing upon his face.

"When will the time come?" he asked. "It has been long and for some their time grows short. Are we not yet worthy?"

"Yes," Simon said. "But *we* are not yet worthy of you. And, there is much to do. Be patient."

Rides-the-Moon nodded, resigned, and returned to his seat. I followed, turning Simon's words over in my mind. The braves made room for me, and I sat between them, separated from Simon by Cornplanter on my left. Cornstalk patiently waited while we greeted the others we knew and when we had quieted, addressed Simon.

"What brings The Chosen to our council?" he asked formally. Simon rose and stepped to the center next to Cornstalk and spoke, slowly turning to include all with his words.

"All know me here," he said, and waited until the respectful acknowledgment of his words had been made. "This battle against the white man should not have been made. He who advised it spoke not with the wisdom of the Master of Life but from the deceiving words of his evil brother Stony Coat. He did not have *orenda* and should not have spoken." He stared for a moment at Handsome Lake who angrily blushed and avoided his eyes. He turned and muttered something to Thayendanegea on his right. The two looked with malice upon Simon, and I reminded myself to watch them carefully in the future.

"The white man has many warriors—too many warriors for the Iroquois and their friends." He paused when Thayendanegea leaped to his feet, angrily interrupting.

"Has The Chosen forgotten the strength of his own people, the *Hodenosaune,* the Six Nations? This is a council for men! Not the fearful pipings of a child mewling for its mother! Do not listen to this man who betrays his people! He has lived too much among the white men!"

"And you have not, Joseph Brant?" Simon said softly, using Thayendanegea's white name. Brant had been educated at Moore's Indian Charity School at Lebanon, Connecticut and fought for the British during the French and Indian War. His eyes narrowed as he considered Simon's remarks.

"Are you calling me a traitor to my people?" he asked, his voice dangerously soft.

"If you persist in this madness, yes," Simon

said. "It is not time, yet. And you know it. As does your 'prophet.'" He nodded at Handsome Lake who blushed, recognizing in Simon's words the suggestion of a false prophet.

"And who will tell us the time? You?" Brant did not try to keep his contempt from his voice. "I know what they claim." He flung his hand in a disdainful gesture at the Senecas. "And others." Angry mutters followed his words. "What do you claim?"

"Nothing more than you are willing to believe," Simon answered calmly.

"And I choose not to believe you!"

"Then, believe in Stony Coat," Simon said. "For I tell you, the time is not right." He contemptuously turned his back on Brant to address the others. "Soon, the time will come when the white warriors will divide themselves and war upon each other in the way the Iroquois and the Huron did in the Trade Wars so many years ago when each claimed to own the rights to trade among the other tribes. Yet, they were brothers for did not the great Huron prophet Deganawidah and his follower Hiawatha of the Mohawks join us together as the Nations? And still the Irquois and the Hurons made war upon each other. The time is coming when the white warriors will war in like manner. Then, will the time be right! But, not now! Not now, I say! And those who would convince you to do otherwise are false prophets and not endowed with *orenda* as they want you to believe. They do not serve the Nations but only themselves. They are filled with greed and envy and thirst for power and glory at the expense of their brothers."

Abruptly, he sat down. Brant started a hot retort, but Cornplanter rose.

"I will speak," Cornplanter said quickly. "Chillicothe is my village, the Shawnee my people. The Mohawk have already spoken." He nodded at Brant who turned away sullenly and sat. Cornplanter waited a long moment, then grunted disgustedly deep in his throat. "I, too, did not believe the time to be right. It was a time to make peace, not war. This, I tried to do, but you," his voice dripped with disgust, "you chose to follow the wishes of Thayendanegea and Handsome Lake. And, what happened? What happened?" He looked into each face as he spoke. "You chose to fight and were beaten. What will you do now?" He gestured towards the outside of the Council House. "The Long Knife is coming upon us, and we shall all be killed! Now, you must fight or we are done." He paused, but nobody answered him save the Mohawks, making clicks of approval in their throats at his words. But, as he continued speaking, I realized they did not understand his intent for he supported Simon without mentioning his name. I smiled to myself as I recognized Antony's ploy.

"This is what you wanted," he continued. "Now,

let us finish what we started. Let us kill all our women and children and go and fight until we die like all honorable men who have wisely begun a war." Again, nobody answered. Even the Mohawks remained silent considering Cornplanter's words. With a theatrical gesture, Cornplanter crossed to the ceremonial tomahawk in front of Cornstalk and lifted it high overhead. "Let us continue now with this war so that the ground and air may weep at our honor, at our bravery. But, let us kill our women and children first to keep them from the Stony Coat's men, the Long Knives!"

For the third time he paused, but no one answered him. He buried the blade in one of the timbers of the Council House and shook his head in mock disgust. "Silence speaks many words. No one speaks with me? Ah!" He sighed dramatically. "Then, I shall go and do your bidding." He stalked from the Council House but not before exchanging a tiny, secret smile wih Simon. I looked quickly at Brant: he had caught the exchange and realized too late how Cornplanter had beaten him. He glared murderously at Simon.

"I think you'd do well to watch your back," I said softly to Simon as we rose to follow Cornplanter from the Council House. He followed my gaze and nodded.

"Yes," he said soberly. "I am afraid we shall have trouble from him. He lost a lot of influence here today, and that is important to people like Joseph Brant."

I followed him outside the Council House to where Cornplanter waited impatiently. His eyes glittered with intensity as he bent to speak lowly with Simon.

"Go, and be quick about it, my friend, for my words will not hold our warriors for long! Tell the leader of the Long Knives that Cornplanter is willing to make peace if the white man stays east of the river they call the Ohio. The Shawnee will not go east of those waters, but the white men must promise not to pass beyond that river. If they do, then shall Cornplanter again pick up the tomahawk and lead the Shawnees against the white man. There will be only this treaty from Cornplanter for there can be no other. Tell him this, and tell him, too, that this is all Cornplanter will agree to. Now, go before my words disappear into air."

We found Dunmore deep in conversation with a mud-spattered and weary Lewis. He weaved slightly and turned red-rimmed eyes upon us as we approached.

"Well?" Dunmore snapped. "What does the chief have to say?" Simon bent to retrieve his belt.

"He's willing to settle for peace as long as the treaty keeps the white man east of the Ohio," he said, buckling the belt around his waist. "In turn, he'll keep the Indians west of the Ohio."

"By God, no!" Lewis said loudly. He

straightened himself with an effort. "These savages are murderers! We undertook this campaign to protect the settlers in the river valley. Many of them have been terrorized and killed by the marauders." He paused to gulp in air. "We have twenty-five hundred Virginians here! There's no need to make a treaty. Just turn the boys loose and they'll solve the problem."

"And create a bigger one," Simon answered coolly. He ignored Lewis and addressed Dunmore. "You have a large village here, it is true, but to massacre them will antagonize the other tribes. You already have a league of tribes with the Six Nations; others would join and soon you'd have a confederacy much larger than the twenty-five hundred you have here. You'd have a war that you could not hope to win."

"Preposterous," Lewis retorted. "You make them sound invincible." Simon nodded.

"Not them, the idea. Oh, yes," he quietly said. "They can be defeated. But only if attacked in small groups. It will make a deliberate and extended war that will take many years to end. A sudden mass extermination such as you advocate, Colonel Lewis, will only serve to drive the tribes together. No, the best thing is to give them the treaty they want."

"Like hell!" Lewis began, but Dunmore interrupted him.

"There is much merit to what you say," he said to Simon. "Tell them that I will give them the treaty if they will give me four hostages as a guarantee."

Actually, I do not think Dunmore was being generous. We had spent far longer in the field than he wanted—the entertainment "season" was almost upon us along with Christmas—and, given the nature of those in Pennsylvania he was trying to impress, the role of "Peacemaker" instead of "Conqueror" had a duality of purpose.

"I will not see this happen," Lewis vehemently retorted. "You did not hear the cries of the men who died in the Indians cowardly attack upon our forces. You did not see . . ." He swallowed heavily to keep his emotions under control, "your brother killed." He breathed deeply. "I, for one, intend to finish the job we set out to do. The rest of you go hang yourselves." He made as if to leave, but Lord Dunmore leaped in front of him, drawing his sword. He flicked the point against Lewis's throat.

"You will, follow my orders, sir. Of that, rest assured. Either with your willing obedience, or with your death. Which will it be?" he said, Colonel Lewis hesitated, looking from the tip of Dunmore's sword unwaveringly held a scant inch from his throat along the gleaming length of the blade to Dunmore's unsmiling face. For a moment, I thought he would act *malgré tout*, but he swallowed his anger, curtly nodded, and strode away. Dunmore watched him go in silence, then slowly sheathed his sword and turned back to

Simon.

"You may tell the Indians that I agree with the one stipulation of hostages, Mr. Girty," he said. He pulled a silver snuffbox from his coat pocket. Simon nodded and gestured towards the departing Lewis.

"And him?"

"Do not worry about Colonel Lewis," Dunmore said. "He'll remember this."

"*Oderint dum metuant,*" I murmured. Dunmore gave me a surprised look. "Lucius Accius, I believe," I added, and followed Simon back to Cornplanter leaving Dunmore staring after us. Simon laughed quietly.

"That may not have been a smart thing to do. Now, he knows you are not a woodsie like he thought. It's best not to reveal too much of yourself."

There was much to his words, but I didn't care. I may have been guilty of *cacoethes loquendi*, but I also remembered my Virgil: *audentes fortuna juvat.* Something good could come of my bragging as well.

Chapter Thirty-two

Cornplanter seemed pleased with Lord Dunmore's quick agreement to a treaty and willingly accepted the conditions. He sent messengers to the outlying villages, demanding their representation at the scheduled council. Shawnee chieftains began to assemble near the place Dunmore had impulsively named Camp Charlotte (after a young lady he hoped to make his mistress upon his return to Williamsburg) along with minor representatives of the Six Nations. A few Mingoes were present as well, but Logan was conspicuously absent and, as no treaty could be concluded without his agreement, Lord Dunmore dispatched Simon and myself to try and convince Logan to agree to the proposed treaty.

We found Logan some distance from his cabin under a great elm tree bare against the gray November sky. He noticed our approach and waited, bronzed, powerful, and gloomily fatalistic. He stood erect, stiff with habitual dignity, but the deep lines of his face betold bitter memories of the deaths of this relatives, his people. Simon informed him about Lord Dunmore's proposal and waited respectfully to hear his answer. I watched Logan struggle with his conscience: seething anger still demanded to be unleashed while cool reason objected, arguing the uselessness of continued war. At last, he spoke, his words harsh and mournful.

"I appeal to any white man to say if ever he entered Logan's cabin hungry, and I have not given him meat; if ever he came cold or naked, and I have not given him clothing!

"During the course of the last long and bloody war, Logan remained in his cabin, an advocate of peace. Nay, such was my love for the whites that those of my own country, pointed at me as they passed and said, 'Logan is the friend of the white man.' I had even thought to live with you, but for the injuries of one man. Colonel Cresap, the last spring, in cold blood and unprovoked, cut off all the relatives of Logan, not sparing even women and children. There runs not a drop of my blood in the veins of any creature. This called on me for revenge. I have sought it. I have killed many. I have fully glutted my vengeance. For my country, I rejoice at the beams of peace. Yet, do not harbor the thought that mine is the joy of fear. Logan never felt fear. He will not turn on his heel to save his life. Who is there to mourn for Logan? Not one."

He turned away and left us standing beneath that great elm. We carried his words back to Lord Dunmore who was delighted and ordered his scribe, John Gibson, to make a copy of Logan's speech "on a piece of clean, new paper" for posterity. The Shawnee subsequently signed the treaty, but I knew the treaty was a sham, and it would only be a matter of time before settlers pushed over the Ohio River. Still, Lord Dunmore had his moment: he was a "Peacemaker", a role that would stand him in good stead with the citizens of Pennsylvania, and he had managed to extend Virginia's borders. Most importantly, he was back in Williamsburg in time for the holiday season with the young Charlotte for whom the camp was named. And myself.

The Renegade by Randy Lee Eickhoff

Chapter Thirty-three

On 22 February 1775, Major John Connolly swore Simon into his battalion as a second lieutenant in Lord Dunmore's militia at Fort Pitt with an oath that signed away any lingering belief of transubstantiation in the sacrament of the Lord's Supper (had he any to begin with) and bound him to undying allegiance to His Majesty, King George III, the sole avatar, the sole legatee, the sole assignee of his soul.

I was not at Fort Pitt with Simon for Lord Dunmore remembered my reference to Lucius Accius and took me back to Williamsburg with his four hostages as a translator and one of his personal secretaries (and a "curiosity" much on the order of an India curio). Dunmore arranged for the hostages to stay in a cabin on the outskirts of Williamsburg where they quickly became centers of attention; a situation that at first bewildered but soon contented them.

I, on the other hand, became a "guest" among the various parties Lord Dunmore insisted I attend. He introduced me as his "assistant chief scout" during his most recent campaign (I imagined Simon bellowing with laughter at this) and at whatever party we were in attendance progressed, would casually mention that I was somewhat of a scholar which often resulted in my being called upon to declaim something from the classics. Knowing this to be Dunmore's intent, I would allow myself to be cajoled into providing entertainment and would usually select Cicero's *Catilinam*, beginning, *"Quo usque, Catilina, abutare patientia nostra."* But only one person, an elderly gentleman with a foot swathed in bandages against the gout, actually understood the allegory being offered, cackling with glee at the knowledge his fellow guests pretended with their vague banter following my recitation. He suggested that sometime I should invent a jargon replete with lenes and dipthongs to give the illusion of a classical language and note how many suggested intimacy with the same. But I never did. It was much easier to recite one of the tracts that my father had made a part of my early catechism.

The Epiphany found me in Philadelphia, delivering a packet of letters from Lord Dunmore to a representative of Sir Guy Carleton, the governor-general of Quebec. I went around to visit my friend Benjamin Franklin but found a black-bordered wreath on his door and did not wish to intrude upon his grief. He would not, as I later discovered, have been home at the time anyway as he was on the high seas returning from England where he had been trying (unsuccessfully as it happened) to get Parliament and King George to listen to American grievances.

All around the city, there was talk of war and a second Continental Congress. Tradesmen went twice a day into the field at five of the o'clock in the morning and six in the afternoon to train as volunteers should war erupt. Reportedly, Philadelphia had three battalions, a troop of light horse, and a company of artillery, although I never saw such members on parade during my stay. My old nemesis, Major Leggett, served as liaison between the various commands and was rumored to be in line for a squadron command should the "army" ever be mobilized. Our paths never crossed during my early wanderings, although I did have occasion to meet his sister, Anne, a time or two at society gatherings.

My fortunes, it seems, had undergone another reversal since my association with Lord Dunmore, and I was no longer *persona non grata* among Philadelphia gentry. The first two times I met Anne she was escorted by a somewhat vain schoolmaster in a poor, but serviceable coat. Nathan Hale and I had a rather spirited argument (not surprising given the fact he was a Yale graduate) concerning his misquotation of a passage from Joseph Addison's *Cato* on the duties a man had to his country which led to a disagreement of Horace's declaration: *dulce et decorum est pro patria mori.* Hale argued the nobility of such an action while I argued that to do so was to embrace the role of *âme damnée.* It was a good argument, but Hale had not had as much opportunity to develop expertise in formal argument as I and was hopelessly over-matched. When I introduced Cicero's *silent leges inter arma* into the argument, he fell silent and withdrew sulkily to a corner punchbowl.

Unfortunately, others had overheard our little debate and, misunderstanding our intent which was purely scholarship (being simply a case of *vox et preaterea nihil* as far as I was concerned), quickly labeled me a Loyalist. At first, I was amused by this for I was highly apolitical, being more concerned with the metaphysical, but my reputation ran a jaunty flag before me, and I found some tempers slightly cooled towards my inclusion within their societal sphere as the weeks, passed. Ah, well! *Forsan et haec olim meminisse juvabit*!

Anne, however, had recognized my intent in the ill-timed debate and, at the risk of incurring the wrath of her brother, frequently invited me to afternoon tea. At first, I was tempted to send my regrets for fear of being the cause of future difficulties between her and her acquaintances, but I was suddenly stricken with an irresistible impulse to visit with her. A wise choice as it turned out, for we became fast friends although I sensed a dark shadow hanging over our relationship behind the gaiety with which she consistently greeted me. Slowly over the weeks, the friendship grew deeper and deeper: the lingering touch of her fingers upon mine when she passed tea, the long silences between us when we contented ourselves with looks into the other's eyes, a sense of comfortable familiarity, happy times at the spinet as she played and we sang *"Greensleeves"* together.

Yet, we had not kissed for I instinctively sensed that to do so would move our relationship immediately to lovers. Although I ached to take her in my arms, for some strange reason, I felt a certain reticence within her to make that adjustment in our relationship although the desire was there. The contradiction was a puzzlement to me, but I reluctantly forced myself to end my visit whenever the temptation threatened to be a more powerful force than reason, taking my lust to the taverns on the outskirts of Philadelphia where I could spend myself in the white arms of the wenches who eagerly waited for gentleman callers.

We kept our times together a careful secret from the world outside the walls of the house she shared with her brother—to this day I cannot call it a "home"—save for the few servants her brother allowed. His temper and stingy wages, however, cost him the loyalty normally afforded the master of the house.

One day, I determined our happiness together far overshadowed the difficulties between her brother and myself and elected to make my feelings known to her. I realized that thoughts of Anne were continuously with me, even lingering on the fringes of my thoughts when I was visiting or conducting business with others.

Would Anne like this? I found myself asking, or would Anne approve? My course of action dictated itself. I determined to ask her to be my wife.

On the day I decided to broach the question, I took especial pains with my toilet, selecting my best wine-colored coat and snowy-white stock, binding my hair with a black ribbon in the style rapidly becoming popular in the colonies, and taking with me a copy of James Thomson's *The Seasons*—a delightful selection of poetry written in blank verse and the Spenserian stanza—for amusement.

I arrived a bit early at the house on Jermyn Street and was shown into the library to wait for her to finish dressing and come down. As is my custom, I looked over the shelved books all bound in new calfskin and showing little wear. I turned to go to the fireplace and the high, wing-backed chair deliberately blocked at an angle to the fireplace to receive the most warmth in February to wait when my eye happened to fall upon the papers left on Leggett's desk. I glanced through a land survey report, then froze as I recognized Lord Dunmore's hand on the paper beneath the one I was reading.

I picked up the letter and discovered it to be one of the letters I had brought north with me and given to Carleton weeks before. It was based on a report from Dr. Connally to Dunmore and contained the descriptions of nineteen men in the Fort Pitt area thought to be sympathetic towards King George. Among the names I recognized were those of Alexander McKee, Simon, and myself. It was a damning letter in the wrong hands. I folded it and placed it into my pocket, determined to discover the means by which Leggett had acquired it.

I started to leave when another letter caught my eye: *To Bryan Fairfax from George Washington.* Boldly, for I sensed that I had little time before Anne's appearance, I lifted it from the blotter and read about Washington's intent to ignore the crown's call to service. A peculiar hollowness settled in my stomach as Washington's words drilled home:

> *"...as to your political sentiments, I would heartily join you in them, so far as relates to a humble and dutiful petition to the throne, provided there was the most distant hope of success. But have we not tried this already? Heve we not addressed the Lords, and remonstrated with the Commons? And to what end? Did they deign to look at our petitions? Does it not appear, as clear as the sun in its meridian brightness, that there is a regular, systematic plan formed to fix the right and practice of taxation upon us?"*

I heard the latch click and hurriedly stuffed the

letter into my pocket to join that of Dunmore as I crossed the room to greet Anne.

"Jonathon!" she exclaimed warmly. She offered me her band. I took it, pressing the palm to my lips, kissing the Venus mound (oh! sweet succulent softness!) and murmuring my gratitude at her thoughtfulness in inviting me to tea: literal mutterings that had quickly become our familiar mating dance. She blushed scarlet high in her cheeks and led me to the parlor where tea had been laid for two.

"Your brother is not at home?" I inquired politely as always. She gave a little nervous laugh that, too, had become ritual and motioned me to a chair. She seated herself opposite in a low, wide-armed chair built to accommodate her wide skirts. A small table stood between us.

"No. He has gone to a meeting with Samuel Adams at the Horse and Spur. I daresay you are not at a loss for all of his absence?" she asked archly. She poured tea into a delicate cup, carefully spooned in sugar, and handed it to me. Her cool fingers momentarily rested upon mine.

(Dare I take hint from this?)

"Not at all," I said. I sipped the tea. "In fact, it is best that we do not meet."

"Yes," she said softly, sadly. "I am sorry for the harm that he has caused you. I heard about your incarceration. I understand Lord Dunmore pardoned you?"

I nodded and took a large swallow of the hot tea, burning my mouth against the memories threatening to crawl back into my mind.

"Actually, it was a friend who first released me then arranged for my pardon," I said. "Simon Girty."

"You are fortunate to have such a friend," she said. (Did I hear a touch of bitterness in her voice?) Her eyes met mine over the rim of her tea cup: green eyes with flecks of hazel reflecting the flickering light of the fire. My hands suddenly seemed damp.

"Very," I said. "Otherwise, I am afraid I would have been murdered. Your brother's jailer was quite a brute."

"My brother's friends are not my own," she murmured, her eyes lowered upon the tea cup held in her hand. A faint blush tinged her high cheekbones. (Did I detect an opening? I pressed what I took to be an advantage.)

"For which I am grateful," I answered. "Such a creature as yourself, though, must have many friends." A hint of sadness appeared over her fine features.

"If you wish to call them that. They are really friends of necessity."

"Necessity?"

"Yes. Those whom my brother wishes to know and who may be able to advance his fortunes, and those who hope to advance theirs by knowing my brother."

She gave a short, hard laugh. "Then there are a few who make my acquaintance with the hope that I have some slight influence with my brother. When they discover how ineffectual I am in this, I do not see them again."

"But surely the ladies . . ." I began, shocked at the harshness of her reply. The pleasant afternoon suddenly seemed bleak and unfriendly. I probed for reasons for the sudden change in her but could find no fault on my part.

"The ladies of my brother's, ah, 'acquaintance' do not associate with . . ." She hesitated, obviously embarrassed. "That is, they find little time for social amenities. As for the others, well, I am afraid I am allied too closely with my brother for many others to extend invitations. And, of course, reciprocating on my part is quite impossible. Few are that socially secure not to fear for their reputations by calling upon me or answering my invitations."

"I fear your reputation has not been helped by having me to tea," I said ruefully. "Ah, well! Fortune's miscreants. Fate has thrown us together."

"Is it fate? I wonder."

"If not fate, then what?" I asked.

"A mischievous god? Pan, perhaps."

"Or Aphrodite," I swiftly added, leaping into the opening she had unconsciously supplied. She looked startled. The tea cup rattled against its saucer as she recklessly replaced it.

"Why not?" I continued, plunging ahead. "Perhaps she has decided two such as ourselves need to find love. Deserve to find love. Is that so bad?"

She drew a deep breath to steady herself. Her hands clutched and twisted the delicate handkerchief in her lap. Tiny muscles bunched along her jawline.

"Will you have more tea?" she asked, our voice strained. She reached for my cup. I caught and held her hand as she tried to pull back. "Anne . . ."

Her lips parted and I moved swiftly around the small table, pulling her to her feet. Her eyes widened, her breath catching in her throat, then, I kissed her.

For a moment, she resisted, her hands pushing hard against my shoulders, then she sank against me and her lips moved against mine. I pulled back momentarily, looking into her eyes.

"The servants," I said.

"Gone for the afternoon," she said thickly.

I picked her up, feeling her softness against my chest and carried her up the stairs to her bedroom.

And, we made love, urgently, passionately, as if time worked against us.

Afterwards, we lay, naked in each other's arms, my head pillowed upon her firm breasts, the rosy nipple as wide a plum, tantalizingly near my lips. Her scent made my senses reel.

"Anne," I whispered. "Marry me."

She suddenly pushed me from her, rolling away

and rising, crossed to the mirror. I rose and followed her, placing my arms around her. She pulled away. I caught her arms, turning her to face me.

"Please," she whispered, breathing heavily. "Do not torture so."

"Anne," I softly said. "Who else is there for either of us? Have you not thought of me since we encountered each other in the street? You do not have to answer; I can see the truth. You are trembling."

"You do not understand!" she cried wildly. "Oh, you do not understand! There can be nothing between us! Nothing! It is impossible!"

"Because of your brother?" I shook my head, tightening my grip upon her arm. "Anne, we do not have to live here. We can go back to Boston. Or New York. Someplace where no one will know us."

"It's too late," she whispered. Tears began to well in her eyes. "Oh! Why couldn't you have left it alone?"

"Do you fear your brother that much?" I asked. She tried to pull away from me, but I held her tightly, wrapping my arms around her, pulling her naked body to mine, but she forced herself free and fell upon a small chair and covered her face with her hands as tears began to flow.

"Anne? Anne! What's wrong?" She shook her head and began sobbing harder. "Anne? I love you!"

"No. No," she moaned, and began to furiously

pull at her hair. Pins fell in a shower to the carpet.

"If it's a question of your brother, we'll move to another colony. Virginia, perhaps. I can find work with Lord Dunmore."

"My brother," she choked back a sob, her lips twisting cruelly. She raised her face to mine, tears sparkling in her eyes.

"Yes, your brother," I said mystified. "Anne, what is it?"

"My lover," she said bitterly.

I reached for her, but she ducked under my arm and ran from the room. I followed her to another bedroom at the end of the hall and tried to catch her, but she threw the door shut and locked it against me.

"Anne!" I yelled, and pounded on the door. "Anne!"

But she did not answer, her sobs coming harsh and loud through the panelling. I stood for a long moment at the door, listening to her sobs and the loud ticking of the clock on the mantel downstairs. Then, the implication of her words filtered through the daze in my mind, and a coldness descended over me, withering my spirit. My mind reeled from twisted images of fiendish tortures imposed upon her by her brother. I turned back to our room and dressed hurriedly, collected my hat and stick, and let myself out, turning my steps towards The Horse and Spur.

Chapter Thirty-four

Several characters in tattered buckskin eyed me suspiciously as I pushed open the door to The Horse and Spur and entered the smoke-filled room. To my left stood the bar, planks nailed to the top of large barrels behind which two unshaven bartenders clad in soiled aprons visibly plied their trade. Several small, rough-hewn tables stood scattered across the floor. On my right, a small fire flickered in a stone fireplace held together with heavy mortar. Leaning against the fireplace stood a man I did not expect to see: Lewis Wetzel. His lips parted in a terrible smile as he saw me, revealing rotting teeth as he raised the mug in his hand, sipping from it. I could tell he was not pleased to see me: the smile never touched his eyes. I turned to the bar and motioned for one of the bartenders. He approached, giving me an impatient look.

"Major Leggett," I said, making it a statement, not a question. His eyes flickered to the shunt staircase at the far end of the bar.

"What do you want with him?" he asked.

"Never mind," I answered, and turned towards the staircase. Two men quickly stood to bar my way.

"Can I help you?" asked one politely. Although

253

clean, his homespun shirt and trousers were ragged and worn.

"I wish to see Major Leggett," I replied, and tried to push my way past them. Like a well-rehearsed troupe, they joined shoulders to block my passage.

"He's in a meeting," the one who spoke before replied, his voice still courteous. The other stared indifferently, but I could tell from the scars around his eyes he was not the least worried about my reply. Anger crawled through my body.

"Then perhaps I'll join the meeting," I replied hotly. His lips thinned into a hard line as he started to speak only to be interrupted by a voice from the landing above me.

"What is it, Jamie?"

I looked up at a square-jawed, unsmiling man wearing a powdered wig and gray broadcloth. He had no lace: a long, narrow collar and thin ribbon knotted into a cravat standing him in lieu thereof. He stared unblinkingly down upon us.

"This feller here thinks he's going upstairs," Jamie answered, keeping his eyes upon me. "But I never seed him before, Mr. Adams. So, I reckon he won't." The man on the stairs gave me a hard look.

"You did right, Jamie," Adams answered. He paused, considering me. "What do you want, sir?" His voice was curt, brusque with its officiousness.

"I wish to see Major Leggett," I said, spacing

the words out. He gave me a cool look.

"I'm afraid that's quite impossible. He's busy at the moment."

"Then, perhaps, he had better make himself unbusy. I wish to see him."

"In regards to what matter?" Adams queried.

"Honor," I replied and took a step towards the staircase only to be brought up short by a calloused hand upon my elbow.

"Still making trouble, eh, squaw-man?" a deep voice asked. I turned to face Wetzel. "I'da thunk you'da larned yer lesson aback at Pitt." I jerked my arm from his grasp.

"Keep your hands to yourself, Wetzel," I said, my voice ringing across the room. Voices ceased as attention turned towards us. Wetzel's eyes flared with delight.

"If it's a fight you want you can have it," I said. "But, face-to-face this time. Not in ambush." His eyes flared with anger. Dull, dark red rose from the collar of his buckskin shirt to mottle his face.

"Is it a coward you're callin' me then?" he asked. "There's no Kenton to get you outter this one."

"I do not believe I'll need Mr. Kenton," I said. Casually, I reached towards my waistcoat where I had concealed a small, single-shot pistol.

"But you may need your border friends," a voice said. I looked up to face Leggett standing on the first landing next to a David Rogers I recalled from several of Dunmore's parties: a self-assured gentleman very popular with the ladies though a bit of a fop. Briefly, I wondered if he was the one who had given Dunmore's letter to Leggett, then I ignored him to concentrate upon his companion.

"Leggett!" I exclaimed. My voice quivered from anger. I drew a deep breath to calm myself. "You foul splash of Satan's dung! It's time for others to be free of your belialism. Choose your seconds!"

His eyes darted to his right towards Adams, deeply frowning at our exchange. His tongue flicked out like an adder's to wet his lips.

"I do not duel with cowards," he stiffly said. "You proved that by firing when my back was turned at the river."

"You are a liar," I replied.

"We do not have the time for such matters as this. There is important business ahead for us," Adams said, his voice hard, biting.

"That well may be," I said. "But first, there is an affair to be settled between Major Leggett and myself."

Rogers nodded at this and stepped away from Leggett, making it clear he considered himself out of whatever conflict might develop.

"Should I handle this, Mr. Adams?" Wetzel asked.

"No," Adams said staring at me. "What is your

quarrel?"

"I am sorry, sir," I stiffly replied. "That, as I said is between Major Leggett, myself, and his sister," I added, turning my stare upon him. His eyes narrowed to pinpoints. Again, his tongue flicked out like a serpent's.

"Ssssoooo," he said, drawing the sibilant out. "You have been seeing my sister again."

"I have," I answered boldly. "And it is in the latter matter I make my challenge."

"In what respect?" he uneasily asked.

"In respect of honor. Or the lack of it, as the case may be," I said. The crowd drew a quick breath at my insult.

"We have no time for such nonsense. We have much to do," Adams interrupted impatiently.

"And what business would that be with a man who wears the King's red and ignores his oath?"

"I take it, sir, your sympathies lie with the King?" Adams stiffly said.

"And if not with King George with whom should my sympathies lie?" I asked. Adams's eyes flickered to the men standing behind me. He gave a slight nod, and hands suddenly pinned my arms to my side. I struggled futilely as my pockets were searched.

"Here, Mr. Adams," my searcher cried in triumph as he found the letters in my pocket. He handed them up to Adams who frowned and silently handed them to Leggett.

"These are from my desk," he said slowly, after scanning their contents. "He's a pawn in the employ of Lord Dunmore." An angry murmur sprang up around us.

"You are in Lord Dunmore's employ?" Adams asked. I nodded.

"Yes. As was Leggett. And Wetzel," I added, nodding at the borderman.

"Yes. Well. I am sorry," Adams said stolidly. "But I am afraid we must detain you for the moment. You have come at a most awkward time."

"And these two?" I spat at Wetzel and Leggett.

"We know about them," Adams calmly said. "You, sir, however, are the enigma."

I started an angry reply but never finished it as Wetzel's brawny fist crashed against my temple.

I awoke to find myself lying upon a pile of filthy flour sacks in a darkened storeroom. Moonlight shone through a barred window high above my head. I groaned and rolled to my back and sat up. Tiny mice scurried wildly away at my movements. My head throbbed. I winced from bruises from blows that had landed after I was unconscious. The room swam, and I ducked my head between my knees for a moment to keep from fainting. My tongue felt thick in my mouth; my throat parched. I gingerly explored my face with my hands, feeling the bumps from Wetzel's beating. I took several deep breaths and pushed myself erect, staggering against the well below the window. I grasped the bars and pulled myself up to look out onto an alley filled with old barrels and crates. I breathed deeply and smelled foul water and knew I was near the Delaware River: an apt place for a man to disappear and leave no trace behind him.

I let go of the bars and dropped back into the room to take stock of my surroundings. A pile of hides lay against one wall. Bottles of wine stood on rough-hewn shelves against the opposite wall. I took one, knocking the neck free, and drank thirstily. I felt better and crossed to the door and gingerly tried it: locked and barred. I slumped against the pile of hides, forcing myself to think, sipping carefully from the bottle of wine.

Obviously, I had accidentally stumbled upon one of the secret meeting places of those calling themselves "Patriots" or "Sons of Liberty." I had little doubt about their plans for me. Secrecy was the watchword that kept them from the gallows-tree. Yet, I knew instinctively my greatest danger came not from them but from Leggett who could not let me live lest I blurt out to my captors his relationship with his sister. His continued good relations with the rebels depended upon not a breath of scandal. The bars, however, were too heavy to bend out of their stone bedding and the door too thick to kick free. I began to consider the objects in the room and their possible use to me.

A scratching at the door as the outside bar was raised interrupted my thoughts. I cast wildly about for a weapon. The door swung open. Immediately, I lowered my fist as a startled Benjamin Franklin peered in at me.

"My dear Jonathon!" he exclaimed. He brushed my reply aside, saying, "Come now! Come now! Let us be away from here." He led me from the storeroom through a back door. I stumbled against the cobblestones of the street as we hurried away from the river.

"How did you find me?" I asked, trying to ignore the pounding in my head.

"We have a mutual friend. A *lady* friend," he emphasized lightly. "One who has an angry brother. You are fortunate she found me. I had just returned from England to find Dorothy dead." His voice caught. I involuntarily glanced at the mourning band around his arm.

"England!" I blurted.

"Yes," he said. "I was trying to convince Parliament and the King's advisors to allow the Colonies representation. But, I am afraid that all my efforts were wasted. Their refusal has played right into the hands of the Hotspurs among us. There will be war."

"War?" I couldn't keep the puzzlement from my voice. "With whom? You have no army."

"That," he said, tapping the side of his nose, "we are in the process of rectifying." He shook his head. "I am afraid you have made a mischief of yourself. Samuel Adams is not going to be happy with your absence."

"I care nothing for Samuel Adams nor his happiness. My business is with Major Leggett," I replied.

"That may be. That may be," Benjamin answered, resuming his rapid walk away from the river. "But right now, Major Leggett is indispensable to our plans."

"*Our* plans?" I exclaimed. "Do you mean to say you are one of them?"

"Oh, come now, Jonathon. That blow to your head could not have addled you that much! Yes," he grimly answered. "I am. I am afraid there will be no place for you in Philadelphia after this night's bad business." His face softened, and he placed a consoling hand upon my shoulder, gently adding, "I am sorry, but it would be best for you to return to Fort Pitt."

"What about Major Leggett?" I asked.

"Forget Major Leggett for now," he said quietly. "He has too many powerful friends."

"Does this include you?" I asked. He shook his head.

"No," he answered dryly. "I indulge Major Leggett; that is all. When this business is over, he will cease to be of value to us. He is an opportunist. For the moment, we are profitable to him for he can run arms to us from the West Indies. But that could quickly change and so could his position despite Washington's endorsement of him. For now, we can do business together. You, however, must leave Philadelphia. I have some influence but not with an assassin's dagger." He took my arm and pointed across the street. "There. In the livery, I have left a horse for you along with your rifle and powder." He pushed a small purse into my hands. "I am sorry, but that is all I can do for the moment. Take care." He squeezed my arm and left me standing in front of the stables.

Again, I felt the bitterness of being an outcast well up within me and fought down the urge to ignore Benjamin's heeding and seek out Leggett. Reason, however, dictated otherwise, and I could see the soundness of Benjamin's advice. We would meet again, Leggett and I, in the near future. Then, I would kill him. For Anne. And myself. Tears suddenly filled my eyes, and I crossed the street and entered the livery.

Chapter Thirty-five

I did not think I had been away from Simon Girty that long, but I was shocked by the change in him when I dismounted, tired and dusty, in front of his cabin at Fort Pitt. It had taken close to three weeks to make my way from Philadelphia to that outpost, and I could feel the strain in the tired knots along my spine and the stiffness in my legs. My mount hung its head, nuzzling the dusty grass by the corner of the cabin.

Simon's face, bronzed from the elements, was scoured with deep lines, his eyes, hard and cold, lips drawn into a tight line that only briefly lifted in a smile at my bedraggled appearance before again falling into the rigid, bitter mask. He stretched forth a hand, took my rifle from me and leaned it against the cabin wall beside the doorway. George and Jim lolled on the cabin steps, sharing a jug of rum between them. Jim lifted the jug in welcome and I took it, drinking deeply of the raw spirits to revive myself.

"You're a sight," George said. His eyes were bright in his face, and I knew he had been a long time at the rum. I handed it back to Jim and took a deep breath. My muscles began to relax.

"I suppose so," I said, and looked at Simon. He

nodded, his face remaining frozen in its mask.

"Trouble?"

I nodded. "A bit."

"That cock, Leggett?" Jim interjected.

"Yes," I said. I took a long look around the post, noticing the absence of regular officers. "Where are Dunmore's men?"

Their eyes flickered involuntarily to Simon. He ignored them and turned to look across the clearing to the dark woods beyond. Jim regretfully shook his head and turned back to face me.

"Withdrawn," he said, a minatory tone to his words. "And no good has come of it. Simon no longer has his commission. The soldiers here are Pennsylvanian and refuse to recognize Dunmore's appointments. Simon," he cast a quick glance at Simon's back before continuing, "tried to work as an interpreter for George Morgan—the new Deputy Commissioner of Indian Affairs?—but that bastard fired him after three months and stiffed him for a hundred dollars expenses. That son-of-a-bitch deserves the stake," he added in a dark aside.

"What does Dr. Connolly say to that?" I asked. He shook his head and took a large swallow of the rum.

"Nothing," he said, lowering the jug. "He's gone, too. Brigadier General Edward N. Hand is in command. Do you know him?"

I frowned: the name had a familiar ring to it.

Then, I remembered: I had caught a glimpse of thet
name among the papers on Leggett's desk. Suddenly,
everything seemed to make sense. If certain people had
already given up on peaceful negotiation or, I excitedly
amended as a new thought twisted the premise of the
old, Hand *never* planned on a peaceful negotiation, then
logically it would make sense to secure the back and
flanks before launching a frontal attack. But before I
could raise the question of *consensus audacium*, I had
to have an *argumentum ad rem*. I looked again at
Simon still staring at the forest and for some strange
reason remembered another document on Leggett's
desk. I had paid no attention to it for it had seemed
completely innocuous. But now I recalled not only the
document, but the date and the name: a survey of forest
lands in western Pennsylvania made in 1752 by a
certain Captain William Crawford assisted by
Lieutenant Henry Leggett. The chief surveyor had been
Geo. Washington with Hand listed as treasurer of the
firm employing the survey. The forest lands in question
were currently protected by a treaty signed by British
negotiators. *But*, if war was declared, then armed forays
could justifiably be made into the interior. *Silent leges
enim inter arma*. If the war was won, then the treaty
would be worthless. Either way, they would have vast
tracts of rich lands. I had my proof: the argument of the
pocketbook. All they needed was a war and Crawford,
Leggett, Washington, and Hand would become *very*

rich men.

"Yes," I said softly. "I know of him."

Simon turned at my words, and I looked deep into his eyes. Tiny fires licked and danced behind the grayness there.

"Make yourself ready," he said. He reached out for my hand. I returned the pressure, a lump forming in my throat.

News about the "difficulties" (the events in Philadelphia and Boston) was eagerly a-waited at Fort Pitt during the coming weeks. The Girtys and myself were treated with great suspicion that grew uglier with the arrival of every dispatch since everyone knew we had once been in the service of Lord Dunmore. Finally, George and Jim left Fort Pitt in disgust for the deep woods. Simon decided to linger at the fort, augmenting the meager wages he received as a sometime interpreter with hunting trips.

I was reluctantly hired as the schoolmaster after my predecessor contracted a fever and died. I elected to keep to myself and not hobnob with the men of the fort, spending my evenings in the little room at the rear of the schoolhouse set on a bluff a few rods from the fort.

I quickly settled into a dull routine, firmly refusing to allow my charges to introduce the subject of the "difficulties" into the classroom. This insistence on my part served me in good stead for it convinced some that I was of a pacifist nature. Gradually, animosity towards me changed into a grudging cordiality. What they did not know was that I was being kept aware of the actions of the Continental Congress and the "difficulties" through a correspondence with Benjamin Franklin.

A few months before the Congress sent Benjamin to Paris in an attempt to negotiate a treaty of commerce and amity, he wrote that there had been a fierce debate among the members of the Congress since the novelty of being a revolutionary was beginning to wear off. Some members were beginning to express doubts concerning the possibility of success with the enterprise of war. Some were beginning to voice vain hopes of reconciliation with England.

One day, I received a bulky package from Benjamin containing a copy of the Parliamentary act removing the Colonies from the protection of the Crown and authorizing the seizure and confiscation of all colony-owned ships at sea. Also in the package was a forty-seven page pamphlet written by Thomas Paine entitled *Common Sense*. Benjamin's message was clear: all opposition had been swept aside in Congress. Parliament, with its own act, had snipped whatever cords of reconciliation might have kept the Colonies and England together. It was, as Paine wrote, "time to part."

Simon took great satisfaction from the news and

again cautioned me to hold myself in readiness while he pretended to work on behalf of the colonists by recruiting men of the settlements for the army under one-year enlistments. Meanwhile, he had George and Jim working to keep the tribes among the Nations away from the various patrols. He found a sympathetic trader in a young Irish lad named Matthew Elliott and used him as a messenger between George and Jim and myself, carefully keeping everyone apart to assuage any suspicion that might have been engendered if we had maintained the relationship we had enjoyed in the past.

Actually, he was most worried about George and Jim and how their actions might reflect back on the two of us—an instance of concern, as it turned out, for they acquired a reputation as border outlaws when they stole some horses from a wealthy settler. Suspicion was kept from Simon and myself, however, as when George and Jim made their ill-timed raid, I was teaching school, and Simon was in jail, having been incarcerated when Hand became suspicious of Simon's past association with Connolly and Lord Dunmore and his friendship with Alexander McKee, the Deputy Agent of Indian Affairs appointed by the Crown before Morgan. The rebellion had cost McKee his position and had caused him to be placed on parole as a person suspected of "seditious sentiments."

Hand, however, still suspicious of Simon, refused to release him from jail. Simon finally broke out of jail and stayed away for a week before returning and surrendering, thinking, he told me later, that the gesture would sway Hand's opinion in favor of Simon. It did not work: Hand threw him back in jail only to have the court release Simon when Hand could bring no proof against him. Hand did, however, take vicious pleasure in declaring Simon *persona non grata* on post. That was enough for Simon. In the early morning on 8 February 1778, Simon led McKee, Elliott, McKee's cousin Robert Surphlit, Seth Higgins, and two of McKee's Negro servants from Fort Pitt back into the woods for the last time.

Chapter Thirty-six

The warm sunlight feels fresh and clean upon my face as I watch the first ship of the early spring cautiously navigate the narrow shoals of the lake below my knoll. I chuckle for I know the pilot has nothing to fear: the lake will easily accommodate the draught of his vessel: the spring run-off from winter snow has provided for that. The deep blue of the waters should tell him that.

Esau whines at my side, his paws scratching against my legs in a eager chase of his dream. The past winter has left its mark upon him in the light sprinkling of rime around his jaws and in his memory. Like him, I, too, spend more time in memory, but far from remembering pleasant pictures from my past, my thoughts require a firm effort on my part to shut out the pain and the horror.

It has been two days since I paused in my narrative for the good Father, and I take a fiendish glee in parrying the gentle hints he makes that I continue. He masks his impatience well behind a concern for my well-being, but I can tell how anxious he is for me to continue. Why, I still do not know unless he is seeking my confession for absolution. But, it is too late, too late! I have spent too much time contemplating the dark joy, the madness, the debauchery of man while civilization stopped its feeble advances to lay siege against the crumbling defenses of the forest. I have resisted that advance far too long, preferring the old gods to the new. Even now, I cling to a passionate defense of my actions. I left my soul on the dark paths of the woods, by the sylvan streams, in the forest glades.

By the good Father's standards, there may be more of the *Satannus Dictum* about me than the *Pater Noatruum*.

Perhaps there is, perhaps there is.

I have only the terrible horror of my deeds with me anymore. Whatever god there is cannot forgive me, for there is no longer a soul to be saved.

Yet, I know my time is over, the ways of my life a thing of the past. It is the time for a new destiny, a manifest destiny. The new God is proving far stronger than the old ones. But I am too old now for the new one and prefer the old ones. The new one seems to be far crueler. I no longer understand the turning of water into wine, a god-son lying to save me, Lucifer as a managing director of an underground wholesale house of souls. The entire theory of love seems self-contradictory with the actions of its followers.

Yet, I have come to cherish our time together and am reluctant to tell the good Father more for fear of causing him pain. In truth, I am also suspicious for when I question his reasons for wanting to know, he becomes somewhat vague and quickly changes the subject to the weather, the food, my health, or else invents an excuse to go to the fort. But if I accuse him of evasion, his face becomes very red, and his lips tighten with anger. He will not speak, yet his stubborn silence is eloquent with angry rhetoric. A great awkwardness comes between us that takes days to disappear. Consequently, I am very careful of late and deliberate about whether to continue or not.

Will he stay if I refuse to finish my history? Will he understand why? Or will he become indignant and angry and leave after accusing me of having little faith in him and his God?

A footstep falls lightly upon the path. Instantly, Esau leaps to his feet, facing behind me. Growls rumble from deep within his chest. I crane my head around, shading my eyes with my hand. O'Meara pauses, his brow wrinkling in confusion at Esau's actions.

"What in the world is the matter with Esau?" he asks bewildered.

"You startled him," I reply. "He was having a dream, and you startled him."

Esau crouches, the growls increasing in volume. O'Meara casts a quick, nervous look to see if I have noticed. I pretend ignorance. Suddenly, the confusion clears from his face.

"Something is wrong," he says gently. "What has happened? If you tell me, perhaps I can help."

Shame and despair overwhelm me and I turn and speak sharply to Esau. "Down! That's enough! Down!"

Esau trembles. His great lolling tongue laps once around his jaws. Slobber drips to the ground. Reluctantly, he drops his haunches to the ground and, grumbling, falls flat beside me. O'Meara cautiously sits down, keeping well away from Esau.

"What is wrong?" he asks again.

I ignore him and stare out at the ship. It has almost made it through the narrows. The pilot has grown bolder, and a second sail has been shaken out.

"If it is something I have done..."

"It is nothing," I say, rudely interrupting him. "Do not make too much of it. You just startled him, that is all."

"Somehow, I do not think that is all," he says thoughtfully.

I cannot help myself: I laugh and lean back against the new grass on the knoll. At the corner of my eye, a small orange flower blooms.

"What is so funny?"

"You. You think you have all the answers. What do you think caused Esau to act the way he did? Do you think he is my familiar?"

"Is he?"

The words come so softly that at first I am not sure they have been spoken. But the intensity of his stare draws that doubt from my mind. I sit up so sharply that Esau rises in alarm, moving forward to stand between us.

Is *this* why O'Meara is here? To exorcise a demon? A warlock?

Suddenly the care and deference shown to me over the past few months takes on new meaning, and I see O'Meara's reason for remaining with me, the patience of his Bishop, the constant attention to his rosary and breviary in new light.

Did I hear faint murmurings of the *Rituale Romana* when the darkness fell upon me a while back?

Angry retorts spring to my lips, but I choke them back. My frame trembles with rage, and a gray fog begins again to fall over my eyes.

"You are a Jesuit," I manage. "Not a Franciscan."

His eyes calmly meet mine. I see the truth in them.

"Why?" I ask. A faint smile flickers over his face.

"I think you know," he says. "It has taken a long time to find you."

"Then, it isn't Simon Girty about whom you seek knowledge."

He shakes his head. "No. It is his apostate, his

274

follower."

I leap to my feet, facing him. "Why?" The word hisses again from my lips. Esau growls and crouches. "We are not devils; only men who fought for what we believed."

"The truth," he says. "We want the truth. We *need* the truth."

I pause, feeling the rage coursing through my body like wildfire. For a wild moment, I am tempted to speak the words that will unleash Esau to tear out his lying throat, but then a strange calmness begins to emerge from a tiny crystal, and I hear a voice: "There's a better way, a better way." I draw a deep, ragged breath, feeling the pain deep within my chest.

"Need? What do you mean 'need?'"

"We have need of you. Perhaps," he corrects himself.

"For what?"

"For the glory of God," he says simply. His eyes meet mine calmly. I almost send Esau again to his throat, but I sense new resolve in him. For the moment, he is strong in his faith and would welcome the chance to be a martyr for his belief. But that can change.

"So, you want to know. Very well. You shall know. Everything. Tonight. Pray to your God for strength, Priest. You shall need it. Come, Esau!"

I turn and walk away from him my steps following the path around the side of the cabin towards the forest. I, too must prepare.

Chapter Thirty-seven

An unseasonal blizzard rapidly moves down from the north as I return to the cabin from the dark woods. When I slam the door behind me, hard crystals rattle against the walls and roof. O'Meara waits calmly beside the fire. Steam rises from a large toddy like smoke from a witch's cauldron by my chair. I smile tightly and take my place in front of the fire. Esau warily settles down beside me. I lift the toddy, mockingly salute him, and take a large drink, then ignore him and stare deeply into the fire, letting the writhing, twisting flames dance through closed doors of memory kept carefully locked for over twenty-odd years. The wind howls, the fire leaps and roars, but I am barely aware of this as the years fall away, and the warmth of vigorous youth slowly heats my blood, driving away the cold of age. I speak.

The sutler handed a parcel wrapped in oil cloth and twine-tied to me when I stepped into his store for supplies. On top of the parcel, I noticed a letter from B. Franklin and retired to a corner of the store to read it. The words, hurriedly scrawled (no doubt to catch a posting), leaped off the page, stunning me with their intensity:

>*"Anne is dead three days this p.m. by her own hand. She was, we discovered, with child. Her brother loudly insists you are the father and a great ugliness has been created through his indignation. I fear for you, my good friend, but I am torn with indecision for I cannot decide your position in this sordid affair. For the moment, though, I can only caution you to be careful and urge you to depart Fort Pitt before word arrives in regard to this business. Knowing the temper of those border ruffians, I do not believe any denial on your part would be rationally considered. I shall, on your behalf, endeavor to discover the true parent, but I must confess that I have little hope for success in this pursuit as I must leave within the week for Paris. She was, by definition, a bit of a recluse, having no suitors and few of her own sex to serve as confidantes. Still, I shall try, rest assured of that. Send word under a pseudonym of your new address when you have settled to me in Paris. In the meanwhile, I remain*
>
>>*yr. obt. servant*
>> B. FRANKLIN

My sight blurred I felt the ache of loss in my

throat as I remembered her softness and kindness, her desire to do good. Then fury replaced despair as I thought of her brother who had stifled her, destroying her with his brutishness, his cold disdain, shredding her sensitivity with his demands.

I leaned back against a post to calm myself and noticed a group of men clustered around the flour barrel, whispering among themselves and casting furtive glances in my direction. In their midst stood Wetzel, and Benjamin's caution leaped into my thoughts. Casually, I stood, thrusting his letter into my shirt, and made my way to the door. I was unarmed, but I did not think I had much to worry about yet. A good three hours of daylight remained before they would come under cover of night. Still, I had not time to waste for I knew Wetzel would follow me.

The thought was chilling. Wetzel was a formidable woodsman, and I would not be able to lose him by skill alone. For that, I would need luck. But, I could slow him down *if* I had enough of a lead.

I felt their eyes like rifle bores upon my back as I needed my buckskins, sack of "possibles", rifle, and powder and shot. I intended to travel light for speed was of the essence. Yet, I had to be careful for if I appeared anxious, they might try to detain me through divers means.

Deliberately, I slowed as I neared my quarters and forced myself to sit on the steps to my quarters and glance across the parade ground: the men had moved outside, casually collecting on the sutler's porch. Apparently, my fears were not groundless. I smiled grimly and rose and went inside. Quickly, I changed clothes. The trick would be in leaving for my quarters anchored against the stockade wall and had only the one entrance. I need not have worried, though, for a wagon passed in front of my door as I pondered this problem, momentarily blocking their view of my quarters.

In seconds, I was out the door, walking beside the wheel. Minutes later, I was through the gate and in the safety of the shadows of the wood fringe. Immediately, I broke into a dog-trot, heading on as straight a line as I could manage to the northwest. I needed distance between myself and the fort before I took time to try and disguise my trail. I moved deeper and deeper into the forest, a fierce joy growing within me as each step took me closer and closer to Simon Girty.

Chapter Thirty-eight

Lieutenant-Governor Henry Hamilton made me feel welcome in Detroit from the moment I first offered my services and asked for the whereabouts of Simon Girty. Hamilton promptly placed me on the payroll as a liaison between his office and Girty's forces although I suspect he had liaisons with other tribes who could have performed that duty in passing with others. My pay was to be sixteen shillings York currency and one and one-half rations per day. In addition, I was given a new flintlock rifle, a saddle and bridle, and three horses. A veritable fortune!

Detroit, at that time, was a large, sprawling fort surrounded by clusters of dirty cabins housing the border people. I appeared to be welcome in either section although the smiles on the lips of the fort ladies seemed tolerant and strained. The cabin women found my elocution flattering although the men grumbled and whispered amongst themselves when I passed. Still, I felt content and safe although I knew my contentment to be the result of an escharotic agent, namely fear. My welcome by the "Hair-Buyer" and dark stories concerning my association with Simon Girty created that, and, I confess, I took a perverse delight in appearing an enigma to all. I had given myself up to the epohistical temptation of Thespis.

At first, I could not understand why Simon had not been assigned to the Wyandots but rather to the Mingoes, a bastard tribe made up misfits, half-breeds, and renegades, cast-offs from all the tribes. But I soon learned that was Joseph Brant's doing in an attempt to keep Simon from exerting any influence over the Six Nations. It was a futile attempt, however, for Simon, with a series of quick raids across the Ohio, quickly proved himself far more capable a leader than Brant. The Mohawks may have made Brant their war-chief, but the rest of the Nations elected to follow Simon.

Brant did not take the loss lightly and constantly sought ways to undermine Simon's authority. Each failure left him more and more bitter, and I resolved to watch Brant carefully whenever he was in camp. Simon was always much too careless about his back, a high belief, I am sure, in his own immortality.

I waited in Detroit for about two months before Simon returned in the early spring, fresh from his many victories and recent election as principal war-chief of the Nations over Brant. I had been sitting lazily in the unseasonal warmth of the sun when my senses pricked at a familiar light step. Rising, I found myself crushed in a huge bear hug.

"Nightwind!" Simon said loudly, bruising my ribs with his enthusiastic greeting "How long have you been waiting?"

"Long enough," I gasped, blinking back sudden tears. I caught a glimpse of George, grinning over his brother's shoulder, then was thrust back and away. "I was forced to leave Fort Pitt not long after you." His eyes narrowed with question, but I shook my head. "Not here. Later. When we are alone and away from long ears. Have you seen Hamilton?"

He nodded, and dropped down on his heels beside the step to the trading post. He began drawing hieroglyphics with his dirk in the dust. I squatted beside him.

"Yes," he said. "Before I came to find you. We are to return to Chillicothe and assemble a raiding party and work our way south through the Ohio Valley. This should pull soldiers and militia from Pitt and other outposts. While they chase our raiders south through the valley, Howe will strike from the northeast with his troops, and Burgoyne will move down from the north with his. After we have pulled the troops below the Little Miami, we are to turn back and destroy the followers in a series of ambushes." His mouth twisted in a wry grin. "We should be able to seize the West."

"And what," I asked, pitching my voice low, "does this do for the Nations?" He remained silent for a long time then softly answered.

"We have been promised all the lands of the Ohio and west, but I do not believe this will happen.

When we turn back to establish the ambushes, we shall, instead, turn north and strike swiftly here. We shall seize Detroit for ourselves!"

His eyes burned with determination, and I thrilled to the savage promise within them. It was a masterful plan and one that would work for no British officer would believe that the savages could possibly be capable of such a plan reflecting the genius of Hannibal.

Chapter Thirty-nine

I felt at home from the moment my foot first fell onto the soil of the Ohio River Valley, and I knew why the Indians so vehemently opposed the white settlers anxious to slip an iron plow blade into the rich soil. A dense forest of mixed hardwoods—oak, ash, black and yellow walnut, wild cherry, coffeetree, honey and black locust, buckeye, beech, shagbark hickory, hackberry, and tulip poplar-underbrushed with stands of dogwood, red bud, hawthorn, magnolia, and pawpaw swept back from the river to cover the ridges. Some red cedar and hemlock broke deciduous lines as did some pine. Yellow butterflies *(I remember it was the year of the yellow butterflies.)* so numerous they appeared like a carpet over meadows of bluegrass, pepper-grass, Virginia rye, wild ginger, peavine, red clover, and Shawnee cabbage. At the edge of the forests, the occasional buffalo grazed contentedly along with wapiti and white-tail deer. The forests were home to wildcats, yellow wolf, black and gray fox, panthers, raccoons, squirrels of many colors, beavers, bears, and mink living beside pure flowing streams filled with catfish, sunfish, spotted perch, some mullet and chubs, bass and crappie, and freshwater clams. In the early morning, the wild turkeys would wake the world with their strange call and be answered by pheasants or partridges or Carolina paroquets *(already extinct, I fear).*

My heart sang with gratitude for the Creator who had made such a place. The entire valley pulsated with life. How could anyone be arrogant enough to demand ownership of this land? This was a place for Abel's people, not Cain's, and I felt a surge of loathing for the followers of the latter.

Ironically, our first efforts in the Ohio River Valley were as saviors, not destroyers. *(Did you know that, Priest? Of course not. Evil and kindness do not mix, right? Like oil and water. But, I tell you this: men are by nature good not evil as you priests would have us believe. Evil is acquired, not the product of birth. There was much good in Simon Girty that was never told but no story as great as that which occurred in the spring of that year in the village of Wapatomica.)*

It was a cool morning when we rode into Wapatonica to begin a five-day council with the Six Nations. It was the formal gathering of the Iroquois, and the rules, laws, if you will, for the governing of the tribes for the coming year would be decided as well as judgment declared on all complaints.

John, Simon's brother, was with us as was John Ward who later died of wounds suffered while with Brant. A large, brawny man lay on the ground within sight of a fire-blackened stake with fresh firewood piled high around it. His hands and feet were tightly bound with wet rawhide and his face had been painted black with charcoal and bear grease—a custom of the Iroquois with doomed prisoners. He looked familiar, but I could not recognize him for his features were swollen from the beatings he had undergone: both eyes pinched nearly shut, a severe cut running down one cheek from ear to chin, lumps across his shoulders and head from having been forced to run the gauntlet. Yet spirit remained within him for even as we watched, a squaw pulled up her dress and tried to defecate on his face only to let out a scream as the man sank his teeth in her rump and tore a chunk of meat free.

Immediately, the children began to beat him with hickory and willow switches as the braves watching laughed heartily at the squaw's misfortune. Simon climbed down from his horse. The children grudgingly gave way as he crossed to the man and squatted beside him. He stared long and hard into the captive's eyes before speaking.

"I know you," he said quietly. Upon hearing his words, I slid from my pony and joined him, staring intently into the man's face. White teeth gleamed in a twisted smile. He nodded.

"From where?"

"I'm from Kentucky," he said. His voice had a familiar twang to it. Memory began to move. Simon nodded and considered him again.

"What's your name?" he asked at last. The man grinned.

"Simon Kenton."

Simon rocked back on his heels and thoughtfully regarded him. Strangely, tears began to flow from his eyes. He reached out and awkwardly shook Kenton's shoulder.

"Did I not tell you that the day would arrive when you would need me? How did you come to be here?"

Kenton grimaced and eased his shoulders back against the ground. "Bad judgment," he said. "We— Alexander Montgomery and George Clark were with me—thought we'd make a little money taking Shawnee horses and selling 'em to the settlers at Boone's Station. We got away with seven, but a storm blew up an' the horses wouldn't cross the river. Clark got away, Montgomery got scalped, and, well," a sheepish look crossed his face under the black, "here I am."

"And they brought you here?" I asked. His eyes shifted towards me.

"No," he said. "First, to Chillicothe where they made me run the gauntlet. Damn near got away there 'cept one Injun caught up with me and slowed me down enough for t'others to catch up. Kept me from reaching the Council House. Figgered if I made it there, I'd have a chance of gettin' free. Anyways," he sighed, "they voted to bring me here after a little detour to Piqua on the Mad River and Machachack."

"They put you through the gauntlet again?" Simon asked.

Kenton nodded, painfully swallowing. I rose to get him a cup of water.

"Yep. Both times. They were a mite more careful this time, though. Reckon they didn't want to show up here without their prisoner. Lose face in front of the chief *sachem* and all. Think thar's any chance you kin git me?" he asked calmly, but I could hear the faint hint of desperation clicking behind his words.

Simon slowly shook his head, his brows furrowing with thought.

"I have little hope," he said. "The council has passed sentence. The business is through as far as they are concerned."

"Ah, well," Kenton said, and sighed. He looked again at the blackened stake waiting a few yards away. His face filled with revulsion, and he shuddered. "A favor. Yer knife. Drop it on the ground and walk away. I'll take my chances."

Simon again shook his head. Kenton's lips twisted ruefully.

"Yep. Thet would mark you, wouldn't it?" His eyes fell on my rifle. "Could you make it quick than? A bullet? From the trees? Who would know?"

"Maybe it won't come to that," Simon said, laying a soothing hand upon Kenton's shoulder. He rose and looked down the street to the Council House at the far end. "Let me see first what I can do in there."

"Girty . . ." Kenton began, and stopped as Simon made a small motion with his hands.

"I'll do my best," Simon said. He hesitated. "I will promise you this: you will not die at the stake."

He strode away, heading for the Council House. I followed, staying two steps to his left and rear, carefully watching the shadows between the lodges. I knew several of our enemies were in the camp for a prisoner of Kenton's stature would draw them like bees to honey. To take part in his death would strengthen their spirit. I had seen Red Jacket's shield before one of the guest lodges when we rode in and knew Red Pole, too, would be there for he was Red Jacket's shadow. Brant's friend, the prophet Handsome Lake, undoubtedly had made the trip down from Erie along with the Deleware chiefs Captain Pipe and Wingemund. Pipe had expressed reservations about us in the past and was a friend of Brant as well.

Simon halted for a moment inside the Council House to allow his eyes to adjust to the gloom. The elders sat on raised platforms along the sides, stoically watching us, wreaths of smoke whispering from their pipes as they waited. My heart lifted as I noticed Rides-the-Moon heading the Seneca delegation instead of Red Jacket. At the far end, Logan sat in the seat of honor, and I felt a faint glimmer of hope for Kenton's fate.

Logan stood upon our entrance and waved us to two empty seats on his left.

"Welcome, The Chosen. Welcome, Nightwind," he said solemnly. "We have waited long for your arrival."

The words were more than a formality in this instance for Logan held the ceremonial knife and eagle feather while a massive war club rested on the edge of the platform in front of him. They were waiting for Simon's words, his *war* words, for it was evident from all around that they believed the moment spoken of in prophecy years before when Simon and I left them to go to Pitt had arrived. That, I feared, might make things a bit more difficult for on the heels of the echoing murmurs of welcome came words of satisfaction in anticipation of white men's blood.

Simon coolly ignored the hot-tempered comments and walked the length of the Council House to the seats indicated. He stood for a moment calmly surveying the others then took his seat without comment. Logan gave him a puzzled glance, then a tiny smile stole across his lips only to be repressed before he turned stern features to the others.

"The council is complete," he said. "The work at hand may now begin. Who will speak first?"

A young brave I did not know at the far end leaped to his feet and gave a long, impassioned speech on the readiness of the Oneidas followed by another brave favorably commenting on the worthiness of the Onondagoes. We heard equally impassioned speeches from the Cayugas, the Tuscararoras, and the Senecas— all minor chiefs earmarked for greatness while the leaders, the great men, waited patiently for the young ones to finish before the main business would be broached. I sighed, and leaned back, easing an ache between my shoulders as a young warrior from the Delewares climbed to his feet. Then the Munsies, the Shawnees of the Scioto, the Wyandots of Sandusky and Detroit, the Ottawas of Lake Michigan by the Great Falls, the Chippewas of the Lakes, Pottewatemies, Pyankeshas, Kickapoos, Muscoutans, Vermillions, and Weotonans all pronounced their readiness through their first-day spokesmen.

Simon waited patiently until all had finished and Logan began the words to close the council before standing and indicating his desire to speak. An excited buzz swept around the Council House at this departure from procedure.

"Yes, The Chosen," Logan said. "What is it you wish?"

Simon waited until the others gave him their attention. His words were soft, but not humble, succinct, but not harsh. He spoke clearly and to the point. He did not beg but simply explained that Simon Kenton was a brother and to kill him was to kill a piece of The Chosen. He spoke of what this would do to him and then cleverly reminded them that as he, The Chosen, was a member of the Six Nations, his family was under their protection as well. To kill Kenton for what he had done would violate their own laws and dishonor him. He asked for another vote, a tally to free the prisoner and place him in his custody.

No one spoke for a long time after Simon finished and sat down. Somewhere a fly buzzed. A lone dog barked. The plaque of jagged light on the floor beneath the smoke-hole had dimmed. Red Jacket started to rise, but Logan caught the movement in the gloom and quickly called for the tally Simon had requested. Red Jacket tried to protest but was sternly reminded of the rules of the council: no debate allowed after a call for the tally by the presiding chief.

An intricately carved and painted ash stick was produced and passed around the council. To strike it on the platform was a vote for death. To pass it, a vote for freedom. Logan made a notch on the ends of another stick to count the votes. At the end, Kenton was spared but barely, much to the disgust of Brant's friends.

Simon quickly removed Kenton from Wapatomica to his cabin at Solomon's Town while he attended the council. It was fortunate that he did for on the fourth day of the council, the day before Simon was to speak, a small band of Shawnees staggered into camp from an ill-fated foray against Wheeling where they had been soundly beaten.

293

The chief who had led the raid—Smoke, I believe was his name—demanded Kenton be brought back for another vote of the council. There was little doubt which way this vote would go despite Simon's citing of Six Nation law: Kenton had been declared *cut-ta-ho-tha* before Simon's arrival and as Brant smugly pointed out, Simon and Kenton shared no blood: their brotherhood was one of spirit only.

Simon gracefully accepted the council's condemnation but then requested that Kenton's death be postponed until the celebration at Upper Sandusky where all tribes were scheduled to gather to receive presents from the British government.

I do not know if it was an attempt to help soothe Simon's feelings or the suggestion of a grander spectacle, but the enraged shouts of Brant and his friends who claimed Simon was plotting aginst the council's wishes rang through the lodge.

The lodge grew silent as Simon stood and leaped lightly to the ground. He crossed to stand in front of Brant. He pulled his knife from its scabbard and dropped it at Brant's feet. Then, he calmly turned, presenting his back to Brant who stared speechless at him. Simon cast a contemptuous look over his shoulder and walked back to his seat as the council exploded in laughter.

Brant's face turned ugly at the laughter. He leaped to his feet and stormed from the Council House.

I let my held breath out slowly: Simon almost had caused his own death for drawing a weapon in council and delivering a challenge. But in a master-stroke of diplomacy, he had turned the challenge into a grim joke that had destroyed Brant's argument.

Kenton was sent to Upper Sandusky where Peter Druyer, a Canadian trader in the British service, claimed Kenton possessed military secrets and bought his life for a hundred dollars' worth of rum and tobacco—just as Simon had planned when he sent Kenton north with his brother Jim as guard.

I pause in my narrative to consider O'Meara. "Now, Priest. What do you have to say to that?"

"A favor returned," O'Meara says. He slips two beads of his rosary through his fingers. "And, what else should I be thinking? If it's to illustrate Girty and yourself as honorable men, you have partially succeeded. But, sure, now, you can see the fallacy. It was not a service freely performed for the obligation rested heavily upon his shoulders."

I feel the blood rising to my head. Esau lays a paw on my knee and whines. Absently, I scratch his head with one hand while I pour a brandy with the other. A strange lull falls over me, and from afar I hear my words damning O'Meara as images gather at memory's door, waiting for me to continue. I drink and stare at the flames, willing myself back.

"You look not for salvation but only for horror," I say hotly to him. He opens his mouth to speak, but I raise my hand to stop him. "Three times I have warned you. I do not make a gift of a man's soul a fourth. Sit. You shall know."

I draw a deep breath and let down the final bar to memory.

Chapter Forty

Simon did not wait long to begin operations: we attacked Butler's Mill near Hookstown in mid-May, then quickly raced south, following the twisting Ohio, sweeping over the outlying cabins and small settlements standing in our way. Runners brought word that soldiers and militia followed us, and we fled even further south, drawing them after us.

The summer flew past, the months blurring into one as we attacked outpost after outpost and retreated ever south with the soldiers and militia stubbornly clinging to our trail. I began to wonder about their urgency, their persistence, for surely by now the officers should have become alarmed at how far they had traveled since May.

Simon, too, was perplexed. I would often find him deep in thought, staring into the burning coals of a campfire late at night, absently drawing strange hieroglyphics on the ground in front of him with a hazel wand. Occasionally during the day, his face would cloud over, and he would mutter rhetorical questions, wondering why the pursuers had not turned back for until they did, we could not make our turn north to strike at Detroit.

Meanwhile, we moved ever south, increasing the distance we would have to travel when we did turn north and diminishing our supplies with every move we made.

Finally, Simon decided to split his force, sending one party under Brant due west while the rest continued south with us. Maybe, he explained, the militia would be reluctant to divide their party and give up the chase. Plans called for Brant to make a wide detour, avoiding at all cost a fight, and rejoin us where the Little Miami emptied into the Ohio. Here, although we did not know it at the time, we would discover the reason for the persistent pursuit.

One cool morning two days after our arrival at the Little Miami in early October to wait for Brant, excited runners appeared in camp to report a small fleet of keelboats, guarded by roughly seventy men, moving up the Ohio where the river bends three miles below the Little Miami at the mouth of the Licking. Simon's eyes flickered, and a grin slowly spread over his face as he turned towards me.

"I believe," he said softly, his eyes beginning to glow, "that we now know why the soldiers and militia do not turn north."

"Supplies," I said. He nodded with satisfaction.

"Yes. And unless I miss my guess, those supplies are badly needed at Fort Pitt. *If*," he added darkly, "Hamilton has managed to get the British forces to move south."

"You have doubts?" I asked, suddenly fearful at his expressed concern. A bleak smile flashed across his features.

"I always have doubts," he said solemnly. "For I know some day I will be betrayed."

His eyes bored deeply into my own, and I shivered and started to protest, but he placed a heavy hand upon my forearm and tightly squeezed.

"Do not worry, Nightwind. What is written, is written."

"Do you know who?" I asked. He hesitated briefly, then nodded.

"Yes."

"Who?"

He shook his head and turned away.

"It is not wise to know too much. I will do what I must and perhaps . . . perhaps . . ." He left the remainder unsaid, intending, I believe, for the doubt to be a comfort to me. But it was not: its absence signaled no hope. Despair hung heavy over the clearing while Simon calmly made his plans despite the eagerness of the Senecas, the Wyandots, and the Delewares and Shawnee making up our party. I forced my thoughts from his revelation to concentrate on his plan. It was brilliant in its simplicity which, as any student of Tacitus knows, can be equally convoluted in duplicity.

Simon sent a small force downriver with his

brother George and Matt Elliott to set up a seemingly innocuous camp on the point of a sandbar as bait. We would encircle the camp like sweeping horns of a buffalo and allow the keelboats to pass and land before attacking. The left arm or "horn" would sweep around behind the attackers, sealing them off from retreat back to their keelboats.

Quickly, we dispersed and settled ourselves to wait, some in tall pepper-grass, others in the thick maze of buckthorn and blackberry brambles running parallel to the river. Still others took to the trees, hiding themselves in the thick branches of walnut and ash. Then, we waited.

A raven cawed a short distance away and was answered by an angry fox squirrel startled in his lunch. A tentative warbling roll from a bunting evoked a reply from a mourning dove, but it was not enough, I worried, for a borderman not to be suspicious. Then, the keelboats edged past, and I forgot about the birds and concentrated on the men in front of me, so close that I could hear their grunts and the *thump-thump* of their poles against the gunwales as they sunk their poles deep in the mud and threw their weight against them to "walk" the keelboat upstream. I recognized the leader in the second boat: David Rogers, a flamboyant colonel in the Virginia militia, elegantly dressed, his only concession to the wilderness a pair of silver-inlayed pistols thrust into a broad, red sash. I saw him start as he noticed George and Matt's camp and the quick sideways motion of his hand and arm as he frantically directed the keelboats to shore.

For a moment, I feared we had been discovered as the rudderman on the first boat hesitated, peering closely into the thick brush, then a savage joy coursed through my veins as he heaved the heavy rudder over and the unwieldy prow gently bumped against the bank only a few yards from our hiding place.

Rogers quickly gathered his men around him and divided them into groups to form a tauriform attack on the camp, an encircling action that would allow his forces to cut off any escape. Quietly, they began to snake through a patch of scraggly willows toward the camp. My heart became a mallet, banging against my ribs. Perspiration flowed liberally from my face, little spidery runnels streaming from my forehead. My bladder threatened to explode. My mouth grew dry as cotton, and I weirdly thought an antilogy: why does the mouth dry and hands wetten in times of danger?

The first volley of our forces drove the thought from my mind and considerably thinned their ranks. George and Matt quickly drew their men into a firing line and delivered a second volley into their bewildered mass, bringing them into a route. Blue chuffs of smoke exploded from rifles behind leaves. No firing came from their flank where Red Jacket was supposed to be waiting with his force. I threw my rifle up, sighting quickly upon a brawny man bellowing orders, vainly trying to rally his men. I squeezed the trigger. A puff of smoke blinded me for a brief second. When it cleared, I saw the brawny man grab his throat, blood spurting high. He staggered and fell. My body swelled with a fierce joy. A red film slipped over my eyes and a scream escaped from my lips. My muscles threw me forward, and I bounded towards the keelboat men, swinging a knife and tomahawk. I sensed braves on my left and right but paid them no heed as I caught up with the slowest of the fleeing men. He tried to ward off my blow, but I trepanned him with a single blow and sped on towards the others.

I saw Rogers and headed towards him but was passed by Simon who suddenly stopped and threw up his rifle. He fired and Rogers crumbled into a ball. A wild-eyed soldier ran screaming towards me, musket raised to bash in my brains. I dodged the blow and slit his throat with a backhand slash. Suddenly, the roaring ceased. I found myself standing in the midst of fallen bodies. Cries of pain and moans rose from the wounded who begged for mercy. But none would be granted. Already Knows-Too-Well, a bandy-legged dwarf, prowled among the bodies, searching out the wounded and finishing them with a fishing spear.

"Nightwind!"

I turned and saw Simon beckoning. I stumbled to him. He was bending over Rogers's body. He straightened and looked with satisfaction at a brace of French pistols, smooth-bored with silver inlay, he had taken from the body. He threw an arm around my shoulders.

"What bravery! Good work! Had you not charged when you did they might have reached the boats." He frowned. "Red Jacket was too slow in cutting off their retreat."

"Yes, " I answered. "But then, he is Brant's friend, is he not? If you had failed, then Brant would be the leader and Red Jacket his Lieutenant."

Simon's eyes narrowed at my words then cleared as he glanced over my shoulder. I followed his gaze and met Red Jacktet's eyes glittering with hatred. He turned away, hawked, and spat.

"They would not have reached the boats," he said sullenly. "Red Jacket was there. And so was Cornplanter." Simon flashed a look at him that made him drop his eyes.

"You were late," he said flatly. "For this, there is no excuse. You were not threatened. You hesitated. Why?" He waited for a reply, but none came as Red Jacket refused to raise his eyes. "Perhaps," Simon softly said, " no answer is needed. Go. We shall talk again of this later." He disdainfully turned his back on Red Jacket and raised the pistols to admire them.

"These really are fine," he said. He stuck them in his belt and faced me. "What do you think?" I pretended to consider them while keeping my eye upon Red Jacket.

"The red sash," I said. Red Jacket glared murderously at us then stalked away. Simon's face looked blank. I pointed at the red sash around Rogers's body. "You need the sash to set them off."

Comprehension dawned on the face. He dropped the beaded belt that held his knife and tomahawk from around his waist and unceremoniously pulled the sash from Rogers's body. He wrapped it around his waist, tucked the pistols into the sash, and re-tied the beaded belt over the sash. The effect was striking.

"Well?" he demanded.

"Yes," I said. He beamed and looked around the clearing. The dwarf caught his eye and grinned and waved. Six powder horns hung around his neck. He clutched a handful of scalps.

"It is good, The Chosen!" he cheerfully called.

"How many have died?" Simon asked.

"We have lost only two and three others claim wounds," Knows-Too-Well answered. "I do not know of the others."

"Forty-two," George panted as he came up. "And five prisoners. I doubt if any escaped, but I sent Rides-the-Moon out with a small party to search just in case."

"All your people unharmed?" George noded.

"Yes. Matt has a knife slice across his hand. That's all. We've been very lucky."

"Or blessed," I added. Simon gave me a faint smile.

"Yes. Or blessed." He turned towards the river. "Shall we see what they were hauling?"

Matt joined us, his hand wrapped in a dirty neckerchief, and together we walked to the keelboats. Indians were already unloading the boats and neatly piling the goods in a small clearing they had made by cutting back the thick underbrush. I counted as they unloaded: several bolts of calico, heavy coats, two hundred French rifles, powder, lead, saddles, bridles, brass kettles, flints, plates. louse combs, razors, coffee, salt, tea, and seven barrels of rum that Simon wisely confiscated. That much liquor would have rendered our men helpless for days.

"I think," Simon said, surveying the plunder, "that now we know why we are being followed so relentlessly."

"Yes," I said. "But now they have no reason to continue. Unless they think they can find us and recapture their supplies."

"Then the trick is to disappear. Right?" Simon said. He turned to the waiting Indians.

"Pack everything," he ordered. "We leave in three hours. Cornplanter!" The tall Shawnee crossed to him. "Take five men and cover our trail as we pass. Be very careful. No one must know which direction we travel." Cornplanter nodded and moved away.

"That's a rather tall order, ain't it, Simon?" George asked. "You know they'll have a borderman with them. Maybe even Wetzel. Won't be able to fool him for long. 'N this here is quite a load for us to carry."

"Not for long," Simon said. "We'll strike out for Brant. Once we reach him, we'll have plenty to help us carry. Then, we should be able to out-run them."

"Which way?" George asked.

"North," Simon said decisively. "It no longer matters if we're followed or not. We have plenty of supplies, and, if Cornplanter and his men can get us a headstart, plenty of time to reach Detroit. I don't think those who pursue us have enough supplies left to cover that march." He looked at me. "What do you think?"

"A bit of a gamble," I answered. "First, you have to find Brant. He should have been here by now." Simon's eyes clouded

"Yes," he said distantly. "That could be a problem." He walked away. George and Matt looked at me and shrugged and hurried off to organize the packing. I collected my rifle and followed Simon. A cloud of melancholy gathered around me. I looked across the river into the woods. Shadows moved among the trees, and I strained to hear the forest murmurings. But none came.

Chapter Forty-one

Two weeks passed before we finally found Brant. Simon's face slowly settled into stern ridges of granite as bit-by-bit we were forced to cache portions of the supplies we had gathered from Rogers's keelboats. Some of our caches went undetected, but the majority of them were discovered by those following us. Our men grew weary from carrying the supplies, and twice we were surprised by early morning attacks from our pursuers led, we discovered, by elements of Morgan's Rangers. Luckily, we escaped, but we all knew that it was only a matter of time before we were finally caught in a place from which we would be unable to extricate ourselves.

In desperation, Simon moved our force in a wide detour a hundred and eighty degrees from our proposed line of march in an attempt to lose Morgan and, quite by accident, stumbled across Brant's camp just below the mouth of the Great Miami.

A low fog rose from the Ohio River when we found Brant late in the afternoon. Simon's frame swelled with anger as we rode through the camp in search of Brant. Most of his men were drunk, sprawled over the forest floor with jugs of rum beside them.

Several were wounded and dying, but even these had their tote of rum. From what we could gather, Brant had stumbled across a force of Pennsylvanian militia led by Colonel Lockry. Brant had elected to ambush them instead of avoiding contact. He managed to catch Lockry in a crossfire when Lochry, landing at a inlet, turned his horses ashore to graze. Brant killed one hundred six of the Pensylvanians before they managed to fight their way clear of the trap and escape, leaving all their stores behind. But the cost was high: Brant lost a third of his men and another sixth were severely wounded.

We found Brant roaring drunk beneath a large oak tree by the river. Even in such a state, he was a magnificent man: six feet tall, finely proportioned, stout and muscular. His eyes were large and piercing, his nose acquiline, his mouth wide. He wore a scarlet frock cut around his middle with a yellow silken sash. He had tucked Lochry's sword in the sash as a trophy. He could hardly walk for the amount of rum he had drunk and all the beads and trinkets and gold epaulets and silver bracelets he wore. Around his neck hung a medallion of His Sovereign Majesty George III.

"Girty!" he bellowed upon seeing us. "Fortune has smiled upon us and frowned on the Long Knives."

He sniggered, and raised a jug to fill a tin cup in his hand, staggering, and nearly falling into the fire. He drank from the cup, then wiped his mouth with the back of his hand. His eyes narrowed with cunning as they considered Simon's stern features.

"Come!" he shouted. "Have a drink!"

Simon ignored the proffered jug and dismounted. He turned slowly, surveying the camp before speaking.

"It seems that you have been busy," he said dryly.

"We have killed many," Brant boasted. He swung his arm to indicate the stores stacked behind him. "And, we have captured many stores. Enough . . . enough to supply us for many months."

"Yes," Simon said, his voice hardening. Tiny muscles knotted whitely from controlled anger at the corners of his jaws."Yes, you have. Especially since you have managed to reduce your force by so many."

Brant's obsidian eyes glittered with hatred then glanced at me as I dropped my hand to the hammer of my rifle held in the crook of my arm. The taut muscles of his bronzed cheeks resisted his forced laugh.

"Yes. But the spoils are great. We have taken many supplies; many trade goods. It was an opportunity that seldom comes. I simply did what any commander would have done when such an opportunity presented itself: I took advantage."

"Opportunity'?" Simon spat, and stalked past Brant to the captured stores. "These? Beads, ribbons, bolts of cheap cotton—where are the supplies? The shot? The powder? You have taken squaw gaudies but nothing of use to us. Our forces have been foolishly depleted and for what?" Brant took a deep, finishing draught from the cup in his hand. He threw it from him and faced Simon.

"For what? You have to ask me that? What is a man made for? Our men fought bravely and I, I fought with the fangs of an adder, the strength of a bear, and the cunning of a fox. With my own hand, I took eleven scalps of our enemies. They pleaded for mercy, but I had none to offer. Kill! Kill! Kill! My battle cry rang over the field and was answered by my followers from all sides. *My* followers! Not yours! It is me they follow! Me! Who captured eight prisoners singlehanded . . ."

"You're a liar," Simon said quietly, interrupting his tirade. Brant stared speechless at him, the color draining from his face.

"What did you say?" he asked in a whisper.

"You are a drunken liar," Simon answered contemptuously. "This," he half-turned away from Brant, "is due only to your greed. Your greed has cost us many dead and of those who live, too many are useless with their wounds. And as for your bravery . . ."

With a scream, Brant whipped Locry's sword from its scabbard and in the same movement deftly struck at Simon. The blade sliced through Simon's scalp, laying his forehead bare to the bone. Simon swayed, then fell unconscious at Brant's feet. Brant raised the sword for a finishing blow.

"Brant!" I sang out, raising my rifle. He swung to face me as two pairs of arms seized me from behind, forcing my rifle barrel down. I strained against them, but I was helpless. A sneer twisted across his lips. He stepped towards me. Blood ran redly down the blade in his hand.

"Ah," he said softly, eyes sneeringly mocking me. "The Follower." He raised his sword.

"No, Brant!" a hard voice cried, followed by a dry click of a hammer being drawn to full cock. "You've done enough!"

I swiveled my head towards the speaker. Jim Girty held a level bead on Brant from twenty feet. Beside him stood Cornplanter, motionless, his eyes glittering at those holding my arms.

"You are one of us!" Brant thickly muttered, lowering his arm. He swayed for a moment, then collected himself.

"Worse," Jim grimly retorted. "I should have stopped you when I had the chance. But I didn't."

"Kill me, and you'll never leave here," Brant said. Jim gave a slight nod.

"'Course it won't do you any good, either," he said. "Best thing for you is to get out while you can. Before Rides-the-Moon or the others find out what you've done," he added, indicating the still form of his brother.

Brant gave him a long, cool look. For a moment, I thought he would challenge Jim, but then George appeared on his right with five of our men. Brant laughed.

"There's much truth in what you say," he said carelessly. He sheathed the sword and lazily waved my restrainers away. "The next time, Follower, you will not be so lucky. I will kill you."

"Maybe," I answered. "But sleep lightly, Brant. Sleep lightly. Listen for me in the night breeze. And watch your trail. One day, I'll be there."

The words felt thick in my throat. My limbs trembled with fury as I crossed past him to Simon. I knelt, pressing my fingers to the pulse in his throat. He groaned. I looked up at Brant.

"Remember: the woods are large and dark and deep. I could be anywhere. And I will."

He laughed and, turning on his heel, strode from the clearing, arrogantly calling his men to the march. I opened my "possibles" pouch and pulled out a wad of soft doeskin and a small needle and thread. Brant's men silently moved into the clearing to collect the plunder under George's watchful eye. I wiped the flowing blood from the deep wound angling to just above his left eyebrow and sewed the edges together, pulling the stitches as tightly as I dared. Mercifully, Simon remained unconscious through the ordeal. When I finished, George helped me move him to a bed of soft ferns under a canvas shelter. Jim shook his head despairingly.

"I should have stopped Brant. When Simon sent me with him, I knew I was to keep him from doing something wrong, but I didn't. I didn't. I'm sorry," he said dejectedly.

"Sorry don't plant the 'taters," George mumbled. "Simon trusted you. You betrayed him."

"I know. I know." The words were almost a wail. Jim brushed the back of his hand under his nose. "Wisht I could change it, but I can't. John: you understand what I'm saying? Brant made it sound so good. Like we couldn't lose."

"I know," I said quietly. "I know. You aren't the first to do that."

Confusion knotted his brow, but I ignored him and settled down to wait as night slowly fell, and the fog grew thicker and thicker. Jim made a dry camp under a tree across the clearing from us while George quietly placed guards around the perimeter. Simon moaned and thrashed and gnashed his teeth against the pain that must have dug a crooked trench in his skullbone. Twice, he called out against whatever floating pictures slipped in and out of his mind, but I could not understand the words. Repeatedly, I bathed his wound but could not bring his fever down.

Two days passed in this fashion. Our force, led by George, slipped away to the southwest to draw

Morgan's Rangers away from the tiny camp. I grew to hate the days in which the sun drove away the morning fog and turned the interior of the shelter an eerie orange shroud, hot like the flames of hell. The air grew stale and pregnant with our own smell for I dared not leave him for long for fear he would fling himself off his bed of ferns and further injure himself. Flies held congress on his wound, a thousand sticky tongues trying to cling fast to the pasty on his forehead despite my efforts to keep them shooed away.

At last, on the third day, he awoke and asked for water. He drank and immediately fell into a calm sleep. Like a fool, I thought the worst was over when I emerged, cramped and spent, from the shelter to relate the good news to Jim and the ten other retainers who had remained with us during the ordeal.

Chapter Forty-two

Two weeks after Brant's attempt to trepan Simon, I judged him ready to move. We had little choice: George had returned alone, our forces, restless from the lack of Simon's leadership, had elected to follow Brant. Morgan's Rangers had increased their patrols. It was only a matter of time before they stumbled upon us.

I sent the retainers out, hoping for a route southward to the Mississippi where we might catch a keelboat to New Orleans where Simon could rest and heal. But the only route open to us was northeast along the Ohio. Resolutely, I assembled our little party, and we set out, hoping to find a way around the ranger patrols to an Indian town where we would possibly find a healer. For a while, I toyed with the idea of visiting one of the tiny settlements, but the risk was too great to gamble on finding a settlement with a doctor.

We slowly moved north, traveling a few miles a day before Simon's condition forced us to halt. After a week, Simon's condition had deteriorated even more, and I grew desperate. Then, I remembered Gnadenhütten, the Cabins of Grace.

Gnadenhütten had been founded by Moravian

Brethren missionaries on the Tuscarawas River and housed about a hundred Indians, mostly Deleware, converted to Christianity by David Zeisberger and John Heckewilder. All living there had insisted on remaining neutral and living in pastoral serenity, confessing their love for their fellow man. We, however, were not favorably looked upon by either Zeisberger or Heckewilder. The latter had run into us earlier at the Seneca camps when he had been stumping the bushes for converts.

At first, he had been friendly and fanatic in his role as savior. A zealous gleam shone from his eye as he saw a chance to "rescue" two white youths from the clutches of the savages. But when Simon informed him that he preferred the physical Eden to the ethereal Eden, Heckewilder became cold and distant, marking us as worse than the savages for we had consciously rejected his moral ethic despite the education to which our "white blood" supposedly exposed us.

I did not know Zeisberger personally as I was not with Simon when he encountered Zeisberger on the trail from Lichtenau to Schonbrunn. Simon offered to share his noon meal with the missionary who readily agreed only to berate Simon after the meal when he suddenly remembered the story of the "white savage" as told to him by his friend Heckewilder.

This, of course, did not keep us from Gnadenhütten: Simon enjoyed his visits there with the

Deleware chief Half King when he accompanied Wyandot warriors making occasional calls to visit their relatives who had embraced the Moravian god. Gnadenhütten was peaceful and serene, and when we took the field from Detroit, Simon warned the Indian leaders among our force to avoid visiting Gnadenhütten and the sister villages of Schonbrunn, Salem, and Lichtenau. He was unwilling to expose the people there to possible recriminatory attacks from the colonials if the visitations were discovered. Their utopia was to be considered sacrosanct despite the presence of Zeisberger and Heckewilder who gladly passed on any information they could to the Americans.

We arrived at Gnadenhütten to find it almost deserted. Elliott, we discovered, had moved the majority of the Moravian Indians to the Wyandot country of Upper Sandusky to stop Heckewilder from acting as an informer to the colonials in Pittsburgh. He had left behind a small number, about a hundred, to harvest the corn.

Snow began to fly as we rode into Gnaddenhutten. I hurried to move Simon into Arrow's cabin where he usually stayed during our visit. Arrow had taken the name of Abraham when he was baptized many years before, but Simon stubbornly refused to call him by his Christian name.

"This is not good," Abraham said, after anxiously examining Simon's wound. Simon lay on a pallet made from corn shucks in front of the stone fireplace. His eyes were dark pools shaded purple with exhaustion. Lines of pain were deeply etched around his mouth.

"Rest," he mumbled. He shivered, and Abraham hastily rose to throw another Hudson Bay blanket over him. Simon's face was shiny with sweat. Abraham shook his head.

"He needs the medicine of the Long Knives," he said regretfully.

"We cannot go there," I said. "This you well know. Where is Hobbler, the Healer?"

"Not here," Abraham said, and quietly explained what had happened to the village.

"When did this happen?" I asked.

"One moon has passed since the move to the Wyandots," he answered. "One week after Thayandencera left."

"Thayandencera?" I asked uneasily. My stomach muscles contracted on their own. "For what purpose did he come?" Abraham eyed me curiously.

"To trade," he said. "And to see Hobbler, the Healer, for his men. What is wrong?" I shook my head, unable to voice reason for the sudden fear surging through me.

"He was forbidden to come here," I said harshly.

"He was in need of help. If you could not go to the Long Knives, how much more difficult would it have been for him to have sought help from them?" Abraham said, his voice gently reproving.

"You have learned your catechism well, Arrow," I said, deliberately reverting to his pagan name. "But remember: this white man's god is newly come to you. You have seen only the good. There is much bad as well. Much."

He remained silent for a long moment, his eyes disfocused in concentration at the window behind me. A shadow flitted across his face. He shuddered, and shook himself, turning his attention back to me. But I knew he had seen a vision, an image from the future that momentarily frightened the pagan still in him.

"What have you seen?" I asked.

"It does not matter," he answered. "Dreams cannot be changed. And, sometimes, it is best not to know."

"You deny yourself?" I asked.

"No, I accept myself as God's child. What bad is there in that?" he answered calmly.

"Because it gives man a chance to change the world to his liking," I answered. I softened the hot rush of words. "Arrow, we make our own sin when we take His name. We can hide the ugliness behind His forgiveness. But that does not mean the ugliness is not there: it is just disguised. Do you understand?"

"No. But there is no need to do this, Nightwind. Your words are great, but I do not understand them because they are not the words I have been taught to hear." He smiled. "I will remember them, though, and perhaps later, after I have understood what is behind these words, we may speak of this again. But for now, it is best if we sleep. There is nothing more to do for The Chosen. We must wait to see what happens tomorrow."

I looked at Simon, face shining with sweat, as he tossed and turned on the pallet in his feverish state, and shook my head.

"I'll stay with him," I said decisively. "He may need me."

Arrow nodded gently and crossed to the far corner where he had built a rude cot against the walls. He bent slowly on aged knees and bowed his head. His hair, a long, silver mane, swept forward across his face, sealing him in like a confessional. Bits of red light from the fire reflected from it. I picked up an oaken bucket from beside the door and stepped outside to gather snow. Simon's fever had to be broken, and I knew only one way to do it: constant cold compresses continuously applied. I had a long night ahead.

Chapter Forty-three

A rough hand urgently shook me from a sound sleep. Automatically, I reached for my weapons before opening my eyes. Arrow stood over me, his face a mask of concern.

"What is it? What is wrong?" I whispered anxiously.

"Long Knives coming through the trees. You must hurry," he answered quietly. I glanced at Simon. His eyes were clear and calm, the fever having broken during the night, but I knew he was far too weak to travel the way we would have to travel. I shook my head.

"Impossible," I said. "It would kill him."

Simon's eyes narrowed with sardonic humor.

"Leave me," he whispered. "Take the others and leave through the cornfields."

"They'll kill you. There's a price upon your head," I said.

"They'll kill me anyway. Even if you remain," he reasoned. "Or take me back to Fort Pitt as an exhibit before hanging me."

"The potato cellar," Arrow suggested urgently. "They may not search there."

He pulled a chest from the corner at the foot of his bed, revealing a trapdoor cunningly laid in the floor to leave no outline. He raised it and gestured, explaining: "We first built it to hide in should the white man not honor his words about his God. But now, we store food for the winter in it."

I helped Simon to his feet and down the narrow ladder to the hard-packed dirt floor of the cellar. I paused on the ladder before following him.

"What about yourself?" I asked. He smiled gently and firmly pushed on my shoulder, forcing me through the opening.

"I shall be all right. There is no need to harm me. I have done nothing but follow the teaching," he answered calmly.

"Tell the others about the soldiers," I replied hurriedly as he refit the trapdoor into place.

"It has already been done," he said. "Even now, they have scattered into the woods. Now, say no more. To do so is dangerous."

I heard him slide the chest over the trapdoor. He crossed to the door and let himself out. I blinked in the darkness of the cellar.

"Simon?" I whispered.

"Here," came the soft reply from my right. Cautiously, carefully, I felt my way along the floor in the direction of his voice. My hand bumped a lantern. I picked it up, fumbling at the chimney. Simon heard my efforts and whispered: "Do not light it. The light may shine through the floorboards and give us away."

I placed the lantern aside reluctantly and leaned back against the wall.

"I hope Arrow knows what he's doing," I ventured.

I heard a tiny movement, then Simon settled next to me. I could smell his sickness still upon him in the stale sweat of the blanket covering him.

"It will not matter if he knows," Simon said. "It is the others that matter. Did George and Jim get away? Cornplanter?"

"Arrow says so," I said.

"Good," he said and fell silent.

A wave of pity washed over me: he was alone—except for me—his dreams shattered. His loneliness, despair, and silent sorrow spoke volumes. I changed the subject back to those searching for us.

"I thought Morgan was farther behind," I said. "He must have guessed where we were heading and took a more direct route."

A long silence met my words, then Simon sighed and softly spoke. "I don't think these are Morgan's men."

"Why do you say that?"

"They're too careless. They allowed themselves to be seen before they were ready. Morgan's even would have waited for nightfall before moving in. I think these are others."

"Who?" I sensed his head shake.

"I don't know. But I do not like this. Something feels very wrong."

"What . . ." I began, then stiffened as his hand clamped warningly on my arm. The cabin door burst open with a loud *bang!* Someone stumbled as he was pushed or shoved across the floor.

"Now, yuh damned injun, I'll ast yuh oncet more: whar's they at?" an unfamiliar voice asked.

"Goddamn you!"

A blow sounded followed by a body falling heavily to the floor above our heads. Dust sifted down. I grabbed my nose to stifle a sneeze.

"Answer me!"

"Best bring the cul-nel up," someone drawled. "He'll be wanting to hear what this injun has to say."

"If he talks," a third voice added. I recognized his voice: Samuel Laurens from Fort Pitt, a minor landowner who exhibited pretensions by awarding himself the title of squire.

"He'll talk," the first voice adamantly assured the others. The sneer in his voice dripped with disgust and hatred. "Ain't no way a dirt-grubbin' savage will refuse to talk to save his skin. Come on. We'll leave him alone to think about it while we gets the culnel."

"Shouldn't someone stay with him?" the second man asked.

"Now, whar the hell yuh think he's gonna go? Ain't but one way in and out. An' yer gonna be standin' by that door," the first sneeringly said.

The door slammed shut and silence held for a long minute until Arrow whispered through a crack in the floor.

"We are alone. Do not make a sound. These are very bad men who search for vengeance. I do not like the looks of them. They may not harm us if we do not resist them. But you must be very quiet for if they find you they will be very angry and punish us as well. I am sorry for you, my friends. Be quiet now! They return! I will tell you when it is safe!"

The door crashed open and booted heels stamped hard on the floorboards above. Simon's hand gently squeezed my arm then relaxed and fell away.

"This be the leader, cuh-nel," the first voice said. "But he won' give us nuthin'."

"What is his name?" I recognized the soft, almost effeminate, voice of Colonel David Williamson.

"Calls hisself 'Abraham,'" came the surly reply.

"His name's 'Arrow,'" another growled. A start of exclamation broke from my lips as I recognized Lewis Wetzel's voice followed seconds later by that of Leggett.

"Good head of hair," Leggett drawled. "That silver would make a fine scalp."

Williamson laughed and moved across the floor

with mincing steps, his spurs softly scraping the planks.

"Why, yes, I do believe you're right, Leggett. It would be quite a trophy back in Boston. Do you understand what we are saying?" A slap followed his words. "I think you do. Perhaps you will consider your answer?"

"What about the others? What shall we do with them?" a different voice questioned.

"Crawford," Girty whispered. "From Pitt." I nodded, forgetting he couldn't see my agreement in the dark.

"Place them in the cabins," Williamson said indifferently. "Then call a meeting of the men. Do we have a count yet?"

"Thirty-five men, twenty-seven women, and thirty-four boys," Crawford answered.

"No girls?" Williamson sounded disappointed.

"Not by Indian standards. Some are around twelve."

"Oh. Well. I see," he said with relish. "Separate the men from the women. Place the women here. With Abraham. They should be safe enough." He giggled. The others politely laughed.

"One other thing," Crawford said. "We've found bolts of calico, beads, and some medallions. Here. Looks like some of the goods Lochry had with him."

A long silence ensued above us. Finally Williamson asked, "Where did this come from?" He waited a minute for Arrow to answer. "Very well," he said, and briskly strode from the cabin. The others followed, and the door slammed. A few minutes passed before Arrow spoke.

"This is very bad, very bad," he said worriedly. "The Long Knives have found the goods traded by Thayandencera and now believe that we are the ones for whom they search: those who raided the white settlement at Raccoon Creek. But it was not us. It could only have been Thayandencera. But this I cannot tell them for they will not believe me. Do not speak! They return!"

Again, I heard the door open, but this time the sound of many feet echoed through the floorboards as Williamson's men herded passive Indians into the cabin.

"Zeb! Looka this one! Gawd, but ain't she sumthin'?" The women, I thought, and listened as the men confirmed my suspicions with raw and suggestive observations. Once I heard fabric rip, and a sudden gasp followed by laughter and lewd suggestions. Someone called from outside the cabin and slowly, reluctantly, the men left, slamming the door   behind them. Immediately, the women began to pray:

"Our Father, who art in heaven
hallowed be thy name..."

I felt Simon tense beside me then angrily move, pushing himself erect. Alarmed, I reached out to stop him, but he seemed possessed of an inner strength and easily brushed aside my efforts. My blood froze as he raised a loud voice over their prayers.

"My children!" he cried. "Why do you waste empty words upon the false god of the Long Knives?"

The prayers ceased amid a gabble of frightened voices then grew quiet as Simon continued in ringing tones:

"Patiently, I have waited as you ignored the ways of your fathers and followed the lies of the white man! Patiently, I waited as you forgot the forests and lakes and streams given to you long before the white man crawled from his cave. Now, you can see the truth of the white man's lies! Where is his God to protect you? The white man teaches the red man to spare the blood of his victim while he drinks it himself into his belly. Pray no longer to such a God! Remember the ways of your fathers!"

"Manitou!" a voice cried, and was quickly followed by others. "Master of Life! Master of Life! *Manitou!* Forgive us! Forgive us!" The voices slipped into the familiar words of the death chant.

"The Chosen! What are you doing?" Arrow cried loudly. "Stop! You must stop this immediately!"

But the chant grew louder and louder, becoming an epithalamium for the common husband Death: the words more ancient than memory, the words that raised hackles and made fierce dogs howl in fear, the words that merged man with the earth and water and sky.

"Have you gone mad?" I whispered urgently as the chant became an ululation, unintelligible words reverting to primal howls. But even as I asked the question, I could feel the chant working deep within me, unlocking ancient memories of extinct demons that once hid in deep forest, roaming only on darkest nights. The dark of the cellar grew lighter from the savage heat coursing through my veins.

"Man . . . i . . . tou! Man . . . i . . . tou!"

A quiet laugh came at me from the darkness, making my flesh pebble. "Mad? The madness is not mine! Not mine! The madness belongs to those who are the robbers of vision, the slayers of the spirit, the remakers of the soul, the slavers who hold men captive with empty promises of a god who belongs only to those who continually mold him to fit their purposes! What truth has been told to them that will not be remade into a lie when the moment suits the teller of the tales? Sing!" he roared to the ceiling. "Sing again the words of the wilderness! Sing!"

Dimly, I heard Arrow's protests, but the fever had caught, and the women ignored his words. Suddenly, the door crashed open, startling the women into silence.

"What the hell is going on?" cursed Williamson.

"They're singing their death song. They feel they're going to die," Wetzel answered gruffly.

"Then," Williamson said, "who are we to disappoint them? But, first, a little fun, eh, Wetzel?" He laughed maliciously. "Which do you fancy?"

"Pleasure yourself," Wetzel answered contemptuously. "I'll tell the men to take care of the braves."

"Not all of them, Wetzel," Williamson answered. "Let those who wish come here first." Wetzel grunted and left. Moments later, the others arrived, and the screaming began.

For over two hours, Simon and I crouched in the cellar darkness as the mass rape continued over our heads. Then, when all were apparently sated, Williamson gave the order to kill the women. Again, we listened in silence to the horror above as Charles Builderbeck began the slaughter, slaying fourteen with a cooper's mallet as Williamson and Leggett urged him on. Blood ran through the floorboards and spattered our faces and clothes. We moved constantly in vain attempts to escape the droplets, but each time they found us, baptizing us anew.

At last, silence. But in the darkness around me, the souls of the slain stared at me with eyes demanding justice until at last, there in the dark, I surrendered my soul to them.

Chapter Forty-four

I pause, my throat dry and raspy from talking. The storm rages outside, the wind driving the snow against the side of the cabin with gale force. The fire leaps high against the blackened stones of the fireplace. Esau raises his head from my foot to contemplate me. O'Meara idly pokes at the logs in the fireplace. I reach for the bottle of brandy and pour a large draught. O'Meara sits and looks with disappointment at me.

"Is that all?" he asks, his fingers unconsciously moving to the rosary at his belt. His eyebrows draw together, his lips prudishly pursing as if about to pronounce penance for a distasteful confession. I laugh at his priest's trick and drink the draught of brandy.

"You know it isn't," I say. A forceful gust rattles the shutters. Esau turns his massive head and fixes yellow eyes upon the priest. I flex my hands: the stiffness has left them. The brandy seems to have given me new life. I feel the old recklessness upon me. Forgotten memories flood back. I hear the old sounds of the forest—the tom-tits, the ravens, the *whirr!* of ruffed grouse—and I hear the other sounds and smell the rich decay of rotting leaves, a heady perfume, and know that if I close my eyes the verdant forest will leap before

331

me, and I again will lose myself in its deep mazes, perhaps this time forever.

But I resist the tempting draw: it is not time for that yet. I still have more to do. I smile at O'Meara, my lips pulling tightly away from my teeth. Uncertainty flickers over his face like a frightened swallow. His fingers close convulsively around his rosary. Laughter bubbles up inside me. Esau's tail thumps against the floor with pleasure as he senses the change within me. I remain silent for a long moment, teasing O'Meara with anticipation. He looks away, nervously, to the fire.

"We need more wood," he says, and makes as if to rise.

"There's plenty," I say, pointing to the wood box. "You filled it this afternoon."

"Oh." Again, he picks up the poker and stabs at the logs. A dull flush creeps up his neck. A low growl rumbles from Esau's chest like an old man's dissatisfied grumbling. O'Meara hears—of that, I am sure—but pretends not to notice.

"What," I ask, "was Leggett to you?"

The suddenness of my question startles him. He recoils, dropping the iron poker on the hearth. Esau leaps to his feet at the clatter, hair bristling, teeth bared, the rumble now a threatening growl.

"Saints preserve me!" he says, his face suddenly ashen with shock. I smile. I feel beatified. "An' sure the devil has been whispering in your ear. How did you know such a thing?"

"Simple. The way you act whenever I mention him and the way you looked at me when I told you about the affair I had with Anne, " I quietly answer. A flush rises slowly on his thick jowls. "It was not Simon you came for. Nor me. There could only be two— Leggett or Crawford. Dr. John Knight has already published his lies concerning Crawford so that leaves only Leggett. Am I right?"

"The dog," he says nervously as Esau gathers his muscles in a crouch. A long stream of slobber runs from Esau's mouth to the floor.

"The truth," I demand. "Why are you here?"

"Your soul," he whispers, his eyes wide with apprehension.

"No," I say.

"Yes," he answers. He holds himself very still. "Listen to me for a moment. Do you know the history of the Society of Jesus?" Despite myself, I reach out a hand to stay Esau.

"Go on," I say. He sighs deeply and pauses to collect himself. His face is shiny with perspiration.

"You know His Holiness Pope Clement XIV dissolved the Society in 1773." I nod but remain silent. "Sure, if a man like you wouldn't. 'Twas the question of property, you know. Many there were awaiting for the axe to fall, as it were, so they could seize the Society's property. But the Society thought His Holiness might bow to the pressure from the Bourbons and other devotees of the Enlightenment, as they called it, and dissolved the Society when the Portuguese Empire banned us in 1759. Quietly, the Society began to transfer its property into the hands of sympathetic friends."

"Like the Moravians?" I murmur softly. His eyebrows twitch in surprise.

"You knew? But, how . . . "

"A guess. Please continue." I pour another glass of brandy. An uncertain respectfulness touches his eyes.

"Fortunately, Empress Catherine II refused to allow the papal bull to be published in Russia, and the Society could still exist. Technically," he amends. I drink and shake my head.

"You are evading the question," I say quietly, taking my hand from Esau's shoulder. He growls again.

"Sure,'n I'm not, I'm not," he says, voice jumping nearly an octave from nervousness. "The Society stayed in Russia and supervised its holdings while we waited for times to change. When Robespierre and Marat and the others started their business in France and the Bourbons fell, we began to move to reclaim our property. Now, it looks well for us since His Holiness Pope Pius VII acknowledged our existence in Russia in 1801. 'Tis not long, we're after thinking, before the Society is restored."

"I see," I say. "And, in light of that, you want to

know what happened at Gnaddenhutten? But, you already have the reports, of Heckewilder and Zeisberger."

"Yes," he says grudgingly.

"I trust, then, that still you have not told me the full story."

"If we are to get the Society's restoration, then we must demonstrate the worth of the Society," he says quietly. "The *Regimini militantis ecclesiae,* our approval, could be amended."

"And one way to 'demonstrate' the worth of the Society would be through converts," I add

"Especially those who are, uh . . ."

"Notorious?"

"'Tis not the word I would have chosen, but it will do, it will do."

"But there is more, isn't there?" I persist. His eyes roll uneasily from mine. He nibbles his lips, then nods.

"What is it?" He shakes his head. I sigh. "You do not have the option of refusal," I say. "Not, that is, unless you wish to die for the greater glory of God."

His eyes flash back to mine, then drop to Esau. He shudders, swallows convulsively, and begins to finger his rosary.

"All right," he says lowly. I strain to hear his words. "All right. 'Tis the whole story you'll be getting. I am to try and convince you and Girty to again unite the tribes."

"What?" I fall back into my chair, stunned by his revelation. "Why? For what purpose?"

"To aid the British," he says. "To establish a second front."

"I see," I slowly say. "The British are going to try to retake the colonies. When?"

"I don't know," he says. "My task was to enlist your aid."

"Why? England has not been a friend to the Catholic since Henry VIII."

"'Tis a gamble," he answers. "If the Society could provide British allies in the west, then the Privy Council would give the Society Ireland and push for legislation recalling the Parliamentary bans on the church. Such a coup would leave the Pontiff little choice but to reestablish the Society to its rightful place in the Vatican. Our Superior General would again be honored as an advisor, and we no longer would be outcasts!" His voice climbs during his recitation until his words ring with fervent conviction through the cabin.

"So to help the Society you were sent to me," I say. A thought dawns upon me. "Why not directly to Simon? Was it because I, too, am an outcast?"

"Partly," he admits. "But, then, 'tis less of a savage you are than him."

"Less of a savage?" Dark laughter bubbles up,

and I let it burst forth. He flushes red at my laughter. "And you thought I would convince Simon? Because I am less of a savage?"

"You are an educated man," he mutters.

"Oh, yes," I say mockingly. "And that does not make me a savage, does it?" I look at the books resting on shelves in the room and wearily shake my head. "You are very foolish, Priest. Very foolish."

"Sure, and what could you lose by helping us?" he asks, misunderstanding my laughter and mockery.

"Nothing. But then I have nothing to gain either." Puzzlement crosses his face, but I do not explain my answer. "Why were you selected to come here?" He frowns and again lifts the poker to jab at the logs on the fire.

"Henry Leggett was my mother's brother," he says.

"Ah. So, it is family and not 'for the greater glory of God' that you have stayed," I say. I shake my head. "That makes you a hypocrite, doesn't it? I believe that is a venial sin. But, then, you are a Jesuit, not a Thomist, aren't you? Or, perhaps the Jesuits find that, too, to be a technicality."

"Perhaps it is a combination of all," he says sourly. "I would like to think I remained for you." I shake my head and let the laughter escape.

"Would you now?" I say mockingly. "Back, Esau! Down, boy!" I push on his haunches. Reluctantly, he sinks to the floor. "Well, let us see which of the reasons is the true one. What are you? A priest of a mountebank? Sit. Sit."

I laugh again as he cautiously eases himself onto his stool near the hearth, his eyes wary, darting back-and-forth from Esau to myself. Esau sags against my leg. I reach for the brandy bottle and begin to place my thoughts in order. The wind wails without. I begin.

Chapter Forty-five

We were at Half-King's on the Sandusky when we heard about Leggett and Crawford leaving Fort Pitt with a large force of men for Mingo Bottom. We knew what that meant: a planned foray up the Sandusky against the villages of Captain Pipe, Wingenund, Half-King, and others. Following the massacre at Gnadenhütten where ninety-four out of the ninety-six Indians (only two boys escaped) were killed, other attacks were made on Coshortan, Salem, and Schonbrunn. The Indians who believed the words of the priests and ministers were pushed farther and farther into the wilderness. The American had grown arrogant with his triumphs against the passive Indians who tried to live according to what they were told.

Brant had contemptuously taken the young braves out in force to fight the Americans and had been soundly defeated in the brakes of Mad River. He limped back home in disgrace, his force in a shambles. But we could take little comfort in his loss of faith among the Nations for he had severely reduced our fighting force with his foolhardiness. Most of the survivors scattered, returning to their villages and families.

Some made half-hearted overtures to Simon, but

he bluntly turned them down, shaming them in the process by reminding them of their broken vow to follow him. Those who remained in Half-King's village avoided him after that, averting their faces on chance meetings, slinking away from our path whenever possible. Even the elders treated them with contempt and no longer tolerated their braggadocio in the Long House, relegating them seats near the slaves at the council door instead of in the middle with the elders. Consequently, the day a runner arrived from the south with the news of Leggett and Crawford's march, Half-King led a small delegation of elders to our cabin. Simon greeted them politely and offered them tobacco. We sat smoking, passing small talk until at last Half-King knocked the dottle from his pipe and carefully stowed it in its beaded buckskin sheath.

"Many Long Knives have left Fort Pitt and even now camp at Mingo Bottom," he began.

"I have heard this," Simon said solemnly. Half-King waited for him to continue, but Simon remained serenely silent, smoking his pipe.

"Perhaps they will come up the Sandusky," Half-King said. "To the lands of the Deleware and the Wyandots, and the Shawnee."

"Perhaps," Simon politely agreed.

"This must not be. We will stop them. We," he paused to include all with him, "wish you to lead us."

"Mm," Simon grunted. "But many have chosen

to follow Thayandencera. Let him lead them for they have already given their voice to him." Brant's followers had successfully campaigned for his election as War Chief while Simon was recovering from his wound.

"That was a mistake. The young forgot the Blessing many years ago," Half-King said apologetically.

"But the elders did not remind them," Simon said. A hard edge came into his voice. "This they should have done but did not. And, now, you wish me to save what Thayadencera has wasted. I do not know if I can. I no longer see what the fire holds for me. I must think." Half-King respectfully nodded and rose. He paused at the door after the others had left.

"Think long, The Chosen. Think long. Perhaps the Master of Life will again let you look into the flames. His people have much need of his Chosen."

"What do you think?" I asked after Half-King had left.

"I don't know what to think," he said. He knocked the ashes from his pipe and began to retamp it with fresh tobacoo. His face grew lined and drawn in the dim light of the cabin, the scar a streak of white across the nut-brown of his forehead. He leaned forward and, taking a coal from the fire, lit his pipe. He drew deeply on the pipe, sending pungent clouds of smoke into the air, drawing deeper and deeper into himself, staring intently into the fire. Silently, I rose and left the cabin.

I was sharing a joke with some hunters around a fire when the door to our cabin opened and Simon stepped out. The whole camp came to a stop as Simon stood for a moment haloed against the blue sky, resplendent in white buckskins heavily fringed. A beaded elkskin belt cinched around his waist held the silver-mounted pistols he had taken from Rogers's body and a short, broad dirk. Around his head, he wore a red silk scarf low over his forehead to hide the scar. In his left hand, he held an eagle feather; in his right, a tomahawk. All eyes remained on him as he slowly walked through the camp to the Long House. He paused before the council door of the lodge, then raised the tomahawk and drove it deep into the wood of the door. He lifted the eagle feather and slipped it beneath the scarf so it trailed behind his left ear. A mighty yell went up and all ran to form a semicircle around him in front of the Long House. He looked over their heads to meet my eyes: I saw a great sadness within their depths and then a wild fire leaped into life as the chanting grew and grew: "Man—i—tou! Man—i—tou!"

Chapter Forty-six

Crawford led four hundred and eight Pennsylvanians on his march north to destroy the Wyandot villages along the Sandusky. The most we had been able to gather, thanks to Brant's indiscretion, was one hundred twenty-two braves, but we had hopes of more warriors from outlying Shawnee towns and a British ranger force supposedly dispatched to us from Detroit. Runners kept us aware of Crawford's progress as he moved up the Tuscarawas towards the Sandusky. Once Crawford's scouts unexpectedly stumbled upon our runners at Gnadenhütten, but the runners escaped before the scouts could do more than fire a quick volley. They did not give chase as evening was almost upon them, and the rest of the detachment had already bedded down for the night.

Slowly, Crawford moved his forces forward towards the Sandusky. It was almost a holiday for them: officers rode in relaxed pairs while the men joked among themselves down the straggling column, unconcerned about the territory through which they moved, secure with their numbers. But, as the march progressed day-by-day and no Indians were sighted, they became restless and wandered off from the column in search of fresh meat.

Still, Simon did nothing except order the runners out and pull his men back to Half-King's town. A few of the younger braves began to grumble but were quickly quieted by their elders who remembered the past debacle with Brant and the reluctance with which Simon had accepted this command.

Crawford's forces finally reached the Sandusky and moved up to where a Moravian town once stood. The cabins were deserted, had been since Gnadenhütten, and only dark rings remained on the grass to show where fires had once been lain. Crawford decided they would march one more day towards the west and, if no Delewares or Wyandots were spotted, they would return to Fort Pitt.

Meanwhile, Captain William Caldwell had joined our small force with his Canadian Rangers. A few northern Indians had arrived at Half-King's town and placed themselves under Simon's command. Their numbers swelled our little group to half again its size, but we were still far outmanned. Half-King had given orders to evacuate the village when Simon suddenly decided it was time for us to attack.

South of the village stood a large oak grove amidst a plain of tall grass. Simon sent an advance party of braves forward through the grass to make contact with Crawford's scouts and drive them back into the main party. Once that had been accomplished, the braves were to withdraw to the oak grove, make a short stand to convince Crawford to commit his men, then retreat, leaving the grove in the hands of the Pennsylvanians. When they tried to leave, they would be met with fire from every direction. They would have no way of knowing how large a force we had. Eventually, we hoped, they would be forced to surrender when their supplies ran out. It was a risky plan for a massive push at one point would show how small a force we had; our survival depended upon our secrecy.

I remember the day: the sun was stifling hot, the air thick like a blanket on the lungs. Thick clouds of gnats and mosquitoes hung heavily overhead. Sweat left thick salt rings on our clothing. I took a small band of Wyandots and Senecas and made a wide detour north around the grove to the West where we concealed ourselves in a shallow dry wash protected from the grove by a small knoll running like a rampart parallel to it. Simon spread his men out in a loose fan along the north while Half-King and Wingenund sealed the west side from escape. Caldwell held his rangers to the side to act as a "swinging gate" slamming shut on the south side after Crawford's men entered the grove.

We panted through open mouths like dogs as Rides-the-Moon cautiously led the decoys forward to meet the scouts. Our bodies quivered with tension as we forced them to remain in the wash when firing broke out. Slowly, Rides-the-Moon artfully drew the Pennsylvanians forward as we waited, our nerves screaming for release. Suddenly, it was quiet. I could hear Crawford's men moving cautiously through the grove. Their voices grew louder as they called to each other in the manner of huntsmen searching for a vanished quarry. Curses flew back-and-forth as they abandoned caution and crashed through the underbrush, ripping their way through briars and brambles. I crouched deeper in the dry wash at the sound of movement in the chest-high brush before the knoll. The movement stopped, and my hand tightened convulsively upon my rifle as I recognized their voices.

"I don't like this," Wetzel growled, the restlessness deep in his voice.

"Where have they gone?" Crawford asked. "Leggett?"

"I don't know," Legget drawled. "I'm not a damn borderman. The reddies seem to have gone to ground. I daresay you'll need hounds to flush them. Forget them, Bill. There'll be other sport later. Let's return home."

"Damn me, if I don't think you're right," Crawford said, disgust evident in his voice. "But I would like at least one decent scalp to show George. Especially from here as this is his land."

"Oh? The survey came this far?" Leggett asked, interest quickening.

"Surely, you knew," Crawford answered. "Your

lands butt up against ours on the south. Mine is the next parcel over."

"I knew we were near them, but I didn't know we were on the parcels." He paused. "It's good land. Almost too good to break apart of others."

"I concur," Crawford answered. "But George's place in Virginia is costing him a bit more than he anticipated what with this war and all. He needs a bit of capital. I must confess that I'll be needing some as well after England withdraws. Cash will be scarce and markets for our crops unstable. But the land will always be worth something. Of course, one can always keep the choice sections for oneself."

Leggett laughed. "And create a barony? I like that. Lord Leggett. Has a certain ring to it, doesn't it? What do you think, Wetzel?"

"I think," Wetzel slowly said, "that we should get away from this place as fast as we can."

"Oh, now, Lewis! Aren't you being a bit overcautious?" Crawford asked, annoyance deep in his voice.

"I've still got my hair," Wetzel said stubbornly. "And there are thems that don't."

"You suspect trickery?" Leggett asked.

"I do," Wetzel answered solemnly.

"Oh, now, really!" Crawford angrily interjected. "I've had about enough of this. Wetzel, you're giving these savages more credit than they are worth. Why, you make them sound positively Machiavellian."

"Or Sejanusian," Leggett suggested.

"Quite," Crawford affirmed. He paused. "Surely you don't mean to suggest these savages to be our peers, now, do you? With their barbaric practices?"

"Cuh-nel, I don't know half them fancy words yer using, but I can tell yu this: some of these here people have received first-rate education. Thayandencera is the brother-in-law of Sir William Johnson. He also is a Mason and been educated in one of them colleges around Boston. His white name is Joseph Brant, and he's the Mohawk leader and principal War-Chief of the Six Nations. But that don't make no matter for he's still an Injun. There are others far worse for yuh to be worryin' about. Men like the one they call 'The Chosen.' He's the worse of them all 'cause he knows."

"What does this 'Chosen One' know?" Legget asked, his voice dripping with derision. But Wetzel refused to take offense.

"Everything," he said, his voice dropping in volume. "It's as if the trees could hear and the 'jays could talk. He knows! Simon Girty, we calls him by his Christian name, though there's far from a Christian bone in his body. Settlers in the Ohio know him as the Devil. Even the Indians walk softly around him, so's I'm told. And his shadow ain't much better: Nightwind. Jonathon Francis Huntington."

"Huntington!" Leggett snapped.

"You know him?" Crawford asked curiously.

"I do!" Leggett said spitefully. "A worse scoundrel I never hope to see. 'Twas him who drove my sister to her early death and him who ran like a coward from my vengeance!"

"I see," Crawford said, impatience creeping into his voice. "But what does that have to do with now?"

"Cuh-nel," Wetzel said slowly, "I think Girty is here."

A long silence followed his words, and I imagined the shocked faces as the heavy implications of Wetzel's words registered. A cold wind suddenly moaned through the oaks, ominously rustling the leaves, the eerie wail pebbling the flesh, raising the hackles. A mourning dove called hauntingly close. The loud voices slowly fell into an uneasy silence. Suddenly, a loud turkey gobble sounded followed by a long scream. Puffs of smoke erupted from the brush. Arrows hummed through the air.

"A line! A line! Form a line, damn you!" bawled Crawford.

"This way!" a frightened voice yelled. The brush crackled as frantic men tried to bull their way towards us.

I gave the signal and rose, my rifle at the ready. A chunky, red-bearded man gaped at me, his eyes rolling wall-eyed at my sudden appearance. I pressed the trigger, and his face disappeared in a puff of smoke, bone, and gristle, a fine spray of blood covering the bushes. I dropped down again to reload, dimly conscious of the cries of pain and fear. I rose again to look for a target. Wetzel stood fifteen yards away. I drew a quick bead and squeezed the trigger only to miss as he dodged back behind the thick bole of a tree. The Pennsylvanians began to mill in confusion.

I dropped my rifle and pulled my tomahawk from my belt and drove into them. A roaring filled my ears. I tasted blood on my lips and smelled the stench of frightened men. A fierce joy raced through my veins. At that moment, I knew I was invincible. Slowly, we drove them back from the brush deeper into the grove. Then, all was quiet, and I stood panting in a small clearing, my clothes covered with blood, pink matter dripping from the blade of my tomahawk.

Bodies lay unmoving around me. Scalping knives flashed in the gloom. I tried to speak but could only manage a croak. I swallowed painfully and tried again.

"Back!" I ordered. "Fall back!"

"But, we can kill them all! Now!" a wild-eyed youth argued. He made to run forward, but I caught his arm.

"They are deep among the trees," I snarled, shaking him like a child. "Have you forgotten their numbers? Fall back! We will do as The Chosen says!"

I threw him towards the rear. Grudgingly, he retraced his steps. The others began to trickle back. I found my rifle and slid into the dry wash behind them. I sat and waited, willing my body to relax.

Night came. Still we waited, but Crawford did not try to push his way out of the grove. He should have for despite his losses, he still outnumbered us. Surprise had been our ally in the first attack, but I knew there would be no more surprises.

Throughout the night, we lay in silent readiness for the Pennsylvanians to venture out beyond the ring of bonfires they had lighted to save themselves from a sudden attack. As night grew darker and deeper, I began to despair for I knew that first light could bring a mass charge by Crawford, and our lines were painfully thin. About two of the clock, Simon quietly slid next to me, his smile flashing whitely in the darkness.

"Since I have not heard otherwise, I guess I can believe you are all right?" he said.

"For now," I answered dryly. "But I don't know for how long when morning arrives."

"You think they'll come then?"

"Yes."

"Why?"

"Because that's what I would do." He laughed and patted my shoulder.

"I think everything will work out."

"If not, they'll attack here. The sun will be

behind them," I said, a bit disgruntled by his cheeriness. "Maybe you had better move more men to this side of the grove."

"And if you're wrong?" he asked quietly.

"Then, I'm wrong," I said stubbornly. "But I'll be alive. And so will others who won't be if you do not make the move."

"I can't," he said.

"Then, I should fall back?" I asked.

"No. Not yet," he answered hurriedly. I sensed a note of hesitation in his voice that had not been there before. "You'll know what to do when the time arrives."

"When will that be?"

He threw back his head and looked at the heavens. I followed his gaze to Sagittarius. He laughed again, a quiet, relaxed sound in the darkness.

"Soon. By first light." He pressed my arm again. Then, he was gone. I rolled on my back and focused on Sagittarius. Vainly, I tried to look through his eyes but saw nothing save the constellation. Wearily, I closed my eyes.

Chapter Forty-seven

False dawn shone grayly through the oak trees when Paul, one of the ex-Moravian Indians to escape Salem, shook me awake. From the grove came the sounds of men trying to be stealthy: soft curses, clink of metal, scrape of twig against buckskin. With a sinking heart, I checked the priming of my rifle and loosened the tomahawk in my belt.

"Warn the others to be ready," I said harshly to Paul. "But they are not to fire until I fire."

He nodded, and slid quietly away. I rose in a crouch, carefully keeping my head below the knoll and crab-walked a few steps to urinate against a bush. The smell of urine was strong in the wash as others followed my example, emptying the fear from their bodies. A lark sang from the meadow behind us. Tiny field mice scurried through the tall grass. The noise in the grove grew, and I knew it would not be long before they volleyed and charged. They had had an entire night to build their courage, and now their numbers would deliver them and crush us.

My mouth tasted bitter with the thought. I dug a piece of pemmican out of a pouch and bit and chewed, recalling memory. I hoped Legget would lead the men

353

out, but that, I sourly thought, would more than likely be Wetzel for he was the madman among them. Leggett would trail last from the grove, relying upon the others to create a living and dying wall of safety for him.

I thought of this and my father and Benjamin Franklin and Rides-the-Moon and my adoption into the Nations.

And Anne.

I felt a great sadness as I thought of Anne and how our love had been a cross too heavy for either of us to bear.

Paul materialized beside me. I gratefully slammed the door shut on memory.

"Yes?" I said. He pointed off to our right. Cautiously, I rose and stared to the south. A large band of mounted warriors—Shawnee, I could tell from their top-knot—rode toward us. I recognized the square figure of Alexander McKee leading them. Another figure broke from behind the grove, and I recognized Simon's white horse loping out to meet McKee and his Shawnee.

Behind me, I heard soft grunts of relief as word swept up and down the wash. I looked over to the grove: all was still and silent as bitter awareness of the change in fortune swept over the men among the trees. Paul threw back his head and gave the long call of the mourning dove.

I settled down to wait. There was no hurry now:

Crawford had lost his chance to escape. They had nowhere to go. It was only a matter of time and we were in no hurry. The elements could do most of our work for us. All we had to do was wait.

Chapter Forty-eight

Simon passed word not to attack but to let nature do its work for us. Soon, their provisions and water would run out. Meanwhile, we would keep them under siege.

The day grew hotter and hotter. Bees buzzed around our heads before scurrying off to water. We heard very little from the grove. In front of me a broken bird's nest lay on the ground, tiny bits of turquoise shell embedded deep among the twisted tufts of grass.

I passed the time musing upon the egg and my soul.

A flock of grackles wheeled over a blackthorn bush a few yards in front of me and suddenly darted away in panic. A small patch of brown moved in the dead air. I centered the sights of my rifle upon it and gently squeezed the trigger. A puff of dirty gray smoke billowed up in front of my eyes and a hoarse scream sounded. The bush jerked violently for a moment then quieted. The brown patch had disappeared.

In late afternoon, a small band tried to break out through the south defenses but none made it through the rangers. Caldwell caught a ball in his chest and two men took him back to Half-King's village. Finally, those in the woods quit trying to creep out through our lines. A couple climbed trees to act as snipers, but our sharpshooters quickly killed them. Soon, they quit even that.

The afternoon grew hotter. Dust danced in the air.

Once in a while, a wood thrush or a meadowlark sang, but no answer came to their calls. Perhaps they sang for a lost mate, their songs ringing melancholically through the humid air, a musical shuttle of notes cascading slowly over the spears of brown grass. Sadness moved over my spirit and I found myself humming "Greensleeves" under my breath. I forced myself to stop, blinking away salty sweat stinging my eyes.

The afternoon slipped into twilight, and then the fog came; a thick, rolling fog smelling of dampness and decay as if it had just billowed up from the depths of a prehistoric swamp, bringing with it odors of rotting flesh and moldering leaves. From the grove came suspicious sounds of men moving cautiously. Hope flared in the night like a white-hot flame creeping out of the woods and over us. I cursed the fog, willing it to stay back, to stay away, but it crept closer and closer. I passed the word to my men to stay alert, but no one tried to penetrate our defenses.

Vainly, I tried to pierce the fog with my eyes, but it was too thick. We waited anxiously for morning to arrive and drive the fog away. Slowly the night passed, and I imagined I could hear the men in the woods murmuring Faustus's plea, *O lente, lente currite noctis equi!*

And this time, Mephistopheles listened to him as the stars stood and fog stood still while time ran slowly. My eyes ached from trying to pierce the grayness, the darkness. I imagined shadows moving through the fog, but when I looked, the shadows stood still and became bushes and limbs of trees.

At last the day arrived and the fog vanished. Cautiously, we moved into the grove only to find it deserted: the Pennsylvanians had made good use of the cover sent to them by their heavenly Father.

In the middle of the grove, I came upon Simon, white-faced, trembling, his eyes burning angrily.

"Send out patrols!" he said thickly. He pulled the silk scarf from his forehead to wipe away sweat from his face. The scar on his forehead throbbed like a great, angry worm. Deep, tight lines streamed from the corners of his eyes to his lips, molding his face into one cursed by God or Satan.

For a moment, I did not move, stunned by the change. I could not compare this Simon to the one I knew the day before: *heterogenea non comparari possunt.*

He tried to retie the scarf, but the knot kept slipping between his shaking fingers. Suddenly, he stopped and seized his head between his hands, pressing hard as if to drive pain away by force.

"They must not escape!" he hissed. "Not . . . escape!"

"There will be other times," I said soothingly. I handed him a skin of water. He took it and drank huge gulps. Water spilled down the front of his buckskin shirt. He breathed deeply and tried to smile.

"No," he said shakily. "This is the time. This is the place. If we allow them to escape, they will have gained another victory. We can't afford that." A tiny bubble of spittle appeared in the corner of his mouth. "Too many of their victories will make us weaker and weaker while they become stronger and stronger from having feasted upon our blood!" He drew deep, shaky breaths in an effort to calm himself. "We must slow them down, make them think before they can counterattack. Do you understand? We've been lucky, so far. But our luck is only as good as long as they believe our strength to be superior. If they find out the truth, we haven't a chance! Do you understand?"

I did. I also understood his anger, but this was not the time to play the Devil's advocate. Simon was reacting spontaneously, taking his logic from the movements of the forest and those moving within the forest.

"I'll find them," I promised, and moved away from the light flashing from the flaming fires deep within his eyes. Swiftly, I put together small parties and sent them off towards all the points of the compass, saving the eastern point for myself.

We moved away from the grove and within an hour stumbled across the trail of a small party of men moving rapidly towards the east and the village of Wingenund. For a moment, I was puzzled, then realized that the trail was the trail of frantic men who had lost direction. We chased after them, pausing only when the trail disappeared into darkness.

For two days, we chased them through the tall grass and woodland. They made little effort to disguise their trail, fleeing towards the East as rapidly as they could, stumbling through stands of fresh willow, battering down brush instead of slipping around it, impatiently wading streams instead of using the running water to disguise their trail.

Finally, on the third day, we caught them as they waded from a cranberry bog, tired, hungry, and thirsty, covered with mud, their clothes ripped and torn. Crawford, muddy and scratched and torn from briars, led them. Exhausted, they made little resistance as we bound them roughly with green thongs that would shrink into their flesh once the heat dried them, and took them to Wingenund's village. We rested there for three days, then borrowed horses and took our prisoners north to Upper Sanduskey and Simon Girty.

All during the trip, Crawford kept himself

distinctly aloof, refusing to react to the taunts of his captors. As we neared Upper Sandusky, though, he maneuvered his horse next to mine and asked, "This place where you are taking us: will Simon Girty be there?"

"Yes," I answered. He moved his horse closer, obviously not recognizing me, and spoke in low tones.

"Look, my good man," he said hurriedly, casting quick glances back at the silent Indians ignoring him. "I know you're a white man. Surely you cannot condone what these savages intend with us. Get word to Simon Girty. He can put an end to this filthy practice before it begins."

I remained silent, guiding my horse along the trail, around a hawthorne.

"Will you help us?"

"No," I answered. A look of disbelief spread across his thin face.

"For God's sake, man," he began.

"God is not here," I interrupted. "Nor is he likely to be. At least, not your God. You killed him back at Gnadenhütten. And as for Simon Girty, well, ask him yourself."

I nodded up the trail to where Simon loped towards us on his white horse. Beside him rode Captain Pipe and Wingenund. White-faced, Crawford drew himself to attention as they reined in before us.

"I am Colonel William Crawford of Fort Pitt,"

he said formally. "My associates are Dr. John Knight, our regimental surgeon, and one of our scouts, Mr. John Slover. We have been captured by these Indians and this . . . this renegade," he spat the word out, "who refuses to help us. We throw ourselves upon your mercy."

"I have none to give," Simon said simply. He checked his horse as the animal danced impatiently on the trail. Simon's eyes were cold and hard, but bright lights burned in their depths, eyes that had once looked upon heaven but now glowed from a horrible dungeon through darkness visible.

Crawford flinched at his words and glanced over at Simon's companions. Captain Pipe nudged his horse forward and peered closely into Crawford's face. Crawford's eyes flickered uneasily away, shifting rapidly back and forth between Simon and me, hoping that one of us would speak.

But we did not, and Captain Pipe gave a quiet, satisfied chuckle and leaned back to take a small deerskin pouch from Wingenung.

"I am very glad to see you," he said. He opened the pouch and inserted three fingers. I translated for Crawford. He visibly relaxed at Pipe's words, then started as Pipe withdrew his fingers and smeared a black, sticky mixture across Crawford's face.

"What . . . What does this, this *outrage* mean?" he sputtered, trying to knock Pipe's hand away. He wiped futilely at the mixture but only succeeded in spreading it further across his face.

"I think you know," Simon said enigmatically. He turned his horse as Pipe finished painting Crawford's face and threw the pouch from him.

"Come," he said, and rode away.

"My God," Crawford said hoarsely, staring in horror from his black fingers to Simon's retreating back. I leaned over and swatted his horse across its withers.

"No," I said. "But His creation."

He grabbed wildly for his horse's mane as the animal leaped forward. I stayed behind him as we followed an old trace leading to the old Wyandot town of Big Spring. The town stood on a low bottom on the east bank of the Tymochtee Creek. Simon drew up as we entered the village and motioned for me to come forward.

"What is it?" I asked. I was tired, my eyes scratchy from lack of sleep. A thin smile smoldered across his lips. Tight lines drew his cheeks into deep hollows.

"A present," he said softly, and gestured.

I looked down to the opposite end of the village where two blackened stakes stood in the ground. A naked, white figure had been tied to one. I frowned and squinted to make out his features as he twisted and strained against the ropes binding him to the stake, recoiling from the sticks and stones of the women and the boys.

Suddenly, he caught sight of us and lunged forward as far as his ties would allow him. He threw back his head and screamed: "Hunt-ing-ton!"

Anger slowly built in me then disappeared as the dancing figures in front of him paused and stepped back from him. A sigh of wind blew from over my shoulder towards him, kicking up a little dust devil along the way. A raven swung low over him, then flapped to a nearby tree to perch and wait. A strange sense of gratitude and, strangely, sadness, but not pity for Henry Leggett rolled through me.

Chapter Forty-nine

The drums. I awoke in darkness to the deep roll of the drums, feeling them throbbing, swelling, enlarging my mind, like the pulse of an immense being beating in my brain. I rose from my pallet and walked to the door. Bold yellow light filled the room, throwing shifting patterns on the roof and walls. Inside its rhythms, the jumpy light bent the logs and worked its spell upon me, leaving reservoirs of black shadow in pits and crevices of the logs.

The warm night laved my flesh as I pulled my jerkin over my head and dropped it on the floor and stepped from the cabin. Heat bathed my hands and face, sifting through my stomach and limbs. A burst of yells greeted me from a whirl of naked bodies swaying, bronze limbs whirling among flickering flames, hands clapping rhythm to the drums.

I looked down to the stakes where now two men had been stripped and tied. I felt myself responding to the terrible frankness of the noise, my body swaying to the primitive beat pounding through me, the shadows grotesquely dancing against the backdrop of woods, the pungent pitch burning from fresh-cut pine.

A sudden hush fell upon the land, the immense

forest, the body of the fecund and mysterious life that seemed to pulsate from the tenebrous and passionate soul of the earth. From the crowd, a tall, wild woman walked with measured stride towards me. Her long, black hair trailed behind her in wild abandon like a pagan bridal train. A small girdle of white doeskin clothed her hips, leaving the rest of her naked save for barbarous ornaments of copper armbands and rows of beads forming a chain from which a polished black stone hung suspended between the hummocks of her breasts. Bizarre charms glittered and trembled at her steps. In one hand, she carried a small pot of vermillion paint. She was savage and superb, eyes black and wild, magnificent, and my soul, my primitive and naked soul, rose up to meet and merge with hers: tenebrous, Stygian, passionate. Her long shadow engulfed me, and when she halted in front of me, the secrets of the wilderness leaped out and danced in her bright, black eyes.

Her hand moved at my belt and my leggings fell away, leaving me naked before her. With a steady hand, she painted red loops and sworls on my body, cabalistic signs heating the flesh. When she finished, she pulled the girdle from her and, naked, embraced me.

Hot flames licked my flesh.

A wild, savage yell accompanied her gesture.

The drums began again their pulsating beat.

Simon stepped forward. He, too, was naked and

painted and a savage woman who could have been the twin of mine stepped with him.

The crowd began a writhing dance around us, oiled bodies gleaming in the firelight, twisting and turning sinuously, a steady stream of naked humans dancing with wild glances and savage movements against the dark-faced and pensive forest.

Simon did not speak. He reached out and placed his hands upon my shoulders. We were one together.

The fire drew us in from its fringes, binding us in rags of smoke, the musky smell of burning wood and grease, stronger than with ropes and chains. Slowly, the crowd separated and drew away, creating a lane between us and the two black stakes. An Indian stepped forward and cut Crawford free from the stake but bound his hands behind him. They tied a rope to the stake and between his wrists, leaving him ten feet of tether in which to move.

"Girty! Girty!" he howled, then flinched and screamed as the braves began shooting powder into his naked skin. He tried running around the post to flee from them only to meet with burning branches thrust against his flesh. He tried to turn, caught his feet in the rope, and fell. An Indian leaped astride him and, with two quick strokes, cut off his ears with a scalping knife.

"Girty!" he screamed. "For the love of God! Shoot me! Shoot me!"

Simon's teeth flashed whitely in the firelight. "I

cannot. I have no gun." He held his hands out contemptuously from his body. He turned to me, his eyes pinpoints of blackness in his face. Tight cords stood out from his throat. Muscles leaped and bunched across his chest. I became aware of the woman beside me, the firelight glinting off her dark breasts, her nipples full and dark.

Crawford screamed. I jerked my eyes back and watched as he stumbled to his feet and moved around the stake again. Women came forward bearing coals in sheets of wet birch. They strewed the coals in Crawford's path and shrieked with laughter as he jerked and hopped around the stake in macabre imitation of their dance. He fell again and another Indian leaped forward to scalp him. He rose to his feet, his face a bloody mask, and moved again around the stake. Knives glinted in the firelight, cutting and slicing chunks of flesh from him. Soon, his body gleamed with blood. At last, he fell and did not rise, and his body lay still on the coals. A woman stepped forward with a skinning knife and cut his penis and testicles free. He did not move. The stench of burning flesh moved like thick perfume over the clearing.

Abruptly, the drums grew silent. Slowly, silently, we turned to Leggett. Urine ran down his legs. His bowels loosened and feces splattered in the dust at his feet.

"No! No!" he pleaded. A man laughed and

sliced off his nose. He screamed from the pain. "Huntington! Huntington!"

Women strewed burning coals around his feet. He wailed and tried to kick them away. "Huntington! For my sister's sake! In her blessed memory! Save me! Save me!"

His face twisted in pain and agony, the arrogant pride crumbling, the sense of ruthless power that had left his eyes drooping and his lips twisted in a perpetual sneer gone. He watched with craven terror as women and young boys approached, their arms laden with wood. They piled the wood around the base of the stake and fanned the coals into flames. He screamed.

"Huntington!"

I moved in front of him. Dimly, I sensed Simon at my side, but I had eyes only for Henry Leggett.

"Remember your sister," I said softly, the words bitter in my mouth like drops of alum.

"Help me!" he cried, tears streaming down his face past the gaping hole where his nose once lifted itself against the world. "God!"

"Don't look to heaven for forgiveness," I said. "There is only now."

A knife flashed through the flames into Leggett's side, cutting deeply and wide. Blood gushed out. His face contorted in agony. Strange words floated from my lips, a chant: *"Stipendium peccati mors est! Maledicat dominus! Maledict Satanas!"*

Screams of pain cut through the pulsing beat of the drums. Simon's hand slipped through the cut in Leggett's side. He pulled out Leggett's liver and held it before his eyes. Leggett screamed again, his face reflecting the unholy horror unfolding before him. A frothy foam appeared on his lips. Above us, dark wings flapped in the night.

The knife flashed again, dividing the liver neatly. Simon extended one half to me. I took it. Leggett screamed.

"No! My God! No!" O'Meara cries. He slams himself back into the nook formed by chimney and wall, his hands clutching his rosary like a shield between us. "*Quod di omen avertant! Ne di sinant! Di meliora!*" He fumbles in a small pouch belted around his waist and removes a small phial. He shakes drops of water from it, fervently chanting, "*Exorcizo te, immundissime spiritus* . . . ."

Esau leaps to his feet. Angry growls rumble from his deep chest. His eyes glow redly, unearthly from the fire. O'Meara closes his eyes and chants louder.

"Oh, stop that gibberish!" I snap. Esau advances two feet and drops to a crouch. "Stop it, or I'll release Esau!"

He shakes his head and violently crosses himself. I draw myself erect, point a finger at him and thunder: "*Sint mihi dei acherontis propitii, valeat humen triplex Jehovae, ignei areii, aquatani spiritus salvete: orientis princeps Belzebub, inferni ardentis monarcha et demigorgon . . .*"

He abruptly stops and stares at me, walleyed with fear and loathing. His fingers automatically pass the black beads of his rosary in an empty gesture of prayer.

"Forbidden," he mutters, but I interrupt him.

"Nonsense," I say sternly. His eyes look unfocused, into mine, a frown folding over his forehead. "You are not here for any of this religious balderdash, are you? Remember: I know why you are here, Priest. Tell me: when is England going to try to capture the Colonies again?"

His eyes widen. "How. . . . Of course. We talked about this. But . . . ."

"You really did not want Simon and I to bring the tribes together again for the British, did you?"

"I told you," he begins, but I wave him silent.

"Yes, you told me many things, but not the truth. The truth is that you want the tribes raised again, but for the French, not the British. Am I right? Oh, do not speak. A simple nod will do. Yes, I know why you came back. Tell me: what has Napoleon promised the Jesuits?"

"How did you figure this out, now?" he asks. His rosary falls unheeded onto his lap. He sits straighter, his hand reaching for his glass of brandy.

"Oh, it wasn't really all that hard," I say modestly. "You remember that my friend visits often from the fort and brings me the news. Did you think because I live here alone that I do not listen to what is happening in the world? I know that the French defeated the British at Corunna two years ago and that the British helped keep the French out of Portugal this year. But, England is having a few problems at home, now, isn't it? The Luddites?"

"What do you know about that?" he asks.

"I know that the Luddites are rioting against the textile people and that George III has been declared insane and the Prince of Wales is ruling as Regent. A good time, isn't it, for the French to mount an attack against the British? Or, at least, keep them well occupied in the Colonies until Napoleon can protect his flanks?"

"My God, you are the Devil! Or, at least, his agent!"

"No," I say. "Just a thinker. One who has little to do anymore but listen to what is happening. What did Napoleon promise you?"

"You know that," he responds. "The right of our order in France. Monasteries."

"If you can produce a third army in the New World, right?" He nods sullenly. "Forget it," I say softly.

He starts. "But . . . "

"No, it's over," I say. "Over. We are only two old men."

"Two old men that others will listen to," he says. "You could do it again. You and Simon Girty. The two of you could raise up the Indians again. You would be amply rewarded."

"With what?" I laugh. "Land? I am too old to do anything with it. I have all I can manage here. So does Simon. No, priest."

He sighs and makes to rise. I make a slight move with my hand and Esau leaps to his feet, growls rumbling in his throat, lips curled back from strong teeth. O'Meara sits back abruptly, staring from Esau to me.

"What . . . ."

"It's very simple," I say. I gesture at my body. "As you can see, it will be very difficult for me to take care of myself. For that, I need you. For the next year or two, at any rate. After I am dust, I will no longer care what you do. But for now, I want you to stay here."

"No," he says.

Esau's growls grow louder.

"You really haven't a choice," I say gently. "If you try to leave, I shall simply tell the British why you came to this island in the first place. You know, Catholics are still not trusted in England. Oh, they're tolerated a bit more now than they were in the mid-seventeenth century, but there's still that suspicion of doubt."

"They won't believe you," he says.

"Oh? Would you be willing to gamble on that? I haven't anything to lose, so it really isn't much of a gamble for me. But if I'm right and you're wrong, then you'll hang from the stockade walls before you get off the island. They don't love you here, priest. They tolerate you, but they do not love you."

His face turns dark with blood. "I . . . could . . . " The words strangle in his throat.

I laugh. "Kill me? No, I don't think so. There's Esau to contend with and I don't think you can manage him." He casts an uneasy look at the huge mastiff. "Besides, killing me would damn your soul to hell, wouldn't it? And, if you're right about me, then I might be there, sitting at the Devil's left hand, waiting for you. Now, wouldn't that be a pretty thing? No, you'll stay. There's no way off this island without going through the British. Resign yourself."

A stunned look passes over his face. For a moment, I feel a brief flash of pity. I force it away for he chose this way when he came to the island seeking to take advantage of an old man for his own use. What was it St. Augustine said? *De vitiis nostris scalam nobis facimus, si vitia ipsa calcamus.* Yes, we do indeed make a ladder out of our vices and climb upon it for our own good.

His face crumbles and he pulls a fold of his robe over it.

"Relax," I say. "This may not be as long as you think. Or, as difficult as you think. In fact, I believe it could be quite pleasant. It has been a long time since I had a learned companion to converse with. Back, Esau," I order. "Let him be."

Grudgingly, Esau backs away and lies at my feet, his head resting comfortably on my foot. I absently pat him and stare into the fire.

Chapter Fifty

The summer days pass swiftly, bringing winter's lowering closer and closer. I sleep well at night, but O'Meara hears stealthy footsteps about the cabin and prefers to pass the night silently huddled before the fire. He no longer is the post chaplain—a younger Anglican has taken his place—and seldom bothers with matins let alone any other church offices. The church no longer has an altar for his worship, no direct voice for his soul. It offers no soothing sanctity: only long, dim naves filled with unheard palimpsestic chants and dusty words absolving empty confessions. He spent too much of his life in the company of divine good. Confrontation with divine evil has left him too shaken and too easily vulnerable to seek sanctuary from a Janus-faced god.

The deaths of Crawford and Leggett marked the end of the Nations. The Indians wanted to kill Knight and Slover the next day, but word came by runner that Williamson had been found. Simon convinced the Council to send Knight and Slover to the next village for the ceremony of death while their warriors rushed to capture Williamson as he fled towards Fort Pitt.

Captain Pipe led a large band of Indians south in a vain attempt to intercept Williamson while Simon and

I left for Piqua with Knight and Slover. As we neared the Mad River, a scout reported a band of Morgan's Rangers moving rapidly towards Half-King's village. Simon had to act quickly if he was to save the village from attack by Morgan and reluctantly let Knight and Slover go free while he led our band to intercept the Rangers. But, by saving Half-King's village, Simon condemned us both. Knight's lurid account of the deaths of Crawford and Leggett was enough to make our names outlawed.

Pipe never caught Williamson, but we drove Morgan and his Rangers away from Half-King's village. It was, however, a hollow victory; we received word that eight months earlier Cornwallis had surrendered to Washington at Yorktown. For all practical purposes, the war was over before Williamson's attack on Gnaddenhutten and Crawford's move against the Sandusky Village had been made for personal glory, a glory that earned him a terrible death. Yet, their names are still spoken with reverence while Simon's and mine draw curses. Strange. If England had won the war, we would have been heroes. Now, we are villains worthy of any in Shakespeare's plays.

Simon tried to hold the Nations together, but the British surrender cut off our supply lines. We could no longer exist as a large force, and Simon knew the colonists would be free to concentrate on the Ohio Valley after the British surrender. Discouraged, he broke our force down into small bands to continue raiding, but in his heart, he knew it was futile: the Nations were doomed. As small forces, they would be hunted down like scavengers and destroyed.

We moved to Detroit and continued to work to halt the advance of the settlers into the Ohio country, but with the exception of St. Clair's defeat and the Battle of Fallen Timbers, we had little success. It was at Fallen Timbers that I took a ball in the chest and was brought to St. Joseph's Island to recuperate. By the time I recovered, the British had surrendered Detroit, and Simon had moved to Amherstburg with Catherine, his wife.

It was fortunate for Catherine that Simon had come to the meeting at the mouth of the Detroit River and found her among a group of Delawares who had slaughtered her family a few years before when they had tried to float down river on a keelboat for New Orleans. For three years, she had been a slave of the Delawares who had been waiting for her to reach maturity before marrying her to Dreamer, a harsh warrior who had already tortured one woman to death.

Catherine had been stripped and stood on a rock by the river, her body glistening and flesh pebbling from a fresh washing in the river. Her young breasts looked like pears, the nipples tiny rose buds rising in the cold air, and a dark shadow grew thickly between her legs.

Simon sat on his horse a long time, staring at her while the Indians poked and prodded at her, then silently rode his horse through the crowd, pausing in front of her. He stared intently into her eyes, then reached up and pulled her from the rock.

Dreamer yelled and tried to attack Simon, but for once I was ready, and put a ball through his head. We left the gathering and rode to Detroit where Simon married her. With sinking heart, I stood up for him and watched as he took her away with him towards Amherstburg. I knew then that our time was over.

O'Meara has become careless with his appearance. His cassocks are spotted with foodstains and the black beads of his rosary are dull from disuse. He wanders around our knoll on St. Joseph Island, venturing only as far as the clearing where he first found me. He seems to have abandoned himself to darkness and vacancy, emerging from this state only to watch me with dead eyes. He waits for my death and prays for it whenever he is reminded of prayers, for he feels that will be his salvation. I know, though, that will never be. His mission has failed and the Jesuits have little patience for failures.

I am still cautious, though, and watch him carefully, knowing that the mushrooms that he cooks with could easily be poisonous, but I have warned him repeatedly that if I feel myself dying in this manner, I will point at him and utter Esau's name with my last breath. He fears Esau more than he fears me. It is not death that frightens him as much as it is the manner of his death. And so, I have my man.

Two days ago, I received a new hunting horn and two eagle feathers. There was also a note from his wife, Catherine Mallot-Girty, asking me to visit their farm near Fort Malden. Simon, she writes, is ailing and not expected to last the winter. It would be good to see Catherine and Simon and their children: Anne, Thomas, Sarah, and Pirdeaux. I have not seen them since shortly after Tecumseh became The Prophet to the Nations and Simon, The Chosen, slipped away to become only legend.

But I am too old, too old.

We no longer have visitors. My soldier friend has married and left the service to work in his father-in-law's shop in Quebec. But the forest still remains; and the lake, and the ships still sail upon the lake. The gulls still cry and swing high overhead in widening gyres, and when the wind blows from the north through the forest, Esau whines and casts longing looks to the woods until I take down my rifle and tramp with him across the meadow behind our cabin and through the forest, following the familiar paths once again.

The End

The Renegade   by   Randy Lee Eickhoff